Zadel Barnes Buddington Gustafson

**Genevieve Ward**

A biographical sketch from original material derived from her family and friends

Zadel Barnes Buddington Gustafson

**Genevieve Ward**
*A biographical sketch from original material derived from her family and friends*

ISBN/EAN: 9783337028992

Printed in Europe, USA, Canada, Australia, Japan

Cover: Foto ©Raphael Reischuk / pixelio.de

More available books at **www.hansebooks.com**

# GENEVIEVE WARD

## 𝔄 𝔅iographical 𝔖ketch

FROM ORIGINAL MATERIAL DERIVED FROM HER FAMILY
AND FRIENDS

BY

### ZADEL BARNES GUSTAFSON

WITH PORTRAIT

BOSTON
JAMES R. OSGOOD AND COMPANY
1882

𝔉𝔯𝔞𝔫𝔨𝔩𝔦𝔫 𝔓𝔯𝔢𝔰𝔰:

RAND, AVERY, AND COMPANY,

BOSTON.

# GENEVIEVE.

(A SONG.)

HAIL to thee, and farewell,
　　Beautiful Genevieve !
Oh, kind for thee be wind and wave,
Thou daughter of the Free and Brave !
Godspeed of English heart and hand
Goes with thee to thy native land.
　　　　Farewell,
　　　　　　Beautiful Genevieve !

Hail to thee, and farewell !
　　Speeding so fast away.
Let not Columbia, eager now
To bind her laurels on thy brow,
Make thee forget that English hearts
First crowned and throned thee Queen of Arts
　　　　And Hearts,
　　　　　　Beautiful Genevieve !

All hail, and welcome home !
　　Over dividing seas
Returning, when the snows are past,
Queen Flower with flowers and spring at last.
Not more victorious than true,
Artist and woman crowned in you !
　　　　Welcome,
　　　　　　Beautiful Genevieve !

---

Words by Mrs. Z. B. GUSTAFSON. The music, by the favorite English balladist Miss ELIZABETH PHILP, is given on the following pages.

# GENEVIEVE.

## A Song.

Words by ZADEL B. GUSTAFSON.     Music by E. PHILP.

**Recitative.**

1. Hail to thee, and fare-well,
2. Hail to thee, and fare-well!

*p moderato.*

Beau-ti-ful Gen-e-vieve! Oh, kind for thee be
Speed-ing so fast a-way. Let not Co-lum-bia,

wind and wave, Thou daugh-ter of the   Free and Brave! God-
ea - ger now To   bind her lau - rels   on thy brow, Make

speed of Eng - lish heart and hand Goes with thee to thy
thee for - get that Eng-lish hearts First crowned and throned thee

na - tive land, Goes with thee to thy   na - tive land. Fare-
Queen of Arts, First crowned and throned thee Queen of Arts,   and

well, fare - well,    Beau - ti - ful Gen - e - vieve! 3. All
Hearts, and Hearts,    Beau - ti - ful Gen - e - vieve!

hail,   and wel-come home!    O - ver di - vid - ing   seas   Re-

turn - ing, when the   snows are past, Queen Flower with flowers and

Beau - ti - ful Gen - e - vieve!

# PREFACE.

IF a book interests me, I always feel I would like to
know how it came to be written ; and, on the sup-
position that this is a common feeling, have prepared
the following little preface for those who may find this
book interesting.

During a visit to the city of Providence, R.I., in the
autumn of 1878, I was present at one of the sessions
of a women's club, then presided over by Mrs. Elizabeth Churchill, — a truly noble woman, who has since
"ceased from her labors," leaving in many grateful
hearts a memory sweet with the eternal fragrance of
good deeds. As we were talking together at the close
of the meeting, she said earnestly, —

"There is one very kind thing you can do for me
if you will. You can help my friend Genevieve Ward,
who has recently arrived in this country. She is an
actress of great talent and admirable training, who has
had an unjustly long and hard struggle for the recog-

ix

nition which was her due from the start. By dint of
genius, invincible courage, and devoted study, she has
at last won grand dramatic triumphs in England and
France ; but this is not enough. She is an American,
and she wants to be appreciated in her native land.
She has ardent personal friends here ; but the large
appreciation of the American public, which such an
artist needs and superlatively deserves, is slow in coming to her."

"What would you like to have me do?" I asked.

"I wish you would call on her, and hear her play
when she comes to Boston in the spring; and, if the
impression she makes on you justifies what I have said,
I wish you would write an article about her, — not a bit
of newspaper gossip, she receives enough of those, but
a careful, critical, and appreciative paper, — and get it
published in an influential quarter. Such a paper
would not only do her a great deal of good, but be
a favor to the fairer-minded portion of the public, who
only need to have their attention called to a palpable
injustice, to rectify it."

In the spring of 1879, when Miss Ward came to
Boston, I called on her, and saw her play. Personally, she impressed me as a lady of pure character and
charming presence ; as an artist, she moved me, both
to admiration and emotion, more than any woman I

had ever seen on the stage, not even excepting Miss Cushman. The few biographical notes taken very hastily *viva voce* during her short stay in Boston convinced me, on examination, that her story was matter for a book, rather than an article.

Before communicating this second thought to any one, what was my astonishment to read in the literary announcements of "The Boston Saturday Gazette," that I was writing a book on Miss Genevieve Ward ! As "The Gazette" was never known to make a mistake, I was determined not to be the first to convict it of human frailty. I wrote to Miss Ward in London for more materials, not then divulging my book plan, being uncertain that a publisher would undertake it — they don't always take a good thing !

Miss Ward wrote back in July, 1879 : —

"I have not had a moment to call my own. We have moved from Paris to London, and furnished our new home. I have taken the Lyceum for the period of Mr. Irving's absence, to produce my new play 'Zillah,' by Palgrave Simpson, formed a company, commenced rehearsals, and generally started every thing. I open the 2d of August, and up to that time can't possibly sit down quietly to give you all the details I must gather together. Mother is delighted with your message, and will take great pleasure in doing all in her power."

Miss Ward had expected to return to the United

States in the fall of 1879; but this plan had been
given up. Meantime I had proposed the book to
Mr. J. R. Osgood, and he had accepted it.

I wrote her that my project had expanded from an
article to a book, and asked for the amplest materials
at her command.

In March, 1880, she replied from Edinburgh, —

"You are a worker yourself, and know how one work often
crowds out another: I therefore feel certain that you do not
attribute my silence to neglect, or want of appreciation for your
kind and noble labors in my behalf; but, as I was not to return
home this year, I thought you would postpone the publication
of your work on G. W. until my return to America should be
decided, when it would have an additional interest. I find I
have not brought with me to Edinburgh all the material I supposed, but I send you what I have on hand. . . . 'Zillah' was
such a failure, I withdrew it after four nights, putting in its
place Victor Hugo's 'Lucrezia Borgia' as arranged for me by
Mr. William Young. This was only until I had prepared another play which I had not yet secured. I also did 'Meg Merrilies.' I spent my days reading plays, and at last concluded
on trying 'Forget Me Not,' a play which had been for seven
years on the author's hands, being refused by all the leading
actresses of England. I produced it with only a week to study
and rehearse it, and playing 'Lucrezia' every night.

"I never played a part on such short notice, and had no time
to analyze it. It was entirely an inspiration. The play made
a hit; but we could not test its drawing capacities, for I could
only have the theatre two weeks. I then took it to the prov-

inces on a very successful tour, and opened the Prince of Wales Theatre, under Mr. Bruce's management, with it on the 22d of February, just six months from its first production. The first two weeks it was uncertain whether it would draw, notwithstanding the encomiums of the press: then it took a start, and the houses have been crammed; many times, ladies and gentlemen in full dress being obliged to go up into the amphitheatre, and they did so rather than not see it. The best test, however, is that the same people come over and over again, and like it better each time.

"The Prince of Wales came twice in two weeks; and as he is considered the best judge of the drama in England, and says there is no acting like mine off the French stage, I have become the 'rage.' They are very generous here; my being an American is no drawback. In fact, when the Prince of Wales asked me if I was not French, and I told him I was an American, he replied, 'I have always thought the American ladies the cleverest in the world,'—a pretty compliment to American women. I herewith send a few items jotted down by mother. I have perfect faith in you, *womanarily* and *literarily*, as I prove. As all the biographical sketches of me hitherto published have been a great mixture of truth and error, I will see that yours is well circulated as authentic. I never wrote so much about myself before, and never shall again ; for I will always refer my friends in future to your complete and comprehensive work."

The "few items jotted down by mother" showed me that Mrs. Ward's memory was my mine : therefore I deferred writing the present biography until this summer of 1881, when, during the latter part of June

and early in July, we were all in London together, and
I received from the Wards the necessary materials,
abundant and rich, but in an unavoidably chaotic state,
which I have taken conscientious pains to reduce to
accuracy and symmetry; and, whatever other defects
may be found, I believe that no error of import to fact
or feeling will be discovered. ·

It goes without saying, that perspective and certain
other qualities and elements characteristic of posthu-
mous biography — obviously much the easiest to write
— are not, and ought not to be, apparent in the present
work. Mrs. Ward furnished me, as I had foreseen
she would, some of the most interesting details from
a well-trained and well-stored memory. From the
masses of letters addressed by eminent men and
women of many lands to Miss Ward, to which I have
had access, I have been guided in my selection less
by the distinguished position of the writers, than by
the capacity to add by illustration or elucidation to
the value of the subject matter. It has not been possible to insert more than a small proportion of letters,
nearly all of which would interest the general reader,
and which form a correspondence, as to source and
character, of which any one might be proud to have
been the recipient.

If this book inspires any talent with the patience

and courage of the profound discipline Art exacts of every votary whom she crowns, and if it pleases its gifted subject and her friends, — a term which must ultimately apply to all lovers of pure art splendidly exemplified, — I shall be well recompensed for a difficult task.

ZADEL BARNES GUSTAFSON.

LONDON, Aug. 27, 1881.

[1] DEAR MADAME GUSTAFSON, — It is with the greatest pleasure that I hear you intend writing the biography of my friend Miss Ward. Such a work cannot fail to greatly interest the general public and especially all lovers of art.

Nature has endowed Miss Ward with precious gifts for the stage. She interested me from the first moment of our acquaintance; and I was glad to have the pleasure of evincing my sympathy by taking part, together with my illustrious friend Frezzolini, in a concert given by Miss Ward in a *salon* of the Hotel de Louvre in Paris.

She was then a lyric artist: and, though possessing much merit, my impression was, that she excelled rather in dramatic power; and when in London, in 1873, she informed me of her intention to devote herself to dramatic art, I encouraged her in every way in my power, aiding her with my advice and instruction.

In December of the same year, when I met her again in Manchester, on hearing her declaim selections from different tragedies, I was convinced that I had not been mistaken in thinking a brilliant career awaited her on the English stage; and, although I have never had the pleasure of assisting at one of her representations, the success she has since obtained in England, France, and America, and the unanimous applause accorded her by the press, have proved to me that my previsions have been fully realized. She has met the just reward for her persevering devotion to her profession. Hoping that I may soon have the pleasure of reading your work, believe me, dear madame,

Yours very truly,

ADELAIDE RISTORI (DEL GRILLO).

ST. MORITZ-BAD, Aug. 28, 1881.
HOF-ST. MORITZ.

[1] This letter is given just as it was written in English by Madame Ristori.

"I CAN conceive of few things more stimulating to a woman, than a gifted mother."

ELIZABETH STUART PHELPS.

# GENEVIEVE WARD.

## (COUNTESS DE GUERBEL.)

### I.

AMONG the "seven hundred and ten distinguished persons, each bearing but one name, who accompanied William the Conqueror from Normandy to the conquest of England in 1066," was Baron Leigh; and in the still-preserved record of their names is mentioned that of "Ward, one of the noble captains, this being the earliest date in which the name is found in English history."

From that period to the present, the Wards and Leighs have intermarried.

John Leigh came with his brother to America from Bruton Street, London, in 1634.

Gov. Morton's memorial, in recording the arrivals from the Old Country, speaks of these Leigh brothers as the younger sons of the Earl of Marlborough. The king had portioned them off with grants of land. The son of John Leigh was sent back in due course of time to England, to be educated, and entered Queen Anne's navy. The descendants of the Bruton-street

3

Leighs settled on the eastern shores of Maryland, and agreed with the Goodenoughs and the Woodhouses — being all stanch republicans — to change their names respectively to those of Lee, Woodis, and Goodenow; names now so widely and favorably known in the United States, synonymes of enterprise, prosperity, and clean repute. The royalist branch of the Leigh family remained good Tories, retained the original spelling of their name, and moved to Nova Scotia.

One of the family, a wealthy bachelor named Horatio Nelson Ward, went to Europe about thirty years ago, and spent about fifteen years, and from ten to twelve thousand pounds, in seeking out the genealogy of his family. He succeeded in tracing them back to the year 700, in Denmark, where the name is still found spelled *Wärt*, and meaning, both in Danish and in German, as in English, — to guard.

Both the Wards and the Leighs have been people of most honorable repute, long-lived, and a notable proportion of them have from generation to generation filled acceptably positions of responsibility and public trust. Besides the long list of families whose names and records are matters of both English and American pride, with whom the Wards have from time to time intermarried, they have continued, as already stated, to intermarry with the Lees in both countries, and the same names have been handed down in the families; William having been usually the name of the head of the family of Ward, and John the name of the head of the Lee family.

Only those who have seen the volume entitled "The

Ward Family," [1] issued in 1851, by Andrew Henshaw Ward, A.M., member of the New-England Historic-Genealogical Society, know what an interesting and proud family-tree it reveals, with branches bearing many of the best-known and best-loved English and American names.

Mrs. Lucy Leigh Ward,[2] daughter of Gideon Lee, formerly mayor of New-York City, widow of the late Col. Samuel Ward, and mother of the beautiful and gifted tragedienne who is the subject of the present biography, is the most remarkable living member of this family, and one of the most remarkable representative women of modern times.

"I am accused of being very proud of my old family," she said to me, one day of this present summer of 1881 ; "and Judge Wayne once reminded me that I was the ninth generation of the Lees born in the State of Massachusetts, and that in Austria ten generations make a noble. But it isn't nobilities, titles, lordships, patrimonies, coats-of-arms, and blue blood, that I care for ; but when you can trace a family back for hundreds of years, and find them, from generation to generation, men and women of splendid bodies and magnificent souls, as the Wards and Lees are to this day, I take it as good proof they have lived after God's own plan ; and I *am* proud of that sort of nobility ; and I think, too, that the family names of such people ought to be spared from public burlesque. When Mr. Browne was here in London, a letter ap-

[1] Published by Samuel G. Drake. See Appendix.

[2] Ever since ascertaining that *Leigh* was the original spelling of her maiden name, Mrs. Ward has adopted that form.

peared in 'The Times,' asking for the correct pronunciation of Artemas.  I replied in the same journal
that I was probably the best authority on the subject,
as there had been several Artemas Wards in my family,
and we gave the accent to the first syllable.  I took
care to add that I regretted extremely that Mr. Browne
should have chosen the time-honored name of Major-
Gen. Artemas Ward of the Revolution as a subject for
derision and laughter.  Mr. Browne called on me immediately, and in a very gentlemanly manner expressed
his great surprise at the fact I had mentioned, and his
regret that in ignorance of it he should have wounded
family feeling, and begged leave to incorporate the fact
in his then forthcoming book."

Mrs. Ward's mother, who died when Lucy was a
baby, was Laura Buffington, who lived in Worthington, Mass., and who was a lineal descendant of old
Jonathan Edwards of Northampton, Mass.  It will
be remembered that keenness, strength, and sterling
moral quality marked the "long-favored" and un-
beautiful Edwards face.  One day, when Mrs. Ward
was little Lucy Lee, one of the Edwards family came
to her father's on a visit.  Noticing the little girl,
caught probably in the first instance by the twinkling
glances of the direct and penetrating eyes, — eyes that
care, experience, and age are powerless to dim, — he
asked, —

"Whose child is this?" and, laying his hand on her
head, he upturned her face for the sort of scrutiny to
which the shyest and most individual souls of children are always being unwarrantably subjected.  She

gave him look for look, and never forgot the pathetic fellowship that came into his face as he released her, and said, "That's an Edwards child!"

She was a prodigy from her birth; interpreting life from the first with an originality, and understanding it with a passion, that belong neither to childhood nor age, but to genius. Her instinct for shams and shallownesses drew blood, like Ithuriel's spear, wherever the lie lay hid. And, though this faculty has kept the circle of intimate friendship thin enough for the freest and happiest grouping of the few who have truly known her, it has not withheld her from entertaining and re-invigorating the social circles of many lands, which her own gifts, and her daughter's beauty, talents, and unique career, have gathered around them.

Major Buffington, a descendant of Lady Buffington, and the grandfather, on the mother's side, of Mrs. Ward, was one of the historic figures of her earliest memories. Lady Buffington used laughingly to call George Washington a "great rascal," relating a little incident somewhat subversive of the popular tradition of the little hatchet.

The Mount Vernon and Buffington estates adjoined; and, according to Lady Buffington, when George Washington builded the wall between them, he made it lap over on her property, thus sparing every inch of his own.

Major Buffington, who served through the whole of the Revolution, is reputed to have been the strongest man in the army, very handsome, and so tall and well-proportioned as to carry gracefully his weight of two

hundred and ninety pounds. His hair when combed
out reached to his ankles ; and his Polish servant, who
took great pride in it, braided and looped it in an
elegant cue. Mrs. Ward distinctly remembers, in
proof of his fabulous physical powers, seeing him on
one occasion go into a stable, lay his hand on a horse,
and push it over flat upon the ground ; and at another
time, when a horse was running away with a buggy,
Major Buffington sprang forward, and catching hold
of the back of the wagon stopped the animal by main
force after a few paces. To Lucy Lee, then not five
years old, he seemed as veritable a giant as any that
Jack the Giant-killer ever slew. At the close of the
Revolution he moved with his family from Virginia to
Massachusetts, where he settled on top of a mountain near Worthington, and devoted his remaining en-
ergies to his horses, which had always been a great
passion with him ; a feeling shared by the whole family, who ride, drive, and manage horses admirably. In
1815 he was offered a generalship, but declined on
account of his sufferings from epilepsy, which had already paled his naturally jet-black eyes to blue.

"Some thirty years ago," said Mrs. Ward, in a recent letter to a friend, "just as I was going aboard the
steamer for Europe, a man addressed me, asking if I
was a descendant of Major Buffington. The government of Florida had sent to know, there being a tract
of land belonging to him in that State, probably given
to him for his services in the Revolution. I sent this
man to my lawyer, who, however, paid no attention
to it. I believe there is an island and a stream in the

West named Buffington for him: I have no papers,
however, on these or kindred matters, as my step-
mother and I were not friends. She had been my
nursery-governess; and she never gave me any thing
after my father's death, which took place when I was
abroad and very ill."

All Mrs. Ward's early recollections are of such men
as Clay, Webster, the Waynes, Gen. Jackson, Gov.
Clinton; all friends of her father's, whom she therefore saw constantly, and to whom she was a never-
palling astonishment, the best of little *bons camarades*,
a fresh-hearted child-sage, never to be driven, bought,
or coaxed from the most courageously truthful
dealings.

Gov. Clinton, who could not get warm at his own
fireside, used often to take his meals with the Lees;
and on one of these occasions, in the course of a
conversation she was too young to understand, Lucy
heard her father suddenly exclaim, —

"If you do that, you'll cut the throat of the United
States!"

The child slipped away, and tremblingly thought upon this announcement. It seemed to her too frightful
to be spoken of, and she was carefully silent though
vividly remembering it. At last, when she had become
a "grown-up," she asked her father about it; and he
explained that Gov. Clinton had wished to be made
governor a second time, which, as it could not be
done without giving a free vote, was a process tant-
amount, in Gideon Lee's mind, to putting the knife to
the throat of the Republic.

Thomas Cooper, the famous elocutionist of Kemble's time, whose powerful "Coriolanus" and "Julius Cæsar" were the models for the English stage of those days, used to visit her father in New York, and took great interest in the marvellous child. He would place her on the table in front of him, and repeat long declamatory passages, which she would recite after him with scarcely the loss of a word, imitating his gesture and accent to a nicety. Her rich voice seemed a miracle in a body so small; but wonder at this was merged in wonder at the memorizing faculty, and at the passionate fidelity of the imitation which fascinated Tom Cooper, and made these scenes great treats to them all; and it was emphatically prophesied that she would grow up to be one of the greatest wonders of the world. When barely old enough to hold a pencil she made little drawings, and painted miniatures on rice-paper, with a sense of color and a notion of management that would have been striking in a much older artist ; and her improvisations in both music and verse were surprisingly graceful and touching.

But, with all her gifts and her quickness, little Lucy was very plain, and was constantly hearing this fact affirmed and deplored, not always as kindly as in Jonathan Edwards's compassionate eyes. This crushed her. Everybody was kind to her, and of admiration she had enough to have turned dozens of heads of another sort than hers; but she did not feel herself loved. To those who know her in these days of her wrinkles and gray hairs, it seems impossible that she should not have been loved in her childhood, if only for the light and quenchless youth of the eyes and smile which make plainness and old age in her so lovely; but the correctness of such a child's instinct can hardly be questioned. She craved for love, always missing it. She carried herself calmly, with the seeming carelessness of her years; but she left people for dumb animals. Horses, dogs, cows, birds, were her intimates. She fed them, caressed them; and they listened to all her confidences, and loved her, each after its kind. Birds, particularly, were very dear and tame to her; and she has never tasted their flesh.

With little notion of the use or value of money, she reaped all the advantages of being an heiress. She became an excellent pianist, played both the harp and guitar, sang, painted, and wrote melodious verse and graphic prose with great facility.

The identity of Mrs. Ward used sometimes to be confounded with that of Medora Grimes, wife of Samuel Ward the lobbyist, for the latter was also very talented. But, unlike Gideon Lee's bright daughters, Medora was a beauty; and by this point of difference the two brilliant Mesdames Ward were distinguished from one another.

But it was as a conversationalist that Mrs. Ward, *née* Lucy Lee, outshone all other talkers, maintaining the nicest harmony between the thoughtful, weighty, and witty elements of conversation; so that her supremacy in this fine art — the most royal and perhaps most exacting of all the arts — was conceded without envy or question. That she was a perfect hostess, follows without saying. An eclectic number of the political,

literary, and musical celebrities of the time gathered
around her, loath to lose a word from her lips; and
Daniel Webster, Calhoun, Clay, and Tom Corwin used
to be moved to tears in listening to her singing of
"The Irish Emigrant," accompanied by the guitar.
For her singing was also something wonderful. It is
said that her voice had a compass of four full octaves;
from the middle register ascending it was a fine, soft
soprano, and below it was a full, strong tenor.

She studied song in Italy, when her daughter Genevieve was a baby; and no less an authority than
Madame Garcia, mother of Madame Malibran, said
that Mrs. Ward's voice was precisely that of Madame
Malibran, only it had greater compass; that their
necks were formed and set alike, with a peculiarity
which she thought would be observable in all great
singers. Mrs. Ward's teacher in singing was Signor
Marchelini, a one-legged Italian of great talent and
taste, who was also the prison-friend of Silvio Pellico,
whose history is so well known.

Once when a guest at the house of Catalini, in Italy,
Mrs. Ward was asked to sing, and, in complying, selected a tenor part. Her singing was quickly inter-
rupted by Madame Catalini's exclamation,—

"No! I cannot believe it! It cannot be you who
are singing: it is a man's voice!" and she placed
her own mouth to that of the young singer to feel if the
notes were really breathed from that quarter. Being
by this process at last convinced, she exclaimed, with
delight and amazement, "But there must be something
wrong here! This is not human!"

She took no lessons in painting, except a few in landscape from an Englishman, and afterward of Miss Viardot in Paris; but she had the benefit of Sir William Newton's advice in London, and in Paris, in miniature, the counsels of the celebrated M. Isabey, miniature-painter of the court of Napoleon the Great.

Mrs. Ward's Friday receptions in Paris were attended by the chief writers and artists of the day. Musset and Balzac were there; the great painter Vernet came, and David d'Angers; but M. Isabey was one of the most interesting of her guests. Imagine a gentleman dressed in the style of the French court during the period when Napoleon affected the richest display for his satellites, — a man over eighty years old, yet with a young and flashing eye, and a most polished bearing, — and you have M. Isabey in Mrs. Ward's Parisian *salon*. He frankly admired her work; and when she applied to him for the address of Madame Mirbel, one of his best pupils, that she might take lessons of her, he begged her not to run the risk of injuring her style, " already combining all that was most finished and precious in miniature, by taking lessons of any one then in Paris."

Since I have seen some of Mrs. Ward's work, I can appreciate the justice of such praise. Her miniature on ivory of Madame Elizabeth, Louis XVI.'s nobly famous "Angel of the Prison" sister, is beautifully worthy of its subject; and her last picture, representing her daughter Genevieve at the age of eight, painted this summer of 1881, with hand and eye of threescore years and ten, is not only one of the fairest ideals of childish innocence and aspiration I have ever seen, but as a piece of work is so delicately fine, it appears rather to have been breathed than brushed upon canvas.

One day M. Isabey escorted Mrs. Ward to see the famous "Battle of the Alma," while in process of painting. She looked at the Duc d'Aumale on horseback, and at the figure of the woman kneeling on the ground in front of him, for some time, with scant comment.

"Well, well, well!" eagerly exclaimed M. Isabey, when they had come out, "how do you like it?"

"Dear friend, I like it very much — all but the drawing of the woman."

"Why! What do you mean? What is wrong with her?"

"Did you really notice nothing?" said Mrs. Ward. "Did you not see that the woman is kneeling on the ground, while the duke is on horseback, yet her head comes up to the top of the horse's back; and if she should rise, she would, while on the ground, be as tall as the duke on horseback?"

M. Isabey, who was personally interested in the artist, heard her in consternation : —

"But if this is so, dear madame, we must go back : we must tell him ; it must be fixed."

"But we cannot go back, now we have come away."

"Yes, we can," persisted M. Isabey : "you can make an excuse. You have lost — yes, you have lost your handkerchief," taking and crunching it in his hand : "I will drop it, and you shall find it."

So they played this friendly little trick; and, to his dismay, M. Isabey found that Mrs. Ward was right, and when they again came out said he must devise some way for getting the artist's attention to such a terrible blunder.

"But I don't think the dear old gentleman found the right time, and the courage, at the same moment," said Mrs. Ward to me; "for the picture with the impossible woman hangs in the palace at Versailles to this day."

During the *régime* of Louis Philippe, Mrs. Ward enjoyed the friendship of the Marquise de Beaufort, whose son was aide-de-camp to the Duke of Orleans. She frequently accompanied the marquise to court, and to the "*intimes soirées.*" The marquise was a great favorite with the royal family, who constantly sent her gifts of fruits and flowers, which she made haste to share with Mrs. Ward. They met daily; and the marquise, always interested in every thing American, was eager to taste every American dish which Mrs. Ward, who added to her other gifts that of being a true *chef de cuisine,* had prepared for the novel delectation of her kind French friend.

When Mrs. Ward was in Italy, Hiram Powers—who was much impressed with her talents—told her that he thought she had even greater genius for modelling than painting, and she moulded for some time in his studio; and when they parted, the great sculptor gave her the instruments with which Miss Genevieve Ward is now modelling.

# À MADAME WARD.

Vous qui réunissez tant de talents divers,
Et dont le cœur unit l'Amérique et la France,
Permettez-moi de dire aujourd'hui dans ces vers,
Que vous aimez surtout à calmer la souffrance !
Lorsque Paris était en proie à des pervers,
Que la bombe écrasait la vieillesse et l'enfance ;
Quand le froid et le faim accroissaient nos revers,
Qu'il nous restait à peine un rayon d'espérance, —
Alors, n'écoutant plus que votre charité,
Votre courage ardent, conduit par la bonté,
Dans bien des cœurs français gravait votre memoire.
Parmi nous votre bon nom sera souvent cité ;
On chérit vos talents ; mais c'est l'humanité,
Qui saura mieux encore consacrer votre gloire.

CHARLES BOISSIÈRE.

## II.

MRS. WARD'S extensive travels have made the whole world her home, and herself a cosmopolitan thoroughly familiar with the manners and customs, and with the languages even to the dialects, of very diverse peoples ; and over a long period the columns of both home and foreign journals have sparkled with her apt descriptions of the scenes and people of her journeyings ; and the energy with which she has devoted her ready mimetic and other gifts — for she has been one of the cleverest of comediennes — to social or beneficiary service everywhere, has been equalled only by the esteem in which the greatest have held her talents and her rare critical powers.

From the striking episodes of her eventful life I have selected certain incidents of the siege of Paris, not only because they afford good illustration of those salient traits which have less defined her own life than wonderfully guided and guarded her daughter's career to its present proud eminence, but because they are of international interest, and have not hitherto been generally made known.

When the Franco-Prussian war was declared, Mrs. Ward was staying in Paris with her son Albert Lee

Ward. Mr. Ward was a young man of unusual capacity, gifted with good sense of the very first order, a handsome person, and elegant manners ; and his acquirements, especially in political science and in the mastery of languages, had already gained him position in the diplomatic service in the city of Bristol, England, as American vice-consul and Austrian vice-consul ; and for a time as consul-general for Portugal, on account of the death of their own consul-general, in which position he gave such satisfaction to the Portuguese government that they wished to retain him in their office, but could not on account of his alien birth. He served also as consul *pro tem* at Cairo, at the time of Butler's ejection. When the siege of Paris was imminent, Mr. Ward gave up his position in a bank for that of secretary to the American Legation ; his linguistic abilities making his services of the most vital importance to Mr. Washburne, then the American minister to France, who was not conversant with the modern languages.

The mother and son, previous to the opening of hostilities, had talked over the matter of staying or departing from the troubled capital, and had concluded to remain in the hope of being of use to the wounded in case of battles, and perhaps of other humane assistance.

One Sunday morning, early in those agitated days, Mrs. Ward, who had lain awake all night on gentle thoughts intent, rose and went to her son's room, and roused him with these words, —

"Suppose we organize an ambulance. Let us go

up to Dr. Evans, and see if he will let us have his tools and things to begin with."

Dr. Thomas Evans was an American dentist, then residing in Paris, and the owner of tents and other appurtenances for sanitary purposes. When the Wards' ambulance-plan was laid before him, he at once begged to be admitted into it.

" Let's unite," said he. " I'll give you a room in my apartments in the Rue de la Paix, and we will form an ambulance ; and Mrs. Ward will have charge of the ladies' sanitary committee, and appeal for funds."

Upon this followed a ladies' meeting, at which Dr. Evans presided. Mrs. Ward nominated Mrs. Dr. Evans for the presidency of the ladies' sanitary com- mittee ; but, as this lady was just about quitting Paris, Mrs. Ward next named Mrs. Anson Burlingame ; Mrs. Burlingame, however, was also about to leave Paris, and proposed that Mrs. Ward, who had initiated the noble measure, should be made president, and at once subscribed with other ladies large sums in support of the project. In a speech, Dr. Evans as chairman declared Mrs. Ward president of the ladies' sanitary committee.

Mrs. Parnell, wife of the Irish agitator, her two daughters, and two other English ladies, joined Mrs. Ward heartily in the labors of getting up the ambu- lance : lint and bandages were rapidly made ready, and all went on smoothly. Dr. Sims of New York, Dr. May of Baltimore, and some other young Ameri- can physicians, assisted the ladies in their enterprise. Dr. Evans, and his secretary Dr. Crane, Mr. Albert

Lee Ward (whom Dr. Evans appointed secretary of the ambulance commission), and Dr. Lamson, one of the American clergy, formed the gentlemen's committee; but, as with this number they had no quorum, Mr. Ward proposed, at one of their meetings, that Dr. Sims should be added to their committee. To everybody's astonishment, Dr. Evans sprang up and exclaimed, —

"No ! *I* won't have him on ! "

Dr. Sims remained tranquil until the meeting was over, then walking up to Dr. Evans, and asking, "What do you mean by saying such a thing?" struck Dr. Evans coolly across the mouth with open palm.

Dr. Evans immediately sat down in the nearest chair, and in a crouching attitude, with his hands lifted, deprecatingly cried out several times, —

"Oh, don't hurt me ! don't hurt me ! "

"Why don't you pick up a chair, and go for him, instead of whimpering like that?" cried Mr. Ward.

"He knocked me down," replied Evans, still cowering.

"No, that's not true," said Mr. Ward.

Meantime the noise of the altercation had reached the ladies' department; and Mrs. Ward, Dr. May of Baltimore, Miss Parnell, and the other English ladies, rushed across the passage into the gentlemen's committee-rooms.

Mr. Ward was standing with his hands on Dr. Sims's shoulders, as in friendly restraint. Dr. Crane had hold of Dr. Evans, from whose nose a few drops of blood trickled. The moment his mother appeared, Mr. Ward turned to her and the other ladies, and led them from the room, saying, "Mother, this is no place for you."

The next morning when Mrs. Ward came to resume her duties in the ladies' committee-room, she found the door locked, and was informed that a Mrs. Conkling had been placed in charge by order of Dr. Evans.

Wishing to reach some understanding with Dr. Evans as to the abrupt and peremptory alteration of affairs, she returned in the afternoon of the same day, and was told Dr. Evans had left town ; but, seeing his carriage waiting at a little distance, she concluded to wait also, and after some time the absent doctor came down-stairs.

Mrs. Ward asked him at once for an explanation of the proceedings ; to which he replied, that he could not give it then, as he was just leaving for Dieppe. He was looking well, showing no traces whatever of the fray of the previous day, and Mrs. Ward congratulated him pointedly to that effect. The very next step in the matter, however, was the prosecution of Dr. Sims by Dr. Evans, damages being set at five thousand francs ; and all the members of both committees were summoned to court.

Dr. Evans testified that he had been severely injured physically by the assault of Dr. Sims, and had lost a great deal of money also, in consequence of being unable to attend to his business.

Dr. Crane denied that he was Dr. Evans's secretary, or had received any salary from him, and then corroborated precisely the testimony of Dr. Evans as to the injuries the latter had received in body and purse.

Dr. May stated that he had just arrived from Dieppe ; that, on the day succeeding that of the alleged assault, Dr. Evans had arrived at Dieppe perfectly well, and had eaten dinner there like every one else at *table d'hôte*.

Mrs. Ward testified that she had seen Dr. Evans the next day after the encounter ; that he was looking just as usual, and had received her congratulations on the fact.

Dr. Sims gave his testimony in accordance with that of Mrs. Ward and Dr. May. He apologized handsomely to the court for having disturbed the laws of a country he so profoundly esteemed ; and, not being familiar with the French language, he made everybody laugh by adding, " I only gave him a *sifflet* " (whistle), meaning to have said *soufflet* (light blow).

The decision of the court was given morally on the side of the defendant ; the damages being placed at three hundred francs, the lowest legal limit.

As the party were going out of court, Dr. Evans shook his fist in Mrs. Ward's face, declaring he would have her up for libel. A New-Orleans lawyer who had been much interested in the case happened to be close behind them, and pulled out his note-book, exclaiming, " What's that ! what's that ! " upon which Dr. Evans disappeared.

At this period Dr. Evans was in communication with the Queen of Prussia, and had shown to the ambulance a letter the queen had written to him ; and he was commonly spoken of as the back-stair friend of Louis Napoleon, which seems to afford some indication of the reason why, when he soon after went to England, he was not permitted to return to Paris while the siege lasted.

It is now reported that he denies that there ever was a ladies' sanitary committee. But the foregoing account can be verified, having been taken from the minutes of the ladies' sanitary committee.

After this suit, and just before Dr. Evans left for England, two English gentlemen arrived in Paris with two thousand pounds they were intending to give to the American ambulance. On talking with Dr. Evans, and finding that he wished to be considered the only person concerned with the ambulance, and to have his name printed on every thing, even to the pill-boxes and straps and toggery of the wagons, these English-men promptly handed over the money to the French sanitary committee at the *Palais de l'Industrie*, which Dr. Sims, Dr. May, and the other physicians had joined.

When the battle of Sedan was thought to be immi-nent, Dr. Sims came to Mrs. Ward, and said they were organizing an ambulance to go out to Sedan, and asked if she would be willing to take part in a beg-ging march from the *Palais de l'Industrie* to the rail-way-station. This procession, conceded to have been the handsomest ever seen in time of war, was formed as follows. First, in double file, came the servants of the ambulance in bright uniform, under the command of the tall and handsome Count Serrurier, vice-presi-dent of the *Société Française de Secours aux Blessés*, an officer who rendered eminent services during the

war. Next came the military band, followed by three
ladies ; Mrs. Carr and Miss Carrie Sims (both daughters of Dr. Sims) and Mrs. Ward. The Sims ladies
declined to carry the English flag, preferring to carry
the French and American banners. To settle this
point, Mrs. Ward heartily volunteered to be the bearer
of the "grandmother's blanket," as the English flag
used jocularly to be called to distinguish it from the
"grandmother's gridiron," the stars and stripes.

Mr. Ward walked beside his mother, then nearly
sixty years old, to help her bear the really heavy standard. Another gentleman walked on the other side
of the three ladies to hold out the contribution-bags.
Then came the body of physicians, followed by the
new and resplendent ambulance-wagon and the led
horses. A thick crowd closed in upon the rear of the
procession, following it all the way.

On seeing this bright and sturdy phalanx pass up
the boulevards, with the three ladies marching in the
midst, bearing the flags of England, America, and
France, the people, officers, and soldiers formed a
dense hedge on either side, and gave them military
salutes. Fired with sympathy in the noble purpose of
the march, they threw off their caps in the greatest
enthusiasm, crying all along the line, "God bless you !
God bless you ! O you dear, brave women ! "

About fifteen thousand francs were taken in this
march.

Later, when the American ambulance was about
breaking up for want of funds, Mr. Ward called a
meeting of the few Americans then in Paris, stated the

situation, pledged every franc he himself possessed to the maintenance of the enterprise in the name of American honor, and even vouched for Dr. Evans that the latter would, when permitted to return to Paris, refund all sums so expended; which Dr. Evans subsequently did.

Mr. Ward's action re-animated popular interest in the project. Contributions poured in: Hon. Stuart Wortley loaned twenty-five thousand francs to Mr. Ward for it; and old Mr. Boucicault of the Bon Marché gave Mrs. Ward five hundred francs, and any article she might require for the ambulance.

Such were the means by which the American ambulance was saved to do great and humane service. Of the situation of the besieged, Mrs. Ward wrote to a friend : —

"At last we were shut up in the siege. Hams were selling at two hundred francs, and every thing else in proportion. We had at the start plenty of tea, and some dried beans and canned cranberries; but they didn't last long. Then the *arrondissement* gave us a card on which we were allotted a certain amount of horse-meat for my son, self, and servant. She would go about ten A.M., and return about four P.M., with the few ounces belonging to us; having been obliged to wait all that time for her turn to come in the long line of applicants.

"At last our allowance was a piece of horse-meat three inches square for all three of us, for three days.

"This was indeed starvation portions. My son was frequently invited to partake of the meagre fare of the generals, most of whom he knew officially; and once Gen. de Maussion, hearing him say he had some salt pork, begged a piece in exchange for a piece of mutton. . . . Once Gen. Appert, knowing that Albert was ill, sent him in from outside the walls a piece of tenderloin, the soldiers having caught a stray bullock. Mrs. Appert had received some little birds caught in Paris. Mr. Hoskier, of Brown Brothers, a brother of Mrs. Appert, sent us some wood; and it was a curious sight to see the Marquis de Jouffroy making charcoal in an iron pot, for we had no means of cooking except with charcoal.

"We had charge of several horses and carriages; but for this care, the horses would have been seized for food. Well, when the wood came from Mr. Hoskier, I put some of it in one of the carriages. It was elegantly lined with blue satin, but I did not once think of that when I was laying in the wood.

"Only the day before, Dr. Gordon had come running eagerly up the stairs with a present for me.

"Some friend had given to him and his coadjutor, Sir James Innes, M.D., two ordinary smoked herring. They had kept one for themselves, and here was Dr. Gordon with the other.

"Dividing my herring, and taking my place on the blue satin along with the wood, I drove to the house of a friend who lay in bed weak for want of food, and without fire. She had four grown-up sons. I sent up-stairs for them, that they might come down and carry up the wood; for, had I left it for a moment, it would have been stolen.

"I called the four youths to me, and made them promise not to touch the fish I had brought, and then went up stairs with the half-herring to their mother. All this may seem laughable now; but no one laughed then. . . .

"During the armistice Dr. Gordon got hold of a piece of white bread and butter, and gave it to me. The butter I ate as if it had been an apple, being quite out of carbon of my own by that time. . . . I made tea every day; and Dr. Gordon, and Hon. Lewis Wingfield, who was attached to the ambulance, and was exceedingly attentive and of great service during the operations, and Sir James Innes, and any other friends who chose, were welcome to a cup when they came in. It was also during the armistice, that Col. Stuart Wortley gave me several hundred bonds for food he brought over for me to distribute among the poor. Albert ate the meat of the horse, mule, donkey, kangaroo, and elephant.

"The elephant-steak was pink, like the inside of a conch-shell, and the flesh of the finest fibre; and Dr. Gordon and Albert found it excellent. Dogs were two prices: Newfoundlands were six francs a pound, and small dogs three francs. Two rats ran into our apartment. The man from the court-yard came and killed them, and begged them of us for food. Rats were then selling for two francs apiece. Yet some people have asserted there was plenty of food in Paris.

"Count Messay asked us to dine on mutton, as he had se-cured a leg. The odor was certainly that of mutton, but the leg was the leg of the Newfoundland dog!

"The Marquis de Jouffroy executed one of the most difficult feats of the war. He knew every tree and rock between Paris and Versailles, where his aunt lived. He slipped out of Paris, unseen, and reached Versailles on foot; took a bushel-basket, filled it with white bread, butter, and chicken, and crept back into Paris, with this heavy basket on his shoulder, unnoticed and unhurt. His escape — for the Germans threw an electric light all the time around Paris — is a marvel to himself and his friends to this day. The contents of his basket he divided between his aunt, the Countess D——, and me."

Mr. Albert Lee Ward's labors during the siege were very exacting, occupying from eighteen to twenty hours out of the twenty-four. Three, four, or five times a week, he carried the despatch-bag to Versailles; leaving at four in the morning during the severe win-ter, and being, during the cold and lonesome journey, always under fire from both French and German ram-part guns and shells.

One day, just at daylight, as Mr. Ward was starting out with the despatches, he halted at a tavern on the road for a glass of water. A bomb-shell struck the house, and covered him with plaster and dirt. His horse ran away with him, and was only brought up by the barricade at the Pont de Sevres. He was the only American incurring personal danger during the siege, except from the bomb-shells thrown into the city, to which, of course, all were exposed.

Mornings and evenings he was at the ambulance, receiving and helping the wounded.

He was deputed by Mr. Washburne to release the Germans from the prisons; and, in discharging this commission, Mr. Ward took many poor but respectable German women who had been shut up with culprits of all kinds, — and many of them had lain in these holes a month without change of linen, — and himself procured the necessaries for them, and placed them in convents.

Among his numerous duties, were those of interpreting between Mr. Washburne and all foreign officials, and of translating Mr. Washburne's speeches and public addresses *viva voce* into French. As one of the three directors of the American ambulance, Mr. Ward had frequent communication with the chief officers of the *Société de Secours aux Blessés*, and, through his friendly relations with them, was able to obtain many facilities and favors. For example, one day when Mr. Washburne had returned to the Legation, after having made unsuccessful application for passes, Mr. Ward asked permission to go and see what he could do, and soon came back with the desired papers. A gentleman at about this time told Mrs. Ward that he had been all the morning engaged in translating German lettters for the Legation, and that these letters all breathed the warmest gratitude to Mr. Ward for his

varied and untiring kindness ; and, by those most conversant with things in the beleaguered city, he came to
be spoken of as "the man of the siege."

At the time of the revolt in October, Mr. Ward
accompanied Mr. Washburne, *incog.*, to the Hôtel de
Ville, where they would probably have lost their lives
but for Mr. Ward's presence of mind. A great tumult
arose just as they were coming out ; and the sentinels,
hearing the cry of "Spies !" crossed their guns to prevent their exit. Mr. Ward sprang forward, and throwing up the guns, cried in a firm loud voice, —

"Attention pour son excellence !" and they were
instantly permitted to pass.

While the son was thus engaged, the mother was
performing noble works of compassion and mercy,
regardless of difficulty or fatigue, and though already
greatly weakened by want of proper food. After
Labouchère had so inconsiderately written to "The
London Daily News," that the London journals could
be read at any time lying on the tables of the United
States Legation, and Bismarck had sent in his em-
bargo that they must thereafter be withheld from
everybody except Mr. Washburne, Mrs. Ward nevertheless succeeded more than once in procuring the
advertising sheet of "The Times," and copied long
columns of messages inserted in the hope of their
reaching the eyes of friends and relatives in the besieged city. These messages expressed the tenderest
solicitude and affection, and pleaded for some good
word or sign in return, if such could by any possibility
be rendered. Having copied these, Mrs. Ward took

them herself to the persons and places indicated.
Many were addressed to the poorer classes; and she
dragged herself up five and six flights of stairs to raise
these loving souls from despair to joy. They hugged
her knees, kissed the hem of her dress, and begged
her name, that they might bear it in their most ardent
prayers to God, while the tears rolled down the
wrinkled faces of the old, and the pale, hollow cheeks
of the young. She did not give her name, but told
them she was the "*carrier-pigeon;*" and often since
then she has been accosted on the street with the
sudden cry : —

"Ah, dear madame, it is you. You are the 'carrier-
pigeon :' may God forever bless you ! "

One young man whom she thus visited had been
married but little over three months when the siege
separated him from his wife; since when, six months
had supervened without his having the least knowledge
of her.

When Mrs. Ward began to read that a son had been
born to him, and that both mother and babe were
doing well, his joy was something beyond description.
He stretched forth his hands, turned pale as death,
then burst into a ringing laugh, sobbing all the while
in deep gasps, "Thank God ! thank God ! "

One very old woman sprang forward with the motion of a girl, and clasped Mrs. Ward to her bosom
when she heard that her husband was alive and well.
And M. Virot, husband of the famous *modiste*, was so
happy at hearing of his wife's welfare, that he pressed
a donation upon Mrs. Ward for the ambulance.

There are many Americans who will remember "old Mother Busque," whose neat little milk-shop in the Rue Michaudière was an American institution in Paris. She was a pale, thin woman, of exceeding kindness of heart. She served her customers with delicious coffee, and chops cooked as only Mother Busque knew how to cook them. Some Americans who were interested sent home for receipts for ginger-bread, pumpkin-pie, mince-pie, molasses-candy, etc., by which receipts Mother Busque soon turned out the real American dishes: her buckwheat-cakes were a marvel, and her shop became the great eating-place for every thing American.

To the poor and the hungry, especially if they were Americans, she gave not only of her wares, but such sums as she could spare besides.

She and her nephew suffered much during the siege. Mrs. Ward, who knew her well and appreciated her, did what she could to make those dark days lighter; and carried her a few beans or a potato now and then, from her own terribly small store, in the hope of keeping her alive. One day, having just come into possession of a little bit of cheese, Mrs. Ward hastened around to Mother Busque, crying out as she entered, —

"I've got something nice for you, mammy!"

The nephew in silence pointed to an inner door; and within lay poor kind Mother Busque, quite dead from starvation. Soon after, on a cold morning, Mrs. Ward in a private carriage, Mr. Huntington the journalist, Mr. Albert Lee Ward, and Mother Busque's nephew followed the poor hearse to the Montmartre

cemetery, where the body of this truly good woman
was laid to rest.

I have seen the little card sent by Mr. Albert Ward
during the siege, to his anxious father and sister Genevieve then in America, dated " Paris, Jan. 27, 1871,"
and marked No. 75. It read, —

BELOVED ONES, — Mother and self quite well. No shells
have yet reached our domicile, and not likely to.

Your loving son and brother,

AL.

and was sent "*par ballon monte*," borne in the little
wind-car out and over Paris ; and, singularly enough,
bears its three distinct postmarks, of Paris, Jan. 27 ;
of London, Feb. 3 ; and of New York, Feb. 17.

Mrs. Ward called on Mrs. Appert one morning, and
found Gen. Appert, Prince Bibesco, and other gentlemen at breakfast, to whom Gen. Appert said as she
came in, —

" Gentlemen, we know we have two true friends
among the Americans, Mrs. and Mr. Ward ; and I am
to tell you " (turning to Mrs. Ward), " from Gen. Tro-
chu, that you are to have the decoration of the Legion
of Honor, and Prince Bibesco is charged with the
order."

Count Clermont Tonerre, *Chef du Cabinet du Mi-
nistère de la Guerre*, said he wished Mr. Ward to have
the cross ; and counselled him to write for it, which
Mr. Ward declined to do.

*La Société des Secours aux Blessés* sent Mrs. Ward
and Mr. Ward a bronze cross with a white ribbon em-
broidered with a red cross, also a letter attesting their

great services; and in 1872 the poet Charles Boissière, president of the Société Philotechnique, wrote
the sonnet to Mrs. Ward, which is prefixed to the
present section of this work. As Gen. Hoffman, in his
able and picturesque account of the siege of Paris,[1]
seems not to have known that Mrs. Ward and her son
were the initiators of the American ambulance enterprise, were faithful and efficient workers from first to
last in its interests, and finally its saviours from total
collapse; and seems also to be wholly uninformed of
Mrs. Ward's unselfish and courageous labors for the
relief of the distressed, as well as of the important
services, both official and voluntary, rendered by Mr.
Ward during the siege, and to which he sacrificed his
health beyond any hope of full recovery; and as in
Dr. Evans's work on the American Ambulance at the
Siege of Paris,—a work voluminous enough to accom-

[1] In examining Gen. Hoffman's account of the American Legation's conduct of affairs during the siege of Paris, I have been painfully surprised to
find grounds for the assertion I have heard from more than one direction, that
the American Legation was a fruitful source of information to the Germans at
Versailles. Notably on p. 205 of " Camp, Court, and Siege," Gen. Hoffman
lightly recounts, that, when at the German outposts, "I met here a young
American, who was living not far from Versailles, and *who was known* to
*Count Bismarck. I gave him a couple of morning papers. That evening
he dined with Bismarck,* and offered to sell him the papers for a quart bottle
of champagne for the big one, and a pint bottle for the little one. Bismarck
offered a quart bottle for both; *but my American* indignantly rejected the
terms. So Bismarck accepted his, and paid the bottle and a half. I record
this as the only diplomatic triumph ever scored against Bismarck."
    At the time and on the very occasion when the Secretary of the United
States Legation gave these "morning papers" to Bismarck's friend, as he thus
publicly avows, the people permitted to leave the besieged city were signing,
by order of Minister Washburne, a paper which forbade the passing of letters,
newspapers, or information of any sort, over the lines, under heavy military
penalty.

modate full particulars, — there is, so far as I could
discover in a necessarily rapid but sincere survey, no
mention whatever of Mrs. Ward, and only a merely
nominal one of Mr. Ward, — it will, I am sure, be admitted that the pages of this little volume are a fitting
place to make good so striking a deficiency.

The Wards live when in London at Corda Lodge,
10 Cavendish Road, St. John's Wood, N. W.   Like
countless other English cottages, Corda Lodge is of
plain and simple construction ; but the arrangements
and effects which depend upon the occupant have
made it a home of art and comfort.   Quiet, informal
habits ; simple furniture ; a few gems among plenty of
good pictures ; music, books, a painting in process
under the mother's hand, a bust being retouched by
the daughter ; political and literary miscellany on the
table of the son ; two wonderfully clever and pretty
little dogs ; a parrot in the garden that never squawks,
but whistles and soliloquizes musically, as becomes a
bird of artistic associations ; a maid with velvety dark
Italian eyes, who comes and goes like a picture carried
by some one else ; a French porter, with hair so duc-
tile-flat he would have been the despair of Traddles,
who is exceedingly courteous to his superiors, but is
overheard indulging in the Flintwinchian propensity
of running up and generally dosing the hapless cook
in the most vindictive manner ; the sound of laughter,
merry and hearty mingling of voices in the chambers
talking back and forth, and from the drawing-room
below ; and, as you enter, a welcome of that frank and
instant sort, such as only the thoroughbred cosmopoli-

tan knows how to make you feel, — these are the spirit and *ensemble* of Corda Lodge ; named Corda for Mrs. Cordelia Sanford, a very dear friend of Miss Ward's, and wife of Col. Milton H. Sanford, the gentleman who first started the notion of taking over American horses to England, to compete in English races, which recently resulted in the brilliant victory won for the American turf by Iroquois.

One very warm day of June, 1881, I was sitting in the drawing-room of Corda Lodge, talking with Miss Genevieve Ward, when I heard a step, light and quick like that of a little girl, coming down the stairs and to the drawing-room door, and looked up to see an old lady come into the room. She stooped slightly, and her hair was gray ; but her motion was that of the freshest youth and unsapped life, and her dark eyes, not large but deep, had the mingled flash and twinkle which we usually see only in the eyes of childhood. She had on her bonnet to go out walking, and lingered only for a few words. But the impression made upon me in those first brief moments, of a nature in which a certain stern Puritan fibre runs like a stem through a moral braid of benignity, energy, and quick broad human warmth, — and all these sparkled over with spontaneous humor, — has deepened with every meeting and conversation, in which I find the charm and depth that was reputed of her conversational powers in her youth.

"If," said the tragedienne to me one day, "if, instead of being left in her youth to drift with her own rich impulses, confused by the multiplicity of her own gifts, my mother had received but half the wise care and training she has given me, she could have splendidly distanced all competitors in any one of the great departments of art or literature."

It is little wonder that her family and intimate friends admire and revere Mrs. Ward as they do; for a heart more young, and a purpose more robust, never in the form of age more calmly smiled at time. Her eye is the quickest to see any thing yet undone for the good or the comfort of those around her, her hand the readiest in the doing of tender and homelike things, and her step the lightest footfall heard in Corda Lodge.

# SONG OF THE SERF.[1]

I KNOW a lofty lady,
  And she is wondrous fair:
She hath wrought my soul to music
  As the leaves are wrought by air;
And, like the air that wakes    ·
  The foliage into play,
She feels no thrill of all she makes
  When she has passed away.

I know a lofty lady
  Who seldom looks on me,
Or, when she smiles, her smile is like
  The moon's upon the sea.
As proudly and serene
  She shines from her domain,
Till my spirit heaves beneath her mien,
  And floods my aching brain.

I know a lofty lady;
  But I would not wake her scorn
By telling all the love I bear.
  For I am lowly born, —
*So* low, and she *so* high;
  And the space between us spread
Makes me but as the weeds that lie
  Beneath her stately tread.

[1] Written to Miss Genevieve Ward, during her visit to Florence, by Buchanan Read.

# III.

ONE of the plainest of babies was the little Genevieve Ward, born on the 27th of the blustering
month of March, on Broadway, New York. She was
a very dark and thin little creature, with a wide mouth,
wrinkled skin, heavy pencilled eyebrows, and thick
black hair.

But a few months wrought a great change, and she
was being carried about from house to house to be
admired; and it was the same in Havana, whither
Mrs. Ward went when Genevieve was nearly two years
old.

Sister Teresa, one of the eighteen nuns of the convent of the Barefooted Carmelites of Santa Teresa, —
the richest cloister in Spanish dominions, — was an
old friend of Mrs. Ward's; and, the fame of baby
Genevieve's beauty having reached the convent, Sister
Teresa begged to be permitted to show the child to
the sisters. So Genevieve and her little brother Robert were placed, like flowers in a basket, in the turn-
wheel chair of the convent, swung within its walls, and
received with tender welcome by the gentle nuns.

Captivated by the fair skin and Oriental eyes of the
children, who were exceedingly unlike, and by their

fearless smiles and prattling graces, the nuns, after
having baptized them in the chapel, — giving to Genevieve the name of Lucia Genoveva Teresa, — made
them presents of rosaries of pearls and gold ; and with
these around their necks the tiny convent guests were
returned to the wicked world, "saved," as the sisters
said, "and sure of everlasting joy ! "

The famous cantatrice Madame Damoreau-Cinti,
then in Cuba, was rehearsing one afternoon in her
own apartments.   Coming to a pause, she was surprised to hear her strains repeated by a sweet childish
voice in an adjoining room.   This continued until the
cantatrice, pleased and curious, crossed the passage,
and, entering Mrs. Ward's apartments, saw a three year
old baby seated in the middle of a bed, with an impassioned expression on her fair little face, and her
mouth still round and open with the last notes.

This pretty episode led to an acquaintance.

"If this goes on," said Madame Damoreau to Mrs.
Ward, "bring her to me by and by, and I will teach
her with pleasure."

When Genevieve had completed her second year,
Mrs. Ward took her to Italy ; and from that time until
she was fifteen, they travelled back and forth from
place to place, from Texas — where her father owned
a great deal of land since lost in the war — to St.
Petersburg.   Her earliest recollections are of Paris,
Rome, and Texas.   The scent of a certain white flower
with a yellow centre (narcissus?) always brings back
to her the very look of the Texan prairies where they
grew.   In her fifth and sixth years she was part of the

time in Texas, studying the piano under a German master, and riding horses, for which she inherited all the family love, and no accident or danger has ever made her fear or distrust them. One day she was riding in company with her father's cousin, Col. George Ward, a West Point officer. Away they went over the Texan prairies, Genevieve on the back of a fiery little mustang. All went well, till they turned homeward; but her horse had the habit, as soon as it saw the stable, of running for it, leaping, hit or miss, over gate, fence, or any obstacle between.

Fortunately the child was thrown just in time to escape being crushed against the heavy beam of the low stable-doorway as the horse went plunging through it to his manger. Genevieve was badly hit in the breast, and picked up insensible; but in the very moment of returning consciousness she besought her cousin to say nothing of the adventure to her parents, as she "liked the little beast too well" to give up riding him.

It was owing to these early sojourns in different countries, flitting from Paris to Italy, from Italy to Cuba, and thence to Paris again, that Genevieve acquired, when so young, not only a knowledge of the French, English, Italian, and Spanish tongues, but an accent in each faultless even in the ears of natives.

Their old family nurse, Madame Cecile Grisel, a Swiss by birth, accompanied them in all their journeyings. She was a large and powerful woman, a Gitana in person and habits, with something of the nature of Torfrida in her proud independence and uncurbed

yet reticent temper. She seemed of no particular
nationality, but compounded of all ; spoke no language
exactly, but used an indescribable *mélange* of variable
*patois* everywhere understood by the body of the people. She was their cook, nurse, courier, interpreter,
confidante, and friend, faithful and capable in all, and,
in their defence from all forms of imposition, equal to
a regiment of Cossacks.

Another faithful servant was Madame Giguit, the
widow of a French physician. She lived in the family
of Mrs. Ward's grandfather, Major Buffington, then
with her mother, Laura Buffington Lee, and lastly with
Mrs. Ward, — a sufficient indication of the nobility of
the service she rendered.

During one of Mrs. Ward's visits to Italy, Genevieve,
then nine years old, was singing Norma by herself in a
garden in Rome. An artist in a neighboring studio,
attracted by the voice, came to his window, and was
surprised to see only a little girl picking violets. After
looking at her a few moments, he asked, "Will you let
me paint you as a little angel?" Genevieve shook
her head promptly in disapproval ; but, giving him a
second look, she added hesitatingly, "Yes, you may —
if you won't put any wings on my back : they are so
ugly except on birds."

He made full-length paintings of her, twice. Her
conversation, showing, as it always did, a quaint blending of direct, almost abrupt, good sense, and sensitive
artistic instinct, tempted him to ask her all sorts of
questions, for the sake of her answers ; and once, when
he asked her if she would have him for her husband

when she grew up, he was plumply rejected in these candid words, —

· "Oh, no, indeed ! You'll be old and wrinkled then, and I like only beautiful people !"

This gentleman was the late talented Marquis of Northampton, then Lord Compton. She was at this time making great progress on the piano, under the tuition of the organist of St. Peter's.

At the age of thirteen, when she was visiting in New York with her mother, she was introduced to Mme. Sontag. The famous songstress looked at the little girl with an expression of reverence.

"*Mein Gott in Himmel !*" she cried, bending over her caressingly, "how beautiful you are ! Will you let me kiss you, my child?"

Genevieve sang to her; and she took at once a warm interest in her future as a singer, advised her as to the right steps and methods, and wrote to Rossini about her; so that when Genevieve in her fifteenth year, and again in Italy, went to Florence to see this great *maestro*, he was so pleased with her beauty, and her noble voice, unformed though it was, he took her musical education under his protection, procured her lessons under Ronzi, then director of the opera in Florence, and at a later date, that he might watch over her progress, he arranged for her to sing to him twice a week, and named her Rossini's "*piccola consolazione.*"

In her sixteenth year Genevieve Ward had grown into a maturity and beauty of the most striking kind, as the bust made of her at this period by Joel T. Hart testifies : no one would naturally suppose it represented the features or expression of a woman under twenty-five.

One day when accompanying her mother on a little journey in the South of Italy, they received much attention from a gentleman, a short time their travelling companion, whom they soon after met again in Nice, where Miss Ward was as much admired and sought for her fine voice, graceful manners, and unusual linguistic accomplishments, as for her beauty; and where he was cordially received by society as the young Russian nobleman, Constantine de Guerbel, bearer, it was reported, of important Russian despatches, and, beyond question, one of the handsomest men in Europe.

He was exceedingly clever, and had the art of impressing himself upon others to precisely the effect and degree that he wished.

He hovered around the beautiful American girl, paying to her and to her mother the most delicate and winning tribute. It was impossible that he should not please ; and he soon made an offer of marriage, by letter. Mrs. Ward consulted with her friends ; and it was decided that letters of investigation should be addressed to Gov. Seymour (of Connecticut), a distant connection of the Wards, who was then United-States minister to Russia.

The replies came that Count and Captain Constantine de Guerbel was a most accomplished member of an old Russian family, influential with the Czar, an officer of the Czarina's guards, and that no unfavorable rumors were connected with his name. Meantime de Guerbel was ardently pressing his suit; and, shortly after the arrival of these fair accounts from Russia, they were married in the American fashion, by civil contract before the consul with witnesses, Constantine especially desiring it out of compliment, as he said, to the nationality of his charming bride.

As there was no Greek Church, either in Nice or Turin, the ceremony which alone could make their marriage binding with him could not be solemnized; and Constantine, with every apparent eagerness, agreed that they should all hasten to Paris, where the Greek ceremony could be performed, and his happiness completed.

Genevieve was too inexperienced to feel any disturbing suspicion of her brilliant and devoted lover: but Mrs. Ward was already tortured with doubts; she had received private intimation that the young Russian needed looking after.

She sought an interview with the Russian ambassador at Turin; but by mistake she was directed to the German ambassador, who, on hearing her account of the affair, assured her that there must be something wrong about the young man, as he could not marry without first having obtained the consent of his superior officer, and without the observance of certain other formalities.

Hastening back to the hotel, Mrs. Ward confronted de Guerbel with indignant reproaches. He faced the matter at first with sóme hardihood, but when Mrs. Ward stopped him with the words, —

"It's too late for all this. I know you now, and you shall never see my daughter again!" he fell into a rage, and treated her rudely.

After this, he avoided Mrs. Ward, but made every opportunity for interviews with Genevieve, and, while expressing great readiness to be bound by the Greek Church rites, endeavored to persuade her that she was quite sufficiently his wife to go away with him until that formality could be observed. Fortunately Genevieve trusted absolutely in her mother, and, though tenderly loving the man to whom she was half-married, would consent to no step not first approved by her.

Foiled by this happy confidence between mother and child, but not in the least abashed, de Guerbel visited the same German ambassador — then acting for the Russian government — who had warned Mrs. Ward of the doubtfulness of the young Russian's proceedings, and in a few moments had so successfully exerted his marvellous personal fascinations that the ambassador became his admiring advocate, and was for the time quite turned from his sympathy with the Wards. And this magic spell was exercised in spite of the ambassador's certain knowledge that some of de Guerbel's pretensions were baseless, notably that of his being intrusted with special despatches; for, had this been true, the ambassador must have been officially notified of it.

With matters in this unsatisfactory state, the two parties set out for Paris. Mrs. Ward, on the truthful plea that water travel made her very ill, insisted on going by land; de Guerbel was equally resolute for a trip by water. The mother and daughter reached Paris first, where they again met with the cantatrice Madame Damoreau, whose singing had been so prettily imitated by the baby Genevieve, in Cuba.

She recalled her promise, and at once received the young girl into her class in the Conservatoire; but, the system being necessarily adapted to a medium grade of talent, requiring years for the completion of its course, Genevieve retired from the class to proceed more rapidly as Mme. Damoreau's private pupil.

Meantime came the season of Lent, during which the Greek Church ceremony could not be performed; and with it the tardy bridegroom, delayed, as he said, by adverse winds and opposing currents.

De Guerbel behaved, however, with so much amiability, and with such an inimitable assumption of being the aggrieved party, that everybody was quite won over to his side, and even Mrs. Ward was influenced, against her well-founded objections, to receive him with something like a return of favor; of all which effect he availed himself to try again, and as vainly as before, to induce Genevieve to go away with him secretly.

Mrs. Ward's youngest son, Robert, the same who was baptized with Genevieve by the Carmelite nuns in the Cuban convent, was staying with his mother and sister in Paris, and used to be even more with the fascinating Russian at his hotel than with Mrs. Ward and Genevieve at theirs; for de Guerbel had done all in his power to attach the handsome and enthusiastic boy to his interests. So it happened that Robert Ward was with de Guerbel in his bedroom one morning, when an officer entered, and arrested him as he lay in bed, — for some offence to the Czar, as it was afterward rumored ; large quantities of blank passports were found in his possession, and he was put beyond the frontier.

Some months of total ignorance as to de Guerbel's whereabouts or movements passed away. Genevieve's spirits, and even her health, had suffered from the strain of a position so anomalous and painful.

While this was the situation in Paris, an old friend of the Wards, M. de Bois le Comte, late French minister to Washington, arrived in Italy on a visit to his daughter, the wife of M. de Soulange, *chargé d'affaires* at Naples. One day, when walking out, M. de Bois le Comte met the Countess Schakoshkine, wife of the Russian ambassador, who, after the usual words of greeting, exclaimed, —

"Wish me joy, for my daughter is going to make a great marriage."

"Indeed ! to whom?"

"To Lieut. de Guerbel."

"Which one?" cried M. de Bois le Comte, electrified.

"To Constantine, of course ; the handsomest and noblest young man in the courts of Europe."

"But Constantine ! why, he is already married !"

"Oh, nothing of the kind," said the countess indignantly. "We know all about that trumped-up story."

"I beg your pardon," persisted de Bois le Comte, very gravely ; "but I, myself, put the young girl — she was Miss Genevieve Ward — into the train, to go to Russia, to look into her husband's affairs."

"It cannot be !" murmured the countess, pale, and deeply disturbed ; "it must be some American trick."

He assured her that it was indeed true, and that the young lady had actually gone with her mother to Russia, to ask the Czar to have the marriage made null and void.

· Countess Schakoshkine hurried to her husband with these terrible tidings ; but, before the latter could reach either the police or Constantine, that dazzling scapegrace was far away in his yacht, leaving a hundred thousand francs of debts behind him.

His personal gifts had served him well ; he had enjoyed the admiration and the confidence of the cleverest and best ; he had been entertained by the royal family : but the *esclandre* was complete ; and another young American girl, lovely and trusting, to whom he had engaged himself in Nice, lay dying for his sake, of a broken heart, in the midst of preparations for her wedding with him.

This at Nice and Naples ; while in Paris, after due waiting, by the advice of our London and Paris ministers, both friends of Mrs. Ward, and of Baron Brunnow, Genevieve, with her mother and brother, had actually set out for Russia in the bitter midwinter cold, to seek justice at the hands of the autocrat.

Papers, letters, and other documents concerning the case had been previously intrusted to a member of our legation, on his representation that he could use them advantageously in seeking Gov. Seymour's and the Czar's interest in Genevieve's claims. Wishing to take these papers to Russia with them, they asked for them back, and were refused; but when Gen. John A. Dix arrived in Paris, his concise message to the gentleman brought back the papers at once.

Being by this partial marriage with de Guerbel put in the singular position of being neither an American nor Russian, Genevieve could not obtain a passport from either the American or Russian legations; and the difficulty was overcome by her going on her brother Robert's passport, he having been made bearer of despatches for the purpose.

The journey was not only attended with great discomfort, but with various kinds of danger. From Konigsberg to Riga they travelled in the intense cold in open boxes on runners, from which they had to change every two hours, so that they barely began to get warm in one of these boxes, before it was necessary to step out into the snow, and climb into another. On the second day after leaving Riga, where they had obtained a carriage, they encountered a long train of sledges laden with iron bars from the immense founderies of Russia. By Russian law a private conveyance has the right of way.

The driver of the first sledge was not on hand: Mrs. Ward's coachman therefore touched the horses with his whip to turn them aside. They reared and backed, and the heavily laden sledge was upset. The serf driver heard the hubbub, and, running up just in time to witness the disaster, flew at Robert Ward, flourishing his whip. Other peasants ran up, and, joining with the sledge-driver, upset the carriage of the Wards. Robert helped up the coachman, and drew a revolver. At this truly critical moment the sergeant of cavalry in command of the sledge-train galloped forward, and cut down the serf driver, and assisted the ladies out of the upset vehicle. The most abject submission, instantly on the sergeant's appearance, fell upon the group of peasants, who fairly tumbled over each other in their eagerness to set the carriage straight and assist the Wards into it.

On reaching St. Petersburg they were most kindly received at the American embassy by Minister Seymour, who already knew not only from themselves, but from Baron Brunnow and the London and Paris ministers, of the conduct of de Guerbel. After consultation, Minister Seymour advised their remaining quiet at the embassy as his guests, and not at once petitioning the Czar. Meantime balls, receptions, and parties should be prepared for Genevieve's introduction to the society of the Russian capital, where her youth, beauty, genius, and noble accomplishments would create for her a public as well as personal sentiment, of great advantage when her real purpose in visiting the city should be developed.

But in the very beginning of this programme a grave difficulty arose.

On hearing the name of Madame Constantine de Guerbel, the chief of police, Gen. Dubbelt, declared there was no such person, and that the lady who had ventured to assume that name must leave Russia within three days.

All was consternation at the embassy ; but then, as always when wisdom, skill, and instant executive power were needed, the mother came forward. Well informed in political affairs, this brave and keen-witted woman knew that Russia, at that date, did not need any more trouble on her hands.

"Come with me," she said to Minister Seymour : "I have something to say to the chief of police."

Minister Seymour went with her, and presented her to Gen. Dubbelt as being with her daughter under his protection. Gen. Dubbelt listened to Mrs. Ward's statement without credence, reiterating that they must leave Russia immediately. Seymour looked exceedingly distressed, feeling that the time was too short for any hopeful action or decision.

"Then," said Mrs. Ward, looking full at Gen. Dubbelt, "it is time for me to say, that, since the simple plea of an unprotected stranger does not avail, I must assure you that this is not what you think. It is a national, an international, affair. My daughter is of an old American family, and has both friends and relatives in positions of influence with our government, who will not be inactive in her behalf. According to American law, she is Madame Constantine de Guerbel, and has an undoubted right to visit St. Petersburg under that name."

The dignity and gravity of Mrs. Ward's words and manner impressed Gen. Dubbelt ; and he made answer, after a few moments' thoughtful silence, that he would think it all over, and see what could be done ; and permission was soon received for Madame Constantine de Guerbel to remain at the embassy.

Soon after, Gen. Sabouroff, brother of the grand chamberlain, gave a grand ball at which Madame de Guerbel appeared. Count Kamaroffski, own cousin of Constantine de Guerbel, was present ; and, pointing her out among the dancers, said to a friend, —

"There is a most wonderful girl here to-night, beautiful and fresh as a damask rose. Where can she have come from? Who can she be?"

The friend, who was informed, replied with a smile, — "Do you not know? She is Madame Constantine de Guerbel!"

"What do you tell me!" cried Kamaroffski, "but Kostia's[1] not married?" and he hurried away from the scene in search of Gen. Daniel de Guerbel, the elder brother of Constantine, to whom, when he had found him, he excitedly exclaimed, —

"Well, have you heard the latest sensation? Kostia's wife — his *wife* — a most beautiful young American girl, is at Sabouroff's ball, turning everybody's head!"

"Pshaw! That's only the hundredth story of the kind!" But the next day Gen. Daniel de Guerbel called at the embassy to inquire into the startling rumors.

Minister Seymour received him, and told him the whole story, and presented him to Mrs. Ward and her daughter. Gen. de Guerbel behaved admirably, expressing to Genevieve his regret that she should have ever met his scapegrace brother, at the same time acknowledging her as his sister-in-law in a very graceful manner.

---

[1] Kostia, familiar diminutive of Constantine.

He did not, however, conceal his hope, that, since it was evident she could neither love nor wish to live with Constantine, she might, for the sake of protecting an old and noble family from public scandal, be induced to forego her original design in coming to Russia. She would certainly receive brilliant offers, and could make a marriage equal to the highest ambition.

But Madame de Guerbel could not consider things in this light. She explained to him that she was a wife in American law; that she and her mother had been abused and maligned by Constantine in the most active, ingenious, and unscrupulous ways. He had everywhere used, and was still using, his irresistible personal fascinations to destroy their claims to consideration. He had avowed that the story of the American marriage ceremony was a pure fabrication; that Mrs. Ward was not even Genevieve's mother, but a clever woman of equivocal social standing, who had secured control of the young girl's fate in order to rise to rank and wealth by means of her great beauty; and that, with this in view, they had planned the bold scheme of the St. Petersburg visit. Thus Gen. de Guerbel could see that it was not only for the sake of having her marriage sanctioned by the Greek Church ceremony that they had come, but because nothing short of that could successfully refute calumnies so artfully and ably disseminated.

The dignity and courage of the young girl charmed Gen. Daniel de Guerbel, who from that moment forbore to press any consideration touching the feelings of his family, and treated Madame de Guerbel and her mother with unvarying kindness and distinction. On one occasion during a grand fête at Pavloffski, the summer residence of the Czar, Madame de Guerbel, leaning on the arm of her brother-in-law Gen. Daniel de Guerbel, passed along the principal promenade in front of the Grand Duke Constantine's party. The grand duchess called the general aside, and asked with much interest, —

"Who is that beautiful girl with you?"

To which he replied so that Genevieve could hear it, "My brother Constantine's wife."

The de Guerbels were originally a noble Swiss family, who went over from Switzerland to Peter the Great; the first of the family being an admiral. Constantine's father was a general aide-de-camp to the late Czar, his uncle Prince Koudascheff was court chamberlain, and he himself an officer in the late Czarina's guards. His mother, the Princess Koudascheff, was the most beautiful woman at the court of Nicholas, where the whole family were in high favor.

It will be seen that patience, courage, and never-failing tact were necessary to the situation in which the Wards were placed, in a strange land with a purpose certain to be felt as at variance with its strictest social precedents and prejudices; and, had these qualities not been possessed in a remarkable degree by every one concerned, the sequel must have been very different.

The weeks flew by. Madame de Guerbel pursued her musical studies with Rubini's nephew, Rubini

Gallinari; her voice, her lovely manners, her exquisitely tasteful simplicity of dress, and the romantic
mystery in which she was involved, made the lovely
young American the talk of the capital; but, so far as
her real object was concerned, things seemed painfully
at a stand-still, when suddenly the court minister, Count
Adlerberg, called on the American minister.

When he was announced, Gov. Seymour with agita-
tion said quickly to Mrs. Ward, —

"Now is your chance. Lay the whole matter
before him."

Count Adlerberg listened to them with attention and
apparent interest, but said nothing to sensibly relieve
their suspense in having taken the initiative step on
which so much must depend. But on a Saturday
soon after Count Adlerberg's visit, an aide-de-camp
was ushered in at the embassy, who approached Mrs.
Ward, and asked, —

"When can Madame Constantine de Guerbel receive Prince Dolgorouki?"

Mrs. Ward observed a change in Minister Seymour's
face : she pointed to her daughter, —

"That is Madame de Guerbel."

Genevieve, instantly conscious by the manner of the
others that the moment was one of great import in her
affairs, cleverly replied, —

"Prince Dolgorouki's hour shall be mine."

As soon as the aide-de-camp was gone they both
said in a breath to Gov. Seymour, —

"We saw how your face changed. What does this
mean?"

"It means that something must indeed be transpiring in your affairs; for Prince Dolgorouki is a very great personage, the nearest to the Czar, and such a thing as his coming here to call on a private individual was never before heard of."

On the next Wednesday, as they sat around the table, Prince Dolgorouki came in. He was a beautiful old man. He walked up to Madame de Guerbel, who had become exceedingly pale, and, laying his hand kindly on her head, said, —

"Well, my little girl, tell me all about it."

They had just received a letter from M. de Bois le Comte, describing Constantine's conduct in Naples, his false engagements to the dying American girl, and to the daughter of Countess Schakoshkine, and of his flight and debts.

"You know of M. de Bois le Comte," said Madame de Guerbel, handing the letter to Prince Dolgorouki. "Will you read this?"

"Yes, he's a sad good-for-nothing," said Prince Dolgorouki, after reading and returning the letter; "and I'm very sorry you ever met him, my little girl; but what is it, the Czar asks, that you now wish to have done?"

"Tell the good Czar," said Madame de Guerbel, with much emotion, "that I wish to have my marriage sanctioned by the Greek Church, so that as a true marriage I may contest it, and obtain a [1] divorce, and be honorably free from this man."

"Well," replied the Prince, smiling very kindly on

[1] All this is in Russian archives.

her, " I will tell the Czar exactly what you say, and
we'll see ; in the mean time have courage."

Their suspense was now the greater for the hopes
of success they could not but feel from Prince Dolgorouki's visit. In a few days he came again, and told
them that the Czar had said it was not in his power,
as head of the Church, to recognize the marriage as it
now stood, nor in his power to dissolve it ; but if she
desired it he would send out a special ukase for Constantine's return to Russia, and insist on the performance of the Greek ceremony.

Madame de Guerbel expressed the deepest gratitude
for the Czar's kindness.

" But when this is done," she added, " I wish it
understood that I will never live with Count de Guerbel. He has endeavored to degrade us in everybody's
eyes ; and I cannot indorse his calumnies by living
with him. Will you tell this to the Czar ? "

Without making any direct reply to this burst of
feeling, Prince Dolgorouki explained to them that
their next step, in the Czar's opinion, was to go to
Warsaw, and there await his majesty's further directions ; and then bade them a kind farewell.

As according to Russian law she would be under
obligation to live with her husband for two years
before seeking a divorce, the Czar's silence relative to
her determination to leave Count de Guerbel at the
altar immediately after the ceremony gave her painful
uncertainty as to the final result of all their trouble.

They lived opposite one side of the palace ; and,
knowing that the Czar and Czarina were about to
leave the city, the anxious girl said, —

" Let's get up early, mother : we may see the departure."

So, looking from their windows early in the morning, they saw the royal family in an open barouche, and the Czar leaning forward to arrange his son's necktie.

At the same moment, as if recollecting that he was near the American embassy, he looked up and saw Genevieve and her mother at their window. He smiled, and waved his hand to them in friendly recognition.

This little omen quieted their fears. " It's all right, I know it, I feel it," they said to each other, and made ready for their journey to Warsaw.

It has been said that Miss Ward gained admission to the Czar, and, throwing herself at his feet, implored him to see her honor vindicated by the Greek Church sanction of her union with de Guerbel. With the exception of the occasion just mentioned, Miss Ward never saw the Czar but once, and that was soon after their arrival in St. Petersburg. They went out walking together, accompanied by their dogs, a King Charles and a Blenheim spaniel. Having heard absurd stories that Russians were hereditary dog-thieves to a man, they were anxious at the notice their pets seemed to attract, particularly at that of a Russian officer driving in a droshky without ornaments or trappings. The horse was jet black, and very handsome ; and the harness as well as the dress of the officer, though simple, were elegant. This officer looked at them in such a way as he drove by, they were quite sure the dogs were the cause of his observation.

Three times they met this droshky, and the last time the officer bowed and smiled from out his muffling furs.

Puzzled and annoyed, they acknowledged his salutation reservedly, but seeing an officer who stood near them uncover with great reverence to the inmate of the droshky, and observing also that several ladies of high position made haste to throw up their ¹veils as he approached, they made inquiry, and, to their confusion, found it was the Czar himself whom they had been regarding as a probable dog-thief!

On arriving in Warsaw, the Wards found that Prince Gortschakoff, brother of the present vice-chancellor, had received full orders from the Czar, and a special ukase had been sent to each Russian ambassador for the apprehension of Constantine de Guerbel.

Meantime a new complication arose in Paris. Madame de Guerbel's father, Col. Ward, had reached that city on his way to them. Soon after being shown to his apartment, he was waited upon by Constantine de Guerbel, who, first expressing in the most graceful terms his joy at meeting the honored father of his beautiful wife, assured him that it was all a misunderstanding, he had been basely misrepresented, and declared himself ready and eager to do any thing a father could ask to prove the sincerity of his assertions, — provided only that Col. Ward would telegraph for Madame de Guerbel to return to Paris, which Col. Ward, quite convinced by and delighted with his son-in-law, forthwith promised to do.

---

¹ In Russia the poor people kneel, wherever they may be, when the Czar appears; and the nobility make profound obeisance, ladies raising their veils.

The very next day Baron Brunnow arrived in Paris, and, calling also on Col. Ward, speedily learned the clever trick of Constantine, and enlightened Col. Ward as to the true character of his fascinating son-in-law. Yet so great had been the impression made by him upon Col. Ward, he was still inclined to think some explanation possible; and, though when a member of the Russian embassy served the imperial ukase upon de Guerbel, he raged, and cursed the Czar and Russia and every thing and body else with violent impartiality, he had the power to induce Col. Ward to fulfil his promise of the previous day, and telegraph to his wife and daughter to come to Paris.

The response signed by Mrs. Ward and Genevieve came as follows : —

"We have passed our word to the Czar : let Constantine obey the Czar also."                      .

Three times Col. Ward was induced to telegraph, but Mrs. Ward held firm. Then Constantine begged Col. Ward to go to Warsaw and see Prince Gortschakoff, and find out if it were the imperial intention to punish Constantine in any way if he obeyed the ukase. If he were not to be punished, Col..Ward was to telegraph for him, and he would come.

Col. Ward hurried off to Warsaw; and, on being assured by Prince Gortschakoff that no orders had been received for Constantine's arrest, he telegraphed to the latter as agreed.

Therefore, on a Saturday when Mrs. Ward and her daughter had been some months in Warsaw, the recreant de Guerbel arrived, and at once sent a note to Madame de Guerbel, in which, for the first time, he called her his wife, and signed himself " your affection-ate husband, Constantine de Guerbel."

He had habitually spoken of her everywhere mock-ingly as " *Miss* Genevieve."

This letter was despatched immediately to the Czar as affording positive proof of the verity of their claims. The next day de Guerbel had a stormy interview with her parents, protesting with astounding effrontery against the proceedings as summary and unfair ; at the same time affecting pleasure at the prospect of meeting his wife again.

In the afternoon he was received by Madame de Guerbel in her mother's presence.

It was a singular interview.

. He approached her with expressions of ardent admi-ration and delight, to which she remained quietly and coldly silent.   At last, subdued in spite of himself, he exclaimed with some chagrin, " But is it not very strange, since you are so cold to me, that you yet desire to marry me ? "

" So far as it has been in your power, you have dragged our names through the mud," she replied. " You shall rehabilitate them ! "

" Well, all right ! " he retorted quickly.   " We shall be very happy.   You are a very beautiful woman. We'll go to my plantations in Little Russia ; and your father can come to see us — not your mother, she's done this !   I have the horses and dogs you like, and you'll be a great card at court."

The wedding had been arranged to take place on the morrow, Monday. Prince Gortschakoff had given directions for the ceremony, and had furnished the usual four groomsmen 'from his own staff, and had given to Madame de Guerbel the Czar's special passport permitting her, as Madame Constantine de Guerbel, to leave Russia with her parents, even in the event of Constantine's not having been found.

In the yard of the hotel where they were staying, their travelling-carriage, strapped with their luggage, stood in readiness for starting the moment they should get back from the ceremony; for, if they had given him any time after that took place, he could, by Russian law, have arrested and locked her up, fed her on bread and water, or beaten her, had he so chosen to do.

On Monday morning as ten o'clock, the hour set for the marriage, drew near, Count de Guerbel called at their hotel to ask if it might be deferred for an hour to make way for a funeral. They assented; and at eleven o'clock, Genevieve, dressed in black silk, with a black lace shawl thrown over her head, accompanied by her parents, entered the Greek cathedral in Warsaw.

The Archbishop Novitzki of Warsaw had received orders to celebrate this marriage. In the vestry, the usual form, pledging that children born of this union should be brought up in the Russo-Greek Church, was signed. The altar was dressed in the middle of the church, which was filled with people. It was a very dark and shadowy interior; from a high window a single veiled ray of sunlight fell, and rested, singularly enough, only upon the bride, leaving the others in more pronounced gloom.

According to the custom, the contracting parties held each a lighted candle. The one held by de Guerbel burned poorly, and was shaking about ; while the one held by Genevieve burned clear and as if in the hand of a statue.

One of the groomsmen whispered to Mrs. Ward, " Why, your daughter is in black, and it looks like a funeral."

" I consider it a funeral," was the mother's reply. The Wards' story had been well noised in Warsaw, during the months of their waiting ; and no one, not even those unprejudiced by Constantine's insinuating slanders, and in sympathy with the trying position of the mother and daughter, had believed that these two American women could get themselves righted thus, alone and in a foreign land. It had been feared that Constantine might, at the last moment, frustrate the Czar's purpose by hiring some one to interrupt the ceremony, in which case it could not have been completed. When this apprehension was hinted to Col. Ward and his son, Col. Ward replied, —

" Well, we are of course nobody in Russia ; but, if Mr. G— tries that, I'll shoot him dead at the altar ! "

" And if father's aim fails, mine shall not ! " added young Robert Ward. " It would be the only way left to avenge my sister."

But in the midst of a stillness so deep it seemed as if the beating of the heart could be heard, the ceremony proceeded to the end. At its close the archbishop came forward, and kindly congratulated the bride. She thanked him in a low voice, and, coldly inclining her head to her husband, took her father's arm; Mrs. Ward stepped to her other side, saluted the groom in the same cold manner, and they moved down the aisle. The crowd of witnesses seemed paralyzed. One of the ladies of the court stepped forward, and whispered to Mrs. Ward, —

" I never thought you could accomplish this : God be praised ! "

They descended the church steps, — Constantine following them as one in a dream, — entered the carriage, and were driven away, while he yet stood on the church steps. And, in less than five minutes after reaching their hotel, they were whirling away to the train, and were out of Russia before the bewildered bridegroom could set about getting a police-warrant to arrest his bride.

Towards the end of their journey *en route* for Milan, they went by night in a diligence down the hill to Trieste. The way was narrow, on one side a deep precipice, and they felt timid.

"But do you go to sleep, dear mother," said they to Mrs. Ward, "and we will watch."

After some time Mrs. Ward waked up to find that the rest were all sleeping, and, on looking out, discovered that they were flying at a mad pace down the mountain, and both driver and leaders were gone.

She roused her husband and Robert, who sprang out, and seized the horses' heads barely in time to stop their plunging headlong over the precipice.

Col. Ward took the missing driver's place, and there was no more sleeping. At the first village they reached, they stopped and waked the people, asked them to search for the poor fellow and horses, who had undoubtedly either been thrown over the abyss, or rolled off in sleep; got new horses and postilion, and drove into Trieste.

When the news of the marriage, and of their immediate flight from Russia, was known in St. Petersburg and Warsaw, and it was seen, that, instead of reigning as a belle in the distinguished circles in which her marriage entitled her to appear, Madame de Guerbel had only sought the single justice of the rehabilitation of her own good name, it was felt that no more than justice had been done, and that her step in coming to St. Petersburg, instead of being unwarranted assurance, had been an act of modesty and heroism.

She never sought for a divorce, because she felt no desire to marry again. She accepted nothing but their friendship from her husband's family, and scorned to make any claims to his estates.

During the year passed in Russia, Madame de Guerbel received eleven offers of marriage, many of them very brilliant; but she was not to be turned from her purpose. She kept a list of her lovers, and when they proved too persistent would turn to it, and ask demurely, —

"Let us see, what number is yours?"

When Constantine de Guerbel was fourteen years of age, his commanding officer said of him, that he had all the vices of a full-grown man, and seemed to know as much. He was so eminently handsome, that the empress made him her page, and a portrait of him hung in the palace.

He bore a remarkable resemblance to the Czar Nicholas, only his complexion and eyes were dark.

When only seventeen years of age, he ran away in a yacht with the wife of Gen. W——, taking goods to the amount of many thousand roubles.

The government, being informed, sent out a steamer and caught him. He was confined in the fortress for three months, but was allowed the society of his friends, and all kinds of luxuries. He seemed always to escape any severe punishment. His personal power with both men and women was something inexplicably great. He was able to embarrass and lethargize the reasoning faculties, while intensifying the emotional. The Saxon minister in Paris, Count de Seebach, who had charge of the Russian Legation, was thoroughly deceived in his favor at the time of his conduct in Paris, and as thoroughly undeceived when heavily cheated by him in some money transactions.

He was a completely dissipated man, and before his thirty-fourth year had lost the use of his legs.

About a year after the flight of the Wards from Russia, a man forced his way into their apartments in the Rue de Rivoli, Paris, during their temporary absence one morning, scared the servants, and opened and ransacked things generally, and went away leaving word that he was Constantine de Guerbel, and should call again that evening.

Mrs. Ward went to her old friend M. de Bois le Comte, and he went with them to the chief of police and then to the Russian minister, to see what could be done. As a result, two gendarmes were placed at the foot of the stairs leading to their apartments; and, when de Guerbel called, he was informed that if he annoyed Madame de Guerbel any more, he would be sent out of France. The next day he sent an *huissier,* commanding her to return to him and live with him as his wife.

But the French court decided the verdict against him on the precedent of a case tried there only the year previous, in which, the contesting parties being both aliens on French soil, neither could be forced by French law to live with the other.

He was told that he must go to Russia if he wished to institute a legal process to oblige her to live with him. This unwelcome advice, together with the prospect of having to pay for the pleasure of annoying his wife, effectually silenced him.

Years later, when Madame de Guerbel was giving singing-lessons in New York, a friend wrote to her from Nice, —

" Who, think you, sits next me at table, but Count Shouvaloff and Daniel de Guerbel? The latter tells me that his brother Constantine died at Pisa."

Of Constantine's four brothers, only one lives. Serge de Guerbel, who was cashiered and entered the ranks as a common soldier, was so brave in the Crimean war that at his death he was re-instated, advanced in rank, and decorated in his coffin.

His sister, a beautiful woman, wife of Gen. Stahl d'Holstein, governor of the eastern frontier of Poland, is living now in St. Petersburg.

# LINES TO GENEVIEVE WARD.

WRITTEN IN FLORENCE.

WITHIN this far Etruscan clime,
　By vine-clad slopes and olive plains,
And round these walls still left by Time,
　The boundaries of his old domains;

Here at the dreamer's golden goal,
　Whose dome o'er winding Arno drops,
Where old Romance still breathes its soul
　Through Poesy's enchanted stops;

Where Art stills holds enchanted state,
　(What though her banner now is furled?)
And keeps within her guarded gate
　The household treasures of the world, —

What joy amid all this to find
　One single bird, or flower, or leaf,
Earth's any simplest show designed
　For pleasure, what though frail or brief, —

If but that leaf or bird or flower
　Were wafted from the western strand,
To breathe into one happy hour
　The freshness of my native land!

That joy is mine: the bird I hear,
　The flower is blooming near me now, —
The leaf that some great bard might wear
　In triumph on his sacred brow.

For, lady, while thy voice and face
　Make thee the Tuscan's loveliest guest,
Within this old romantic space
　Breathes all the freshness of the West.

　　　　　　　　BUCHANAN READ.

# IV.

THE romantic story of her Russian journey and marriage had reached Italy, where, on her return to Milan, Madame de Guerbel was warmly received by many new as well as old friends. It was· known that she had not only defeated the schemes of a very bad man, at the same time winning the esteem and friendship of his proud family, but that in rejecting every right to which her marriage entitled her, and retaining only her vindicated name, she had given indubitable proofs of her noble singleness of purpose.

Col. Ward, having seen them comfortably settled, returned to his business affairs in America; and Madame de Guerbel resumed her singing lessons under the direction of San Giovanni (the same who sang in America with Madame Alboni): she also took up drawing and painting, and in all these arts made such rapid and certain progress, that Mrs. Ward, in the somewhat unusual despair of having to choose between a diversity of splendid aptitudes, brought the matter to a point by telling her daughter that she might take a week to choose which study she would devote herself to.

"For you can only do one of these arts justice," said she. "Therefore make a choice, and avoid my mistake. I have absolutely excelled in nothing, because I was allowed to dabble in all."

At the end of the week Madame de Guerbel said, "Music!"

The Italian poet Uberti, of Milan, an original bristling all over with characteristics, a mad republican, whose brain, seething with revolutionary instincts, germinated class and national imbroglios; a man also, or perhaps one should say consequently, of kind heart and mild personal impulses, and a vivid interpreter of artistic ideals, — was engaged by Mrs. Ward to teach Madame de Guerbel the physical part of declamation.

"I remember Signor Uberti so well," said Miss Ward to me. "He used to prepare little pieces, idyls, expressly for me. He would first read them to me, teaching me the proper look and gesture by his own manner. Then I studied these scenes by myself; and at lesson-time he would read them, leaving the look and gesture for me to do. One of these scenes was about a corsair, who sails away from his lady-love: a terrible storm comes up, and his little boat is wrecked; he is washed ashore, and she is in utter despair. I used to get along all right, until the moment when her woe and horror are to be expressed in one frenzied exclamation: here I disappointed him, until one day he stamped his foot, and glared at me; and perfectly desperate, the blood rushing into my cheeks and the tears into my eyes, I wrung my hands, and made the very cry he wanted. 'Ah!' he cried excitedly, 'that's the corsair's bride indeed.'"

By this method he taught her three operas, " Norma," "Lucia," and "Semiramide." At last, one day, he came to Mrs. Ward, and said, —

" My dear madame, I am not a thief, and I can't go on taking money for giving lessons to your daughter. I can't teach her; no use ! " and was going away as abruptly as he had come.

But Mrs. Ward detained him, exclaiming indignantly, " Why, — why can't you teach her? I know she's bright ! "

" Bright ! " cried the old poet, turning back, a tinge of chagrin blending with his genial smile. "Ah, yes, madame ! she is bright, — so bright that Uberti can teach her nothing more. She already interprets for herself better than any one can teach her."

She was now just entering her eighteenth year, and her determination to go upon the operatic stage met with some opposition from her family, who still thought a divorce should be procured, that the way to a happy and fitting marriage might be open ; but Madame de Guerbel was permanently impressed against the marriage idea ; and Gen. John A. Dix, Baron Brunnow, and other friends, wisely supported her in her choice of a career for which her superb physical vitality and her rich mental and vocal endowments so well qualified her.

It was at this date, that the Archduke Maximilian saw her one day at the opera. He gazed at her for a long time as if no one else were visible ; and, when he passed her in going out, he bowed with an air of genuine homage, murmuring, —

"*Belle comme un ange!*"

Wishing to secure a first-class, unprepossessed, critical judgment, to determine whether or not she could
become a really great singer,· she talked the matter
over with her mother, and it was agreed to put it tc
the test in a novel manner.

Madame de Guerbel dressed herself in the gar-
ments of a poor girl of the people, and completed the
disguise with a pair of ugly green goggles. Mrs. Ward
made herself up as an old family-servant, and they
went to the rooms of the great Lamperti.

As they entered the master's *salon*, a class was still in
attendance ; and Lamperti in a rage was banging about,
striking his piano with such force that the wires rattled
and twanged, and shaking his pupils by the shoulders.

These proceedings filled the young girl with apprehension : but there was no turning back ; Lamperti had
seen her, and was already advancing.

"Well !" said he, pausing directly in front of her,
"who are you? and what do you want?"

Preserving an easy exterior, she looked straight
through her green goggles, and replied, — speaking
artfully in Italian *patois*, —

" I can't pay you well, signor ; but I must learn to
sing, to sing perfectly, so as to support myself.    I
*know* I can *act!*"    ·

"So, so?" said Lamperti.  "Who's with you?  You
did not come alone?"

" No, signor :  my nurse is waiting for me."

" Why do you wear these things?  Take them off"
(pointing to the goggles).

"No, I cannot do that yet, — not till my eyes are stronger."

Lamperti turned over some music, and gave her a little air to sing. When she had finished, he stood a few moments looking at her in silence, and then said, very brusquely, —

"Yes, you can sing: I'll teach you;" then, after another pause, he asked, "What part of Italy do you come from?"

"Ah!" she replied quickly, "you know by my accent, but of course study will correct that."

He perceived that his question was parried, but did not for a moment imagine her *patois* was not genuine, or that it was with American wit he was fencing.

She came regularly to her lessons, dressed in her plain, poor clothes, with scrupulous care, and attended by her nurse. Her progress pleased him; but she mystified him, especially when she insisted on paying the full tuition.

"I thought you could not pay so much," said he.

"I must pay you," she replied, "because, when my tuition is completed, I must belong to myself: I must be free to make my own terms for my voice."

She was exceedingly diligent, and this had made him habitually milder to her than to his other pupils; but one day, when he was particularly irritable, he struck her suddenly across one hand with the pencil he held. He had been accustomed to see his pupils, some of them girls from old and noble families, cringe and weep under his severity, with no notion of resenting it. Madame de Guerbel rose from the piano, drew herself up, and looked at him quietly, with an air almost of contempt. He bowed, — for him an apology, — and said, in a low voice, with a satirical yet respectful accent, "You are a lady !"

The lesson went on without further comment. The next time she appeared without the goggles, but otherwise maintained to the last the *rôle* she had assumed. Whether her eyes enforced the mute rebuke of the previous lesson, or not, Lamperti never again treated her uncivilly.

The next year, in the midst of her brilliant successes as the cantatrice Madame Guerrabella, — for into this flowing word the Italians had changed the name de Guerbel, — she met her old master, and told him the whole story of the way in which she had made sure of his unbiased opinion of her powers, and obtained the benefit of his instruction.

"I always knew there was something," said Lemperti ; "but you kept it perfectly, — only once when I lost my temper."

"Ah ! you were very wrong, because I did not deserve it," she said quickly. "I was careful : I obeyed you exactly."

"Then, suppose you *had* deserved it " —

"Not even then : you forget that I am an American."

She sang first in Milan, at La Scala, in "Lucrezia Borgia." When the curtain rose, and Madame Guerrabella came forward, to the surprise of every one not in a certain high box, she was greeted with hisses. She walked to the footlights, and, folding her arms, looked up to the box calmly in silence.

She had finished her vocal studies with Lamperti, unquestionably the greatest teacher in Milan. Her former teacher, San Giovanni, meanly irritated by this, had taken this box, and, with the party hired to assist in the expression of his spleen, now stood up, and redoubled the hissing. The audience seemed spellbound, until an old gentleman in the pit sprang up and exclaimed, " For shame ! " The audience emphatically applauded this protest. With a fine color in her cheeks, Madame Guerrabella slowly unfolded her arms, and began to sing in a silence stirred by no other sound until, with the closing cadences, the audience broke into enthusiastic cheers, and the high box was discovered to be vacant.

But her real *début* was at Bergamo, where, during the carnival season, her appearance in Pacini's opera, "Stella di Napoli," inspired one of the most splendid popular ovations ever tendered to a young artiste ; and on her return to Milan she was engaged on proud terms to sing in the chief theatre at Trieste. On reaching Venice, *en route* for Trieste, she was met at the railway-station by a secretary of the director with whom her contract was made, who said, in a matter-of-course way, —

" We have, after all, been unable to secure the theatre at Trieste ; but we hope you will kindly open the opera here in Venice instead."

The Italians of the kingdom of Venice were at that time very generally united in their determination not to support, either opera or other gayeties, because of the unhappy situation of the Venetians under Austrian dominion. Madame Guerrabella, perceiving at once what lay behind so considerable and abrupt an altera- tion, and that she was to be used to trick the Vene- tians out of their patriotic resolutions, referred to her contract, and replied, —

" My engagement is for Trieste, and I must decline to alter it."

" Do not refuse, madame," said the secretary, losing his studied indifference, "but accept upon your own terms: make them what you will, and I am author- ized to assure you that the governor of Venice, Count Toggenburg, will come himself, and ratify any proposi- tion you may choose to make."

" My engagement is for Trieste," she repeated ; and, as no train was returning immediately to Milan, she went to a hotel.

The persistent secretary soon followed, and, on being admitted, again urged her with every variety of argument, and splendor of inducement, to reconsider her decision.

Madame Guerrabella, who loved Italy and the Ital- ians, remained firm ; and the secretary, losing temper, manners, and honesty also, seized the contract lying on the table at her side, and tore it in pieces, exclaim- ing, —

" You will be obliged to sing, madame, — you shall see ! "

" Very well," said Madame Guerrabella : " I will do what I am obliged to."

At four o'clock the next morning, hours before the secretary had any idea of calling on her, she felt "obliged" to take the train for Milan, where she was received with acclamation. Count Correr, of the Committee of Venetian Emigration, together with Count Meroner, called to thank her, in the name of the committee, for her brave fidelity to Italy's cause, and made her citizen of Venice. Messages of affection and gratitude flowed in from known and unknown sources during the day: she received an immediate engagement to sing at the Carcano (Milan); and, on the night of her appearance, her reception was not unlike such as a liberated people might render to a queen-liberator.

Her success was complete. She continued at La Scala, and at concerts in Milan and Paris. At one of these, given by the Baroness Von Meyendorff, the Parisian critic Jules le Comte wrote: "A lady whose real name has been Italianized into Guerrabella was heard with great surprise and delight. She is remarkably beautiful; and, when we could no longer listen to her exquisite voice, our eyes were still bounden subjects to her beauty."

During this visit to Paris she went to see her kind friend and protector Rossini, who was at his country-seat in Passy. She rehearsed "Semiramide," he accompanying her; and at the close, when she timidly asked the great composer, —

"Could I venture at the Italiens?" he kissed her forehead, and, taking both her hands in his, replied, —

"Tell them Rossini says no one can sing it better, and no one look it so well, *regina mia !*"

This was the last farewell: she never saw him again. Her *début* at the Italiens was successful. She sang in "Semiramide," "Il Trovatore," "I Puritani," " Lucrezia Borgia," Elvira in " Don Giovanni," in " La Traviata," etc.; and the French and Italian journals wrote glowing encomiums. Once, when she was singing as Elvira with Mario in Paris, he retreated before her instead of attacking her. "Why did you do that?" asked Frezzolini; to which Mario replied, —

"I could not stand the fire of Elvira's beautiful, angry eyes."

She studied with Moderati (now in New York, and the delight of the Coney-Islanders), and Mrs. Ward took her to Madame Persiani. The latter, having listened to the young girl's singing, — who had given months of practice to acquiring the famous Persiani trill, — exclaimed, —

"She is already perfect. I can teach her nothing. I can only give her my *fioraturas!* "

Rubini-Gallinari passed the same verdict. Madame Persiani, who was not only a great artiste, but a woman of lovely character, became Madame Guerrabella's firm friend, and one of the most true and discriminating admirers of her talents.

In July of the same year, of Col. Ward's appointment to the United States Consulate at Bristol, England, "The London Illustrated Times" announced that, —

"Madame Guerrabella, a young singer, with an admirable soprano and a perfect method, has just arrived, and is to sing at Madame Sala's[1] private concert with the 'English skylark,' Miss Louisa Pyne, and other eminent vocalists."

[1] George Augustus Sala's mother.

She sang also at the Queen's Concert Rooms for the benefit of the Warwick-street schools, but she made no public *début* in England at this time : her singing, however, made a permanent impression of the highest character on the comparatively few who heard her.

The next season she was again singing in the capitals of Italy and France, and with such triumph that the entire Continental press found space to signally comment thereon. Her pronunciation of the Italian and French languages was such that she was claimed in both countries as a native, and her American origin scouted as a fiction.

The French and Italian art-critics, Fabien, Fitali, Chadeuil, and Fiorentino, the great critic of the world at that time, and regarded as the scourge of artists, all wrote sparkling leaders concerning her grand and versatile powers. "The London Spectator" then took up the cry : —

"The French and Italian papers are very demonstrative in favor of Signora Guerrabella. It is only two years since she began her career ; and already she is an established favorite, and is greeted with the utmost enthusiasm wherever she makes her appearance. At Turin and Milan she has recently been the reigning star ; and the reports of her success have been followed by substantial offers of engagements from several quarters, — among others, from Constantinople. The Italian critics say that since the days of the great Pasta, no one has equalled La Guerrabella ; and the praise they lavish on her voice, acting, and personal beauty, is confirmed by private letters."

Poets wrote verses to her. Artists followed her

from place to place, petitioning to be allowed to paint her; sculptors prayed for the honor of modelling her arm and hand, which were especially and classically beautiful.

One fine model of her hand,[1] in marble, rests on a little velvet cushion in a cabinet at Corda Lodge.

One of the most unique personal tributes received by her at this period was paid by the venerable Maximilian, Count de Waldeck, painter to Napoleon the Great. He told her that seeing and listening to her recalled to his memory the ancient ode to Sappho, which he had not seen for over fifty years. Seating himself at her writing-desk, he wrote as follows: —

### SAPHO.

*(Reproduit de souvenir.)*

Written at the age of one hundred and eight by Count Waldeck, who was painter to the first Napoleon; after not having seen the verse for over fifty years.

Heureux qui près de toi pour toi seul soupire
Qui jouit du plaisir de t'entendre parler
Qui te vois quelquefois doucement lui sourire
Les dieux dans ce bonheur peuvent ils m'égaler?
Je suis heureux enfin sitôt que je te vois
Et dans les doux transports où s'égare mon âme
Je ne saurais trouver de langue ni de voix
Un nuage confus se repand sur ma vue
Je tremble et je me sens interdite éperdue
Et puis partout mon corps une brulant flâmme!
Je circule, et je tombe en de douces langueurs
Un frisson me saisit! je tremble! je me meurs!

And, handing it to her, said, —

[1] By Joel T. Hart, the American sculptor, who did her bust.

"Here it is as you make me recollect it." When he went away he took the paper with him, and copied the verse correctly from the printed text, on its other side, as follows : —

*(D'après le texte retrouvé.)*

Heureux ! qui près de toi, pour toi seule soupire
Qui jouit du plaisir de t'entendre parler ;
Qui te vois quelquefois doucement lui sourire
Les Dieux dans son bonheur peuvent ils l'égaler ?
Je sens de veine en veine une subtile flamme
Courir partout mon corps, sitôt que je te vois ;
Et dans les doux transports, où s'égare mon âme,
Je ne saurais trouver de langue ni de voix.
Un nuage confus se répand sur ma vue ;
Je ne sens plus ; je tombe en de douces langueurs
Un frisson me saisit . . . je tremble . . . je me meurs ![1]

MAX., CTE. DE WALDEK.
À MADEMOISELLE WARD.

and returned it to her. A graceful attention from an artist *one hundred and eight* years old !

In autumn of the same year, an English journal published in Bristol relates that —

"Madame Guerrabella of Milan, being at Clifton on a visit, and feeling her heart glow within her as she heard of the sympathy displayed by the English in behalf of beautiful but too-long-oppressed Italy, generously offered an evening's services in aid of the fund being raised for the illustrious liberator; and the proffered favor being gladly accepted by the friends of Italian independence resident here, other aid was asked and secured, and the concert was arranged."

[1] Traduit et défiguré par Oussius. Louis XV. possédait l'original, trés ancien, écrit sans distinction de vers, sans ponctuation, et sans ortographie.

"The London Chronicle" commented thereon, —

"The Bristol papers are emphatic in reporting the appearance of Mlle. de Guerrabella at a concert in aid of the Garibaldi Fund in Bristol. The occasion was indeed remarkable. Mlle. Guerrabella is by birth an American: she is barely twenty years of age, but she has already achieved for herself a distinguished name as a prima donna at La Scala. Speaking of her performance, a local paper says: 'She sang in a manner we have never heard surpassed; and her vocalization quite equalled Sontag or Alboni. Her voice is much more extensive than either, including three octaves ; and her constant flights, 'do, re, mi,' above the lines, took her audience manifestly by surprise, and proved her to be of that rare class now to be found — a pure soprano.

"She has been distinguished in Italy, not only for her noble singing, but for her determined refusal to sing under the patronage of the Austrian government at Venice, which resorted to curious manœuvres for the purpose of securing the young singer."

Soon after the Garibaldi concert, which, as will be shortly seen, was not the only favor Madame Guerrabella showed to the Italian patriot, she left England to fulfil a three-months' winter engagement at Bucharest. While sailing down the Danube on the way thither, she noticed that the captain of the steamer, an Englishman and an exceedingly kind and courteous gentleman, seemed abstracted and depressed. At the outset of the trip she had also observed five Hungarians on deck, who had after a little time disappeared. When the voyage was about half accomplished, she made an opportunity to approach the captain.

"You are very anxious about something," said she. "Is it about the journey? If it is any thing about which a woman could help you, I should like to try."

The captain smiled with a momentary look of relief; but his kind face quickly clouded over as he replied, —

"I have five Hungarian noblemen on board : you observed them, of course, by their costume. They wished to join Garibaldi. But we shall have to change steamers to go over the rapids at the next frontier town, my steamer is so large, and the water is unfortunately very low."

"I noticed the gentlemen," said she; "but I haven't seen them for some little time."

"Yes, that's it. They have got to go back, poor fellows; and I had agreed to do my best to pass them off as stokers. They are down in the stokers' hole now."

"Oh! I don't think they'll have to do that," said Madame Guerrabella. "Just wait, and let me talk with my brother."

It was her young brother, Robert Ward;[1] and he had his despatch-bearer's passport. When they had consulted together she returned to the captain, and said quickly, —

"We've arranged it : we'll take them over with us."

"Impossible! It can't be done with so many," exclaimed the captain.

"Yes, it can," cried she. "Listen. They are my brothers: they are all going with me on our American passport. Go tell them. Send them to me."

---

[1] This young man, who possessed rare talents for music, painting, and drawing, died of consumption at Algiers, whither Mrs. Ward went with him in tenacious but vain hopes of his recovery.

The captain shook his head, but carried her message to the refugees in the stokers' hole, who received it with delight, and, resuming their Austrian costumes, rushed up on deck to thank their young benefactress.

She at once unfolded her plan.

"I am your sick sister," said she; "and you are my brothers. I will teach you a few phrases and exclamations in English. Don't utter a word beyond — especially not a word of German, which would betray us all."

She then gave them a little well-adapted lesson in English, training them sharply; and after having assisted them with cloaks, hats, and other items of disguise, put a copy of "Bradshaw" in the hand of one, and taking the arm of two of the five Hungarians began walking the deck slowly, as if feeble and weary.

"Now," said she, as they approached the frontier town, "your rôle is solely this, — devotion to and anxiety for me; and attend to the cue I have given you. If you don't, you'll get your sister into prison!"

The officials came on board at the town. The ruse worked smoothly for the disembarkation: but when they were told it would be some hours before the other boat started, Madame Guerrabella feared the delay might prove a strain too great, and asked permission to go at once on board with her brothers, who did not speak German; as she felt so ill, she desired rest in her cabin. She asked this favor with so winning a mixture of timidity, respect, and physical weakness, that it was granted with little hesitation. The officer, who examined her passport just before the boat started, could make nothing of it, and seemed inclined to quiz her : she answered him, however, in bad German, with a sweet and sad expression, so that he went away quite satisfied.

When they started, it appeared that the new captain was more suspicious ; and Madame Guerrabella, instantly perceiving this, feigned an access of illness, and went down into the ladies' cabin, peevishly demanding the attendance of all her brothers.

"This captain suspects," said she in a low voice. "I must keep you here as long as I can ; but I shall have to flirt with him desperately before we are through with this affair ! "

Presently they went again on deck, Madame Guerrabella supported by two of her brothers, another held her wraps, the rest were occupied with pillows, cushions, and books. She affected to be too ill and nervous to be left for a moment.

As they passed the captain, who was observing them very gravely, Madame Guerrabella almost imperceptibly paused, and threw him a glance, half petulant and languid, yet altogether of such dazzling sort, that the good captain was lost from that moment.

" How very beautiful your sister is ! " he said the next day to one of the Hungarians, who in his whole-souled admiration and gratitude was near to spoiling all by a fluent panegyric in German. A darting rebuke in the eye of Madame Guerrabella warned him just in time to enable him, with an awkward " Um — um " and a deep bow, to turn away. She took care, with never-failing vigilance, to keep them employed with

her countless invalid wants, and to be always scolding
and fretting at them semi-affectionately when any one,
especially the captain, was near; contriving at the same
time to thoroughly captivate and bewilder that gentleman with her beauty, her smiles, and her prettily-
murmured bad German, to such an extent that it was
a wonder they ever, by his guidance, came straight to
Giurgevo.

As they approached this point, she saw they could
ill repress their joy: so she had them all into the cabin
once more, and lectured them soundly on the too little
care they were taking of their faces.

"It is not yet Bucharest," said she. "Here you've
been looking solemn as Moses all the way, worried to
death for your sister; and now all at once you look as
if you had come in sight of the promised land! All
will be lost if you are so careless now. Besides, the
captain is a clever fellow; and I'm not at all sure what
he thinks, or means to do."

But, whatever the captain may have thought, he
parted with them kindly at Giurgevo, having evidently
felt that any oversight on his part had been fully com-
pensated by the fascinating presence of the beautiful
invalid.

From Giurgevo they went by diligence to Bucharest.
There they were safe; and there the five Hungarians
fell on their knees in the street, and thanked her, cov-
ering her hands with tears and kisses of gratitude.
Had this daring ruse failed, all would have been sent
to prison.

As soon as Mrs. Ward learned of this incident, she

wrote to her daughter, charging her to be sure, if trouble came of it, to let the Hungarian government know that the blood of the "good king Matthias Corvinus" flowed in her veins.

In explanation of this : One day, years ago, Hon. Tom Corwin called on Mrs. Ward, then in Washington, and claimed relationship with her through the Wards, with whose ancestors the Curwens, or Corwins, of Salem, Mass., had intermarried. During his call Mr. Corwin related that he had just been visited by two Hungarian officers, who had been sent by the Hungarian people to offer him the crown of Hungary. It seems, that, in the archives of Hungary, there had been found some letters addressed to their beloved sovereign, Matthias Corvinus, known in history as the "good king Matthias," by a cousin of his majesty's, who settled, under the name Curwen,[1] in America, and founded a family there.

The Hungarians felt, that, in their heavy struggle with Austria, a leader of the house of the "good king Matthias" would indeed be of happiest augury for their cause ; and the discovery of these letters resulted in the invitation to Mr. Corwin, as the most distinguished living descendant of the Corwin — and Ward — intermarriage, to assume the crown of Hungary.

The offer was twice made, and twice declined ; Tom Corwin deeming it to be the greater honor and nearer duty to be the head of his party in America.

Hence Mrs. Ward's advice to her daughter, in case

---

[1] The Curwen house is still standing in Salem, Mass., or was within a few years.

the latter should find herself in any danger from her unselfish services to the Hungarian refugees fleeing to the service of the flag of Garibaldi.

Of her visit to Bucharest, a letter, dated there and published in a New York journal, said, —

" We have been more than fortunate this winter in securing for our opera the beautiful and gifted prima donna, La Guerrabella. She made her *début* in the 'Traviata,' and is thought by all here to be the best Traviata ever seen. Her success was great. The reigning prince evinced his admiration by applauding loudly; and the audience, by their repeated calls, proved her to be already their favorite. She next sang 'Elvira,' and such a furore is rare : she was called out innumerable times, and covered with flowers. The cavatina was a perfect triumph; and after the last trio the public did not seem to know how to express sufficient admiration. She is a splendid dramatic singer and actress. She next sang 'Rosina,' in the 'Barber,' and had another ovation ; such a lovely, piquant, Spanish girl is difficult to find. She introduced Rode's air, which was given most exquisitely; and when you heard her singing like a bird, and recalled the powerful, thrilling notes of 'Elvira,' you could hardly believe it was the same person. In a few days we shall have her in the 'Torquato Tasso.' The great point of this young lady's acting (for she is very young) is, you never see *her*, but the character she personifies. Her voice is essentially dramatic, and is of such a rich, telling character that in the *ensembles* it towers over all. I have not said much of La Guerrabella's beauty, for I believe she enjoys a European reputation. I will only add that her smile is something wonderful. It fascinates, it sinks into your heart, and makes you feel joyful; and long after she has passed from your sight you feel it still. She sings in five languages, is highly accomplished in painting, and, withal, is simple and unaffected in manner, always doing some kind and generous act. May Heaven bless her wherever she goes ! "

From Bucharest she returned to England, and studied oratorio with the great oratorio-contralto, Mrs. Martha Groom, who had been a *protégée* of Mrs. Siddons. Mrs. Groom, like all Miss Ward's teachers, was delighted with the earnestness of her pupil, who studied with an industry only the best health could have sustained. At the close of her lessons Mrs. Groom presented Madame Guerrabella with a lock of hair she had received from Mrs. Siddons, who had clipped it herself from among her soft white locks.

The next year Madame Guerrabella's *début* in English opera was made at the seventh Philharmonic concert of the summer season. The programme comprised Beethoven's symphony "Eroica," and Mendelssohn's in A, known as the Italian; together with concertos, overtures, and vocal music, admirably selected. Professor Sterndale Bennett conducted; and in the audience sat the venerable Ignace Moscheles, friend and contemporary of Haydn, Beethoven, Mozart, Hummel, Weber, and Spohr, most of whom had composed musical works expressly for the Philharmonic Society, then in its forty-ninth year of well-merited success and fame.

"The vocal music was specially interesting," said a leading journal the next morning, "inasmuch as it introduced to the London public a prima donna of great Continental celebrity, — Signora Guerrabella, who sang the beautiful aria 'Qui la voce' from the 'Puritani' with undeniable grandeur of style and rare command of vocal resources. . Her voice is remarkable for its power, and her feeling and expression are eminently dramatic. In quality, this lady's voice reminded us very much of Grisi's in her palmy days, whilst her execution is equally true and facile. A more successful *début* has rarely been made in this country."

Three days later she sang in St. James Hall, at the, annual grand concert of Mrs. Anderson, pianiste to the Queen and teacher of the royal children, and a classic performer of great ability. Her concerts were always considered the most brilliant and fashionable events of the London musical season; and on this occasion, besides her own superb pianistic display, there was singing by Giuglini, Mlle. Titjens, the well-remembered and beloved Parepa, and Madame Guerrabella, the *débutante* who was heartily applauded and encored.

Then came the eighth and last Philharmonic concert of the season, at which the aged Moscheles appeared as a performer. His playing "of his own concerto in G-minor" (said George Augustus Sala in "The London Illustrated News"), "one of his finest works, was followed by acclamation and thunders of applause from every part of the crowded room, prolonged several minutes after he left the orchestra, and quite exciting enough to have overpowered one less accustomed to public enthusiasms. . . . Rossini's great air from 'Semiramide,' ' Bel-raggio,' was superbly sung by Signora Guerrabella, the young singer newly arrived in England, who made a furore at the last Philharmonic, a still greater furore at Madame Anderson's annual, and last night materially increased her growing fame. She is an embodiment of the most charming characteristics of literature and art, speaks nearly as many languages as Pic de la Mirandole or Cardinal Mezzofanti ; and, besides singing, draws, paints, sculpts, and dances with genuine merit, and is the young and beautiful heroine of one of the strangest and most romantic dramas of real life which could be matched anywhere in ' Les Mystères de la Russie.' "

The " Daily News," " Morning Chronicle," and other journals were equally cordial in her praise. All opinions concurred as to her great dramatic talent ; and her familiarity with the stage was assumed and asserted as a fact accounting for her astonishing ease and grace, though she had in reality never played, except in opera. The press were not alone in their courteous welcome to the young *débutante*. Letters of congratulation and invitation poured in, and she was invited to sing at the Duchess of Northumberland's and at other distinguished private gatherings. At one of these, Hogarth, the secretary of the Philharmonic Society, and the operatic critic of the day, was asked for his opinion.

" What do I think of her? " he repeated. " Why, what every one must think. It's not enough to call her the new Grisi ; for she is a better singer, and far more beautiful, than Grisi ! "

She *débuted* in Royal English Opera at Covent-Garden Theatre, as Maid Marian in Mac Farren's opera of " Robin Hood." Her success was established as an opera-singer of the very first quality and rank. Her audiences, both select and large, applauded her to the echo ; and the daily press continued to indorse the public verdict. Even "The Athenæum," notably incapable of enthusiasm, remarked that "a lady more elegant in appearance than Madame Guerrabella is not on the London stage. Her voice is a soprano of sufficient compass and power. She sings with refinement and feeling, and appears to have been trained according to good methods. Her action, too, is graceful and sufficient."

It was noticed, that she played the famous heroine Maid Marian, not as it had been conceived in previous representations, as a country girl, ill qualified to rouse men to admiration and consistent action; but as a lady of rank and station, filled to inspire the ambitious love of Robin Hood.

This quality of interpreting character on the highest plane compatible with the artistic limitations of the case has, from first to last, admirably distinguished Miss Ward's dramatic conceptions: as in her latest achievement as the Marquise de Mohrivart, in "Forget Me Not," we have not the vulgarly artful, quasi-pretty, and wholly *blasé* woman of the *demi-monde;* but the far more subtle interpretation of a thoroughly and skilfully bad woman, who is at the same time a perfect lady, graceful, finished, and dangerous not by ill-concealed vice, but by penetrating charm and refinement.

Her impersonation of Maid Marian brought her many private congratulations.

Mrs. Hogarth, wife of the critic, wrote : —

"I must congratulate you on your splendid success last evening. Mrs. Dickens and Helen were with me ; and we really did not know which most to admire, your lovely singing, energetic graceful acting, or *yourself.* We were talking it over at breakfast this morning, and saying what a splendid career is before you, and how many parts you will do beautifully."

A word came from Mrs. Cropsey, wife of the American painter : —

"I have heard of your great success in 'Robin Hood,' from several friends who were present. They say you were splendid. ·I am so delighted when any of our countrywomen or men make a success in London I "

The celebrated actress Fanny Stirling, who taught Madame Guerrabella in "Maritana," wrote cordial congratulations, closing with : —

"You are on the high road to fame and fortune, all that makes life pleasant. There is but little left to do for you by any one, or by yours truly."

The following : —

"DEAR FRIEND, — I cannot allow many hours to transpire before I congratulate you on your great and decided success last night. Our party — six in number — expressed the same opinion. Indeed, I do not see how it could be otherwise. I had *all* my eyes open, both mentally and bodily, as well as my *opera-glass,* so as to *find fault* — but all in vain. All you have now to do, is to go on and *prosper,* which is a sure *result.*"

was written by W. J. Newton, miniature-painter to the Queen. He presented his painting in ivory, of the "Coronation," to the National Gallery.

At this period her father's consulate at Bristol expired, and "The Daily News " said, —

"The retiring consul leaves Bristol with the regret and the respect, not only of his own countrymen, but of the numerous friends to whom he has endeared himself by his courtesy and gentlemanly bearing, — his tact and ability in the discharge of duties often delicate and difficult. During Col. Ward's residence among us, the American trade has increased to an unusual extent. In the nine months ending September last, the value of cargoes imported at Bristol has exceeded four and one-half millions; the number of vessels has been 105, and the tonnage 67,026. The total imports of the Bristol Channel for the same period reached to $5,266,680; the vessels were 406, and the tonnage 261,999. As many as 6,500 seamen have come under the care of the consulate, and we do not recall. an instance where the interference of the magistrates has been necessary. To Col. Ward, indeed, belongs the credit of having raised the consulate to a position of dignity, efficiency, and importance, which has surprised every one acquainted with the circumstances. He will especially be missed by the poor seamen in sickness or distress, to whose needs and wishes he was ever kind and attentive ; paying for them always at the general hospital instead of giving, as he might, a subscription only for their admission as patients."

Madame Guerrabella's success as Maid Marian was followed by an equal triumph in "Maritana." During the holidays she sang in "The Messiah," at Exeter Hall, appearing for the first time in oratorio. The hall was hung in black for the death of the Prince Consort, and the audience was composed of the most distinguished people then in London.

Moved deeply by the solemnity of the occasion, Madame Guerrabella sang "I rejoice greatly" with such passionate animation and power, her thrilled audience gave way before it, and she was tumultuously encored, being the first artiste who ever received that honor in singing this part at Exeter Hall, where encores are never allowed.

"The News," "Musical World," "Chronicle," "Telegraph," "Post"—all the journals—were unanimous and emphatic in their praise. She appeared in Dublin, Manchester, and the provinces during the winter and ensuing spring, singing with increasing favor in "Lucrezia Borgia," "Semiramide," and "Maritana;" her "Qui la voce" and "Bel raggio" especially drawing unbounded approval from all critics and all publics.

There is abundant testimony that there was a peculiar quality in her singing, apart from all that art could lend it, that endued it with certain singular and special memorable effects. Madame Colmache, with whose both strong and brilliant pen the readers of French and English journals have been familiar for the last quarter of a century, tells me that these effects were produced in people of the most differing temperaments and occupations. Only recently a gentleman of studious and æsthetic tastes, a listener to Grisi, Parepa, Alboni, and Lind, asked Madame Colmache if she knew what had become of a Madame Guerrabella who used to sing in London.

"Of all the fine singing I have ever heard," said he, "the tones of that lady's voice remain with me."

To their surprise, a blunt Scotch body turned from the trellis he was repairing, to say, —

"Ay, ay, thet wer' a braw lass, wi' a voice to mak' a mon greet, — the bonniest i' the warld!"

In March, on the splendid occasion of the celebration of the fiftieth season of the Philharmonic Society, she sang Mozart's "Parto ma tu ben mio," and during April appeared in Dublin as Mary Wolf in Balfe's opera, "The Puritan's Daughter," and in May *débuted* in Italian opera at her Majesty's Theatre as Elvira in Bellini's famous "Puritani."

The great tenor Giuglini was announced as the Arturo of this occasion. At the moment when Madame Guerrabella was to appear on the stage as Elvira, she was seen, just within the wing, to press her hands upon her temples with a gesture almost of despair.

She had only at that moment been told that Giuglini was ill, and that Signor Bettini, with whom she had never sung or rehearsed, would take his place.

" That she appeared at all under such circumstances," said a London journal, "was most creditable. As the opera proceeded, she had again and again to prompt Bettini, who honorably did his best in the trying situation into which he had been thrust at a moment's notice. The manner in which she passed through this ordeal elicited hearty approbation from all quarters, and proved that her qualifications for the lyric drama are too great for opposition, if intended, or misfortune, if unavoidable, to exclude her from her place."

It was generally rumored, and credited, that the sudden indisposition of Giuglini was due to an ungenerous attempt on the part of persons envious of Madame Guerrabella's unexampled successes. The attempt, if such it was, served chiefly to render conspicuous the invincible energy and courage of the young singer. Giuglini soon afterward sang with her in " Don Pasquale," in which, as also in " Les Huguenots" and "Robert le Diable," she was received with enthusiasm.

At last, wearing her double crown of English and Continental laurels, she went to be heard in her native land. She opened the autumn season in the Academy of Music in New York, — her native city, — singing with Brignoli in "La Traviata," "Figlia del Reggimento," "Il Trovatore," "Ballo in Maschera," and "Favorita." Then to Philadelphia, and again in the spring at the Academy in New York, singing with marvellous success in "Ione" and "Semiramide."

From New York Madame Guerrabella went to Cuba, to inaugurate the grand opera house at Matanzas, and afterwards appear for the season at the Tacon in Havana. Her repertoire during this season included Norma, Martha, Traviata, Leonora, Amelia, Elvira, etc. She repeated her European triumphs, and was honored with the diploma of the Philharmonic Society of Cuba.

But the unsparing service to which she subjected her vocal powers, singing always four, often five, evenings in a week for three months, through the exacting warmth of Cuban weather, proved too much.

Suddenly, in the midst of her prosperous engagements, her voice gave way, failing abruptly and totally.

No trouble, admitting of an active course, could have been half so terrible as this passive submission to silence, for this buoyant young singer.

In alluding to this heavy period, she speaks with strong feeling of the kindness of her personal friends; of Mrs. Cordelia Sanford, — to whose nephew George Riddle is chiefly due the nobly adequate representation of Greek tragedy, lately witnessed at Cambridge, Mass. ; and whose niece, Kate Field, has lent lustre to journalism and the platform, — of this lady, for whom Corda Lodge was named, Miss Ward says, —

"She is my dear friend of long years standing, abiding by me in all my fortunes, changelessly true. And Mr. Sanford is just the same : when he was here in England, all who were interested in the turf, from the Prince of Wales down, were delighted with him. Aunt Corda was both a pupil and friend of Miss Charlotte Cushman, who taught her singing; and she, in her turn, for friendship's sake, taught Adelaide Phillips when she was a little girl. Her continual and incessant kindness to me, her sweet patience under illness, her generous, unvarying, faithful belief in me, have been an immense inspiration and moral support. Whenever I have needed help of any kind, they have helped me. They are always doing good in the quietest but most real and untiring way; helpers of artists, of any one who needed help."

She speaks also with great warmth of Mrs. Reed of New York City ; of Miss Field ; Miss Adelaide Phillips, whose friendship commenced in Cuba when they sung there, and has always been of the most devoted kind ; of Mrs. Mygatt ; and of many others, whose faithful sympathy has been her chief encouragement.

Her fine bust of Milton H. Sanford (now in bronze), intended for Mrs. Sanford as a souvenir of grateful affection, was finished by Miss Ward in July of the present year, 1881 ; and Miss Ward, wrapped in a huge blue apron, seated before it giving the finishing touches, was a charming illustration of artistic animation.

# À MISS GENEVIEVE WARD,

*Tragédienne,*

QUI M'AVAIT OFFERT DE LIRE QUELQUES VERS DE
MA COMPOSITION.

MES vers paraîtront beaux sortant de votre bouche ;
    Comme accompagnement vous leur prêtez vos yeux,
Le son de votre voix dont le charme nous touche,
    Et cet accent du cœur qui rend tout merveilleux !

Grâce à votre talent tout est délicieux ;
    Que le regard soit vif, tendre, dur ou farouche ;
    S'il se voile un instant, c'est l'astre qui se couche,
Et resplendit encor dans l'ocean des cieux !

Tout paraît noble et beau quand vous versez la flamme
Que Dieu comme un foyer mit au fond de votre âme,
    Afin de la transmettre à tout le genre humain !
Heureux cent fois l'auteur de votre choix, madame,
Vous êtes grande artiste et séduisante femme,
    Et c'est vous qui de l'art nous tracez le chemin !

CHARLES BOISSIÈRE.

20 NOVEMBRE, 1876.

## V.

WITH the loss of her voice, came other cares. Her father had sustained severe reverses owing to the war, by which they were reduced almost to poverty. He was out of health, and mentally depressed.

Knowing that she could never again take a first place in song, it was not in her nature to accept a second. Adelaide Phillips, divining what the high-spirited girl was suffering, advised her to go on the stage, reminding her of the verdict universally passed on her dramatic powers in opera. Acting on this truly friendly and wise advice, Madame Guerrabella went to see Lester Wallack, who gave her a difficult scene in "Wonder," saying that when she had learned it he would hear her recite it.

She tried to learn it, but she was doubting and despondent.

"I had never believed," said Miss Ward to me, "that I could commit long parts to memory. I had never known any thing by heart, except the Lord's Prayer and Pope's Universal Prayer, — to me the most beautiful ever written, though many people seemed to think it wicked. These I did know, because we used to repeat them *en famille*, when we were children, at the breakfast-table. Well, I gave it up, and did not return to Mr. Wallack; and in this way, by not hearing me at once in any thing to which I felt equal, and so giving me a little encouragement, he unconsciously kept me for the time from the stage."

At this time Miss Ward was in the country, endeavoring to recruit her health, and recover her voice; but finding it did not return sufficiently, and discovering a capacity for imparting readily what she knew, she accepted a position to give singing-lessons at Miss Haines's well-known Twentieth-street School in New York City. The senior teacher, Mrs. Seguin, was exceedingly kind to Madame Guerrabella, as was also Miss Haines and her partner Mlle. de Janon, who now carries on the school since the death of Miss Haines.

She succeeded well in these labors; but it was, after all, a forced and not a natural occupation, and wore terribly on her nerves.

Miss Phillips again came to the rescue, and insisted on her quitting this drudgery, and trying the stage. Mrs. Sanford, the Doremuses, Kate Field, and others coincided warmly in this counsel; and at last, plucking up heart, Madame Guerrabella went to see Miss Fanny Morant, and engaged her services as dramatic teacher; at the same time continuing her own singing-lessons during the day, and keeping house for her father (Mrs. Ward was then in Paris), and sitting up nights to learn what was assigned to her.

"I began with Fazio," says Miss Ward; "and I did actually commit fifty lines at a sitting. When I announced this feat to Adelaide, she thought it marvellous, and predicted that I would soon learn thoroughly two hundred lines a day. A good actor must be letter perfect, but cramming is injurious to the artist. My method of study has always been to acquire the whole, so that from the whole the part may appear. Then I play a part by myself till I conquer it. If a part conquers me, — and I've often been overcome by the feeling I was portraying, — I continue to play it until I have conquered it. I have never deviated from this.

"For Shakespeare, I have always read every thing that great German and other critics have· said, and thereafter formed my own views, and acted solely thereon ; for, chiefly in consequence of my interest in and attendance on opera, I have never seen any of the great dramatic *rôles* played until after I had created and played them for myself; although I have been repeatedly spoken of as Ristori's pupil, and she herself calls me '*La mia Doppia*' (my double)."

After six months of study, together with teaching at Miss Haines's, and housekeeping for her father, — rising at six A.M., and not retiring till midnight, — she was prepared with the following fourteen parts : —

Lady Macbeth.
Beatrice. ("Much Ado.")
Hermione. (" Winter's Tale.")
Portia.
Lucrezia Borgia.
Adrienne Lecouvreur.
Medea.
Actress of Padua.

Peg Woffington.
Juliana (in " Honeymoon ").
Madame Fontange. ("Plot and Passion.")
Queen Catherine.
Sheep in Wolf's Clothing.
Bianca (in " Fazio ").

Miss Morant arranged a private rehearsal at Bry-ant's Opera House, kindly lent by Mr. Bryant for the purpose, and invited about forty persons, friends and critical judges, to listen to Miss Ward in scenes from " Macbeth," and Julia in " The Hunchback." Her little audience expressed warm admiration and flatter-ing prophecies, but nothing came of it : she received absolutely no encouragement to attempt the stage in America.

With spirits hardly recovered from the terrible blow of the loss of her glorious voice, further saddened by the failing health of her beloved father, by the wear-ing labor of an uncongenial occupation, and the fatigue of severe dramatic studies pursued in hours due to sleep, — to be confronted with " *nil* " as the result, was a test for the bravest fibre.

She met the crisis as conquering spirits do.   Deter-mined, that, if there was no room for her on the stage of her native land, she would seek recognition else-where, she resumed her maiden name, — having just learned of the death of Count de Guerbel, — and went to England, where her first step was to give private rehearsals to one auditor, a critic of the first quality, — her mother.

Satisfied that her daughter was right, Mrs. Ward set about finding or making the proper opening for her dramatic career.   She went to the managers of the best London theatres, and to dramatic agents, and stated her daughter's qualifications.

Each had all the stars he wanted ; tragedy was out of fashion : one replied, " What we want nowadays are young girls with fine physical development."

Mrs. Ward next went, accompanied by her daughter, to Mr. Bateman of the Lyceum; and he, after hearing the case, wished Miss Ward to begin at the lowest rung of the ladder, and play comedy. Miss Ward laughed.

"That laugh is worth a thousand pounds," said Mr. Bateman, "but as a comedienne!"

"I'm a tragedienne," said Miss Ward, "and not a novice. I have sung in opera, and have always been *attrice cantante*, and I mean within three years to be an acknowledged great tragedienne."

Mr. Bateman laughed this time.

But Miss Ward laughed best and last, when, in less than three years after that time, "The Manchester Guardian" pronounced her "the best Lady Macbeth since Mrs. Siddons"!

One day when Mrs. Ward, who had, all to no purpose, tried every manager of any standing in London, was considering, nothing daunted, what to do next, a visitor was announced, — the Hon. Lewis Wingfield, brother of the Earl of Powerscourt, a cultivated English gentleman, a very clever playwright, and the gentleman mentioned by Mrs. Ward as having been of first-rate helpfulness upon the American ambulance during the siege of Paris.

"Do you remember, when we were in Paris, how I used to talk to you about the beautiful daughter I had in America?" said Mrs. Ward.

"Perfectly well," replied Mr. Wingfield; "and I hear from Palgrave Simpson that she's not only a beauty, but a fine actress."

"So she is; but what's the use, when she can't get a hearing?" and Mrs. Ward related the story of her rebuffs; and Miss Ward, entering from the garden, was presented to Mr. Wingfield, who assured them, that, notwithstanding the ill success thus far attending their efforts, he felt sure she could obtain a fair and proper hearing, and he would see what he could do.

He went with them to the Haymarket, where he had himself formerly played, Miss Kate Field accompanying them. Mr. Chippendale, the stage manager, was exceedingly genial until Mr. Wingfield led up to the real object of the visit, and proposed that Mr. Chippendale should hear Miss Ward rehearse.

Mr. Chippendale instantly lost his genial gracefulness, moved uneasily about on his chair; had no doubt of the lady's qualification, but he had so very little time, and could not see of what use it could be —

"But," persisted Mr. Wingfield, very much astonished, "she wants a hearing: she can't possibly make an engagement without being accorded the opportunity to manifest her claims."

"Certainly, certainly," the manager agreed; "but there is no vacancy at the Haymarket now; and while I do not, I assure you, entertain the least doubt of Miss Ward's qualifications, as there could be no immeate purpose served," etc.

"Do not be discouraged," said Mr. Wingfield, turning to Miss Ward. "It shall not be said, if I can prevent it, that you could not get a hearing in England, — a courtesy due to any aspirant anywhere."

He was as good as his word. "Determined that

the prominent London critics should hear the talented American," said Miss Kate Field, who was there, and knew all about it, " Mr. Wingfield invited them to meet her at the charming studio adjoining his house in Maida Vale. The critics assembled, and partook of a delicious breakfast : and then Miss Ward went through a trying ordeal ; she recited from Lady Macbeth. Her sleep-walking scene was the best I had ever witnessed, Ristori's excepted ; and Ristori has since seen and applauded it."

The critics were taken by surprise ; and within a few days Mr. Wingfield was able to give Miss Ward a batch of letters which, when viewed as the deliberate expression of the effect produced by her acting, — without stage support, and previous to a dramatic *début*, — upon stage-worn critics not her. personal friends, are certainly remarkable, and must have given more than pleasure to Miss Ward.

The critic of "The Hour" wrote : —

"DEAR WINGFIELD, — Miss Ward has unquestionably a large share of dramatic power. I do not altogether like her rendering of Lady Macbeth, but that may be prejudice. She possesses both force and pathos, has a good stage face and figure, and makes her points carefully and effectively. In a part where she could take her own line, without running against foregone conclusions of her audience, she might be expected to make a decided success."

The dramatic critic of "The Echo," after thanking Mr. Wingfield for the opportunity of witnessing Miss Ward's acting, wrote : —

"It struck me as a decidedly interesting performance, --

interesting for the cultivation of its style, and for a most unusual command of gesture.  She seems specially to have studied balance and harmony of movement.  To pass an opinion upon her dramatic prospects, upon one performance under circumstances necessarily so trying, would be difficult; but I think she would quickly take her place above most of the actresses now on the stage."

"Of the genuineness of Miss Ward's qualifications for melodrama [wrote the critic of "The Morning Post"], there can not, in my opinion, be any doubt.  With ample store of passion for that particular province of art, she unites grace of fancy and poetic fervor of sentiment.  Her voice is bright and sympathetic; and her action — wholly free from the vulgar vice of redundancy — is, to my thinking, exceedingly picturesque and impressive.  She is perfect mistress of her text; and her general manner strikes me as being very ladylike and unaffected, invariably bespeaking that valuable quality known as stage-repose, which, intimating in the actress complete acquaintance with the range of her powers, 'begets a smoothness' in her performance, and enables her to achieve the highest amount of effect at the smallest possible cost of effort.  These and other merits, combined with her manifest personal advantages, fairly entitle her to success.  Such, at least, is my judgment, after carefully observing her acting.  Perhaps I should add, that, not having the pleasure of knowing Miss Ward, my opinion, be its value what it may, is at all events unswayed by considerations of friendship."

To these, Mr. Wingfield added a word of his own as dramatic critic of "The Globe :" —

"I think, dear Miss Ward, that your reading of Lady Macbeth showed marked intelligence of a very high order, combined with unusual command of gesture and picturesque movement; I think that you possess a fine presence and sonorous voice, very well adapted to the higher walks of serious drama, and that when opportunity offers you will take your stand among the small group of our best English actresses."

As a result of this timely and most perfectly performed kindness on Mr. Wingfield's part, Miss Ward was able, after a delay of some months, to arrange with Mr. E. English, of English's Dramatic Agency, to make her *début* as Lady Macbeth in the grand Shakspearian revival at the Theatre Royal, Manchester, Oct. 1, 1873.

George Augustus Sala, one of the first and firmest of her London friends; Mr. Wingfield, one of her wisest friends; Tom Taylor, the famous playwright; and Wilkie Collins, — had told Mrs. Ward that two favorable·lines on Miss Ward's performance, in "The Manchester Guardian," would make her.

Mrs. Ward was supposed to be in Paris, on the night of Miss Ward's *début*; but she crossed the Channel without notifying anybody, and, reaching Manchester just in time, slipped quietly into the theatre, took a seat in the back part of the pit, and watched the play through with probably the most critical pair of eyes there.[1]

When it was over, she went with others to the tragedienne's dressing-room. The latter's maid thought it was Mrs. Ward's ghost, and was exceedingly scared; but Miss Ward said, without any expression of surprise, "Well, mother, was it good?"

"Some of it, very," was the reply. Mrs. Ward then

---

[1] An envious attempt was made to disconcert her, by leaving out the table on which the candle is to be set in the sleep-walking scene. She saw this just at the moment of going on, and exclaimed, in despair, "Oh! what shall I do?"—"You can drop it," was the taunting reply; but, seeing a three-legged stool in the wing, she quickly placed it where the table should have been, and was just out of sight in time as the curtain rose.

pointed out to her certain blemishes, Miss Ward's after-avoidance of which was observed and praised by the critics.

Of course everybody was interested to see "The Manchester Guardian" next day; where, instead of the "two favorable lines" on which her case could stand, was found a column of noble, critical recognition : —

"Miss Ward is to be congratulated on a self-control and a thoroughness in the work of rehearsal which form a phenomenon in themselves. Perfect ease, and a most scrupulously exact knowledge of her part, must be conceded to the *débutante*. . . . She has a voice of great power; and it may be presumed that she is indebted, for some of her skill in managing it, to her training as a singer. She has, besides, a good accent and a fluent utterance; her features are expressive; and she gesticulates with ease and grace. . . . In her murderous exhortations to Macbeth, she was savage and soothing by turns; and thus, as it were, made the one manner serve to show the other in stronger relief. The burst almost of invective, —

> ' What beast was it then
> That made you break this enterprise to me! '

was all the more terrible because of the womanly softness of the utterances immediately preceding it. Her hissing whispers, again, in the scene following the murder, made a similarly effective contrast with the full-toned horror of Macbeth's, —

> ' I have done the deed! '

"This scene was, indeed, admirably rendered throughout. Artistic perception of light and shade marked the whole of the performance, which, from first to last, was as well received by a large and discriminating audience as even the actress herself could have wished."

The "Examiner," "Courier," and other journals,

spoke to the same effect; and private congratulations
flowed in. One hearty little note said, —

> "Just a few lines, dear friend, in a great hurry. I saw 'The
> Guardian,' and am delighted. Wrote of your success to
> America. Hurrah! Yours sincerely,
>
> CARL ROSA."

After playing Lady Macbeth for several weeks, Miss
Ward next essayed Queen Constance, in "King John,"
with like results. Charles Sever, whose articles over
the signature of "An Old Play-goer" were esteemed
among the ablest dramatic criticisms of the day, wrote
in "The Manchester Examiner and Times : " —

> "It is obvious that Miss Ward is endowed with great men-
> tal powers, to which high culture has imparted a refinement
> now somewhat rare on the stage.
>
> "Her perceptive powers enable her to seize and appreciate
> the most subtle phases of passion and sentiment; and her pol-
> ished — I may venture to say, almost faultless — elocution, and
> forcible dramatic expression, to deliver the text so as fully to
> realize her conception. Her by-play, too, is equally intelligent,
> expressive, and illustrative of the stage business in which she
> is taking no actual part, and which always shows the true artist
> as much as the more distinct efforts. Her dying scene, as
> Queen Constance, in 'King John,' is one of the finest pieces of
> tragic pathos now on the stage, or within my recollection."

But the harvest she reaped was solely of laurels;
Mr. English having stipulated in advance that the
entire proceeds of her labors must be paid to him in
return for securing her the opportunity of a first
appearance. For the sake of this opportunity, Miss
Ward accepted these preposterous terms, before beginning her engagement, which, as a dramatic *début* in

Shakspearian *rôles*, was an almost unprecedented triumph. Mr. English had the hardihood to exact his Shylock's bargain to the full, and, after its termination, was quite ready with further offers of service.

She *débuted* in Dublin, Nov. 17, 1873, in the English version of Victor Hugo's "Lucrezia Borgia;" and the critics praised her warmly. "The Irish Times" said, —

"An imposing presence, a distinguished bearing, a musical and sympathetic voice, excellent elocutionary powers; fine features, mobile and expressive, capable of at once depicting intense passion or deep pathos, — with such advantages as these, it can easily be understood that Miss Ward's representation of the character of Lucrezia Borgia was very impressive, and highly successful: she worked out the dramatist's conception with consummate ability."

And "The Dublin Daily Express" thought that she "manifested, all through, a depth and intensity of feeling, an earnestness of expression and action, fully equal to Mlle. Beatrice or Miss Bateman, and little inferior to Ristori."

Among the kind things said of her labors at this time, a most peculiar compliment was paid her acting as Lucrezia, at Newcastle-upon-Tyne. A man in the audience, who was very much intoxicated, began by applauding her with offensive frequency and abruptness, but gradually became silent till, suddenly clinching his hands in his hair, he cried out in in a very different and startling tone, —

"By God! that woman makes me sober!"

Of her playing as Adrienne Lecouvreur, "The Irish Times" said, —

"Of the acting of Miss Genevieve Ward, the gifted American tragedienne who has been with us the past week, we could hardly speak too highly. In the many scenes which call for the exercise of the power of representing the extremes of passion, she has proved herself fully able to impersonate the agony of grief, the expression of offended and rejected love, and the rapid transitions of that mysterious and unanalyzable feeling, which mixes itself in nearly every transaction of human life."

The "Journal" and "Mail" spoke at length to the same effect; and "The Irish Echo" compared her Medea favorably with that of Ristori's recent performance at the same theatre in the same *rôle*. "The Times" said, "Miss Ward's Medea rose to the highest level of histrionic art;" and "The Mail" thought "her acting in the last scene faultless and singularly striking."

She appeared as Thisbe in Victor Hugo's "Actress of Padua," successfully; and as Medea, in Hull, she won great triumphs.

All this victory in the provinces, however, meant nothing previous to a London verdict; and her friend George Augustus Sala wrote the following letter to Mr. Chatterton, manager of the Adelphi : —

68 THISTLE GROVE, BROMPTON,
March 10, 1874.

MY DEAR CHATTERTON, — I venture to write to you as strongly as ever I am able, in the hope that I may interest you (managerially, now you have taken the Adelphi really in hand) on behalf of my friend Miss Genevieve Ward. This lady has been, I believe, already made known to you; but she is anxious that I should personally place her views before you, since I have known her from her girlhood, and should be thoroughly acquainted with her dramatic capacity. She was at the outset of her career a prima donna, and as such has appeared with applause in all the great opera-houses of England, the Continent, and America, and in our own Exeter Hall oratorios.

Subsequently she studied sedulously for the stage, and recently has made very successful appearances in Dublin, Manchester, Hull, etc., in tragic parts such as Lucrezia Borgia, Adrienne Lecouvreur, Lady Macbeth, etc. She is an intimate friend of Ristori, and, for the matter of that, could play as well in Italian, French, or Spanish, as in English; but this is beside the point.

Tragedy is now her forte; and for this she has an admirable countenance, figure, and bearing.

Still I think there is likewise a genuine vein of comedy in her, and that under Adelphi influences there is all the making of a first-rate melodramatic actress in her, of the calibre of Miss Kelley and Mrs. Yates, whom I can just remember, but whom you perhaps cannot recollect at all. Besides this, she is a thoroughly intelligent, accomplished woman, who has seen the world, and mingled in it, in every phase, — an artist, a linguist, a musician. She wants a *working début*, that she may let you and the public know of what stuff she is made. If you can do any thing practical to meet her views, you will place me under a real obligation to you.

The immediate result of this letter was the engagement of Miss Ward to play at the Adelphi, as Unarita in "The Prayer in the Storm," a melodrama originally called the "The Sea of Ice." This play was booked for a fortnight as a stop-gap; but Miss Ward's inimitable Unarita kept it on the stage before crowded houses for six months, and the critics had not written with such warmth and unanimity for many a day. She was pronounced fully equal to Madame Celeste, who had in the first instance made the part famous. "The Mayfair" said it had —

"But one word of praise, and that is for Miss Ward, whose skilful acting saves from utter condemnation a drama not worth redemption."

Besides the congratulations of her English friends, she received in pleasant letters from America — among others a very kind one from her old friends of the Haines School, Anne Seguin, and Mlle. Janon — proofs that many in her native land rejoiced in her hardly-earned triumphs. Her valued and valuable friend Hon. Lewis Wingfield wrote, —

"I congratulate you on your notices. Out of seven that I have seen, all are favorable, — a very unusual thing in London ! The result is, that Chatterton will of course want to make a fixture of you."

Miss Ward's pay for having made such a success of a piece intended only for a stop-gap was not increased.

In October, 1874, she played successfully at the Crystal Palace, as Julia in Sheridan Knowles's "Hunchback." Meantime the press began to comment earnestly on the fact that such an artist as Miss Ward was compelled, in order to secure a foothold on the London stage, to accept parts so in every way inferior to her capacity. Of her expected advent at Drury Lane, "The Era" said, —

"We see that Miss Genevieve Ward, who has been playing with great success in London in the regular drama, is to appear at Drury Lane on the 15th of February, 1875, as Rebecca, in the grand spectacular drama of 'Ivanhoe.' The character is admirably suited to the lady; her strongly defined Asiatic features, graceful action, and splendid diction, all promising to render her impersonation the perfect realization of Scott's ideal.   There is no actress on the English or American stage, at present, whose talents and accomplishments warrant so wide a range of parts as this actress can undertake.   Her tragic powers are of the highest order, as was shown by her Lady Macbeth and Lucrezia Borgia, in Manchester and Dublin; and in high comedy she has few rivals.   No better evidence of versatility can be adduced than her resuscitation of the old worn-out melodrama, 'The Sea of Ice,' at the Adelphi, and which, owing to her remarkable impersonation, had a six-months prosperous run during a period of unexampled theatrical dulness.   She accepted the part to obtain an appearance in London, and rendered it so profitable, that the management with difficulty consented to her playing high-comedy parts at the afternoon performances at the Crystal Palace."

Great praise, seasoned with some carping, accompanied her acting as " Rebecca," concerning which Mr. Wingfield wrote : —

"I called in at the Arundel, late, to hear how the performance had gone, and was glad to find a satisfactory verdict from all the critics present. They are, by education, a phlegmatic set; but said your performance was very striking indeed, picturesque, better than Miss Neilson's; that where you erred was always on the right side, — I mean, in avoiding clap-trap and rant, — which, from so cold-blooded a set, is no inconsiderable compliment."

She was warmly received in Newcastle, where she played at the Tyne Theatre.   At Dundee she made her first appearance in May, as the Countess Thecla, in Mr. Wingfield's play, "Despite the World."   The story concerns the court and period of Frederick the Great, "and was written," says Miss Kate Field, "at

Ristori's suggestion. When Miss Ward expressed a wish for something new, the great Italian recommended one of her pieces, ' *Cuore ed Arte,*' — 'Heart and Art.' Finding the Italian play utterly unmanageable in English, Mr. Wingfield, to whom the task of adaptation had been assigned, turned to the Italian novel on which 'Heart and Art' was founded, and evolved an infinitely better comedy-drama."

Miss Ward's impersonation of Sappho, in Mr. W. G. Wills's play of that name, received the highest encomium. She played this in Dublin, and also appeared as Portia, and as Pauline in "The Lady of Lyons," and in "Lucrezia Borgia;" and on the night of June 18, 1875, she played Medea, and the two last acts of "The Merchant of Venice," in honor of the American Rifle Team, at the Gaiety, Dublin.

" As the Americans entered the theatre, the orchestra played 'Hail Columbia;' and Miss Ward, dressed in a complete ancient Irish costume of white, robe and mantle, trimmed with green and gold, with tiara, brooch and armlets complete, and having in her hand the wand and ring which Moore has rendered famous," recited the poetical address composed by Dr. S. D. Elrington for the occasion : —

"Robed as Hibernia's daughter, lo ! I stand,
Like you, a guest in dear old Ireland.
Ye riflemen, by favor of our guns,
Columbia's daughter hails Columbia's sons.
Had I ten thousand hands, with all I'd meet ye,
Had I ten thousand tongues, with welcome greet ye ;
Though time and space may seem to interpose,
And 'twixt our shores a cruel ocean flows,

With magic wand I touch the electric springs;
An instant a responsive answer brings,
Which proves, however distant be each land,
Both nations are united heart and hand.
Our sires, by famine and by wrongs opprest,
Found ever shelter in the glorious West;
And in their children's hearts left still enshrined
The love of home, that distance could not blind.
Then, by their honored ashes, by their graves,
We greet you brothers from across the waves, —
Brothers in blood, as well as hearts and speech,
Brought here together by our favorite *leech.*
Welcome, then welcome; and a happy time,
Marred by no weeping from our tearful clime,
We wish propitious skies; yet still we deem
The reigning favorite, the rifle *team.*
Come to our feast; with love our hearts are full;
The fatted calf we'll kill, — it is a bull.
Soon, when arrayed in contest, you may try
The metal of that bull, — but mind his eye.
Ye strive in friendship; if you win, you'll meet
No heartier cheering than from those you beat.
And, if your brothers win, you won't despair !
You still have left a younger brother's share.
Ireland, in either case, is doubly blest:
She wins the most, in losing to her guest.
Oh, may the spirits of the blessed dead —
O'Connell, on whose tomb warm tears are shed,
And Washington, with all that noble throng,
Whose names are ever an unceasing song,
Who strove for liberty, — now by you stand,
And silent bless each patriotic band !
And so we welcome you, with hands, hearts, eyes, —
*Cead mille failthe,* echoes to the skies."

"None but genius of the highest class can touch or attempt
'Medea' without failing [said " The Dublin Mail"].  The play
is a touchstone; and the hush of silence, the shudder of sym-

pathetic fear, and the enthusiastic bursts of applause, that marked the progress of the piece, leave no doubt of the fact that not here alone, but in America, Miss Ward's reputation as the first tragedienne, the successor of Miss Cushman, is made. . . . 'Yankee Doodle' was played by the orchestra as a closing air, and the *team* left the theatre amidst a vast crowd and tremendous cheering. To-night the team will again visit the theatre on the occasion of Miss Ward's benefit, when 'Medea' will be again performed, and 'The Honeymoon,' in which Mr. John H. Bird will take a part. We expect Mr. Bird, an American barrister, will show the Irish bar what amateur acting may be."

Mr. Bird fulfilled the expectation brilliantly.

"The distinguished American advocate, Mr. Bird, who is regarded as the best amateur actor in his own country [said "The Dublin Mail"] gave us the best Duke Aranza we have seen. He has the merit of being a gentleman in all his minor actions, and this gives to his playing a finish and perfection ¯ rarely seen on the professional stage."

During June she was also playing in Manchester, with splendid success, in "Despite the World." Of the play itself, a critic wrote : —

"From a careful perusal we do not hesitate to pronounce it a production of rare merit, well conceived, admirably written, and with a noble purpose. Such plays as this lift the stage above the category of mere amusement, and rank it with institutions of popular education."

Ristori wrote to her from America : — ⌜translation⌝

"We've received the papers, and all been in your happiness ¨ with you. We see your great future, dear. You so deserve a happy fate, that in truth you will not have stolen it when it comes. Just think of your delight in having your mother with you! Oh! if I could only be with you two months, I'm sure I should learn the whole part of Macbeth. Others have offered to teach it me, but I have not the confidence that they would be like your mother. She is so patient, intelligent, correct, artistic, and I will say mechanical, because no other word will express my idea. To teach a tongue as difficult as that of the ancient English poetry, you must know the system of the movements of the throat and palate; for which I do not use ill the word 'mechanical.'"

While playing in the provinces in the summer and autumn of 1875, Miss Ward was in negotiation with Max Strakosch for a tour of the United States. She accepted his terms ; but he failed to send the contract in season, and she continued to play in the provinces. Of her Bianca in " Fazio," which was strongly praised, Mr. Wingfield wrote : —

"Just a word, dear Miss Ward, to say that Clayton and I were delighted with your Bianca. . . . Nothing could be more charming than the series of attitudes; and in the pathetic portions I am quite certain there is no one on the stage who could at all touch them."

In December she filled the exacting *rôle* of Antigone, at the Crystal Palace ; and the " Figaro " said, —

"It was upon Miss Ward that the weight of the burden mostly lay. How deeply and conscientiously she must have studied the part, was most manifest. Not once did the lady falter. Her delivery was correct and refined; and the depth of pathos, and the poignancy of grief, were contrasted at the proper moments with the power of religious determination, and the most heart-rending representation of utter despair."

The correspondent of "The New York Tribune " said, —

" The production of Antigone has given that handsome and

clever American, Miss Genevieve Ward, an opportunity to show power in the ungracious character of a sketch from the antique. She plays Antigone with the serious grace, reserve, and occasional force called for by the text; and her stately figure, large fine features, and deep contralto voice, suit well the sad and queenly heroine. By dint of quiet yet passionate simplicity she has succeeded in making Antigone's lament, before her living entombment, a really affecting piece of acting, and that is not an easy thing to do."

Early in 1876 Col. J. W. Forney, United States Centennial Commissioner in Europe, received the following letter : —

21 PRINCES ST., HANOVER SQUARE.
Jan. 18, 1876.

MY DEAR SIR, — Before your departure for America, I have great pleasure in offering my professional services in aid of the Centennial Fund. Should this proposition be agreeable to you, I will organize a performance of " Macbeth " at Drury Lane on Friday, Feb. 4, Mr. Chatterton having generously offered his theatre for the occasion.

Yours sincerely,

GENEVIEVE WARD.

To which Col. Forney replied, —

FENTON'S HOTEL, Jan. 20, 1876.

MY DEAR MISS WARD, — Your letter of the 18th was an agreeable surprise, and is particularly welcome, not only as showing your praiseworthy patriotism, but your readiness to follow the example of your distinguished countryman, Mr. John S. Clarke, who, more than a year ago, contributed a large sum to the Centennial Fund. Your liberal proposal is particularly appropriate, as being the first Centennial dramatic representation in the great city of London. Of course I gratefully accept your proposition; and I am much gratified to add, that, since the receipt of your letter, I have consulted Robert S. Schenck,

American minister, and Gen. Adam Badeau, American consul; both of whom have cordially undertaken to recommend your praiseworthy enterprise to the public."

By the kind co-operation of Messrs. J. S. Clarke, J. B. Buckstone, J. Hare, H. Neville, F. C. Burnand, C. Rice, W. R. Field, Parravicini, W. Corbyn, and F. B. Chatterton, all leading managers of London, an admirable cast was secured, and the play was presented under the invaluable personal superintendence of Mr. Edward Stirling.

Though it was unintelligently remarked that with such support Miss Ward could hardly fail to appear to advantage, it is obvious that she could have given no prouder challenge to a public slow in receiving the new, but magnificent in its recognition when once convinced. To shine in such a setting, was to prove herself a star of the first magnitude. Her triumph was grand, artistically and financially. Some of the critics praised grudgingly ; but the more effectively for that very reason, since unwilling admiration proves the power that compels it. Motives underlying covert opposition to success are never far to seek.

"The Daily Telegraph" said, "Miss Ward's Lady Macbeth is unrivalled." "The Dublin Telegraph" thought —

"The whole conception of the character by this gifted actress was strictly in accordance with the idea by which it must have been originated in Shakspeare's mind. Nothing could be more refined or dignified than her whole *tenue* at the banquet-scene, — no hurry, no fussiness, no weak fear of consequences either. But the assumed calm, which the audience was allowed to see, was only assumed, as she tried to divert the attention of the guests, called down thunders of applause, and really established Miss Ward as the first emotional tragedienne of the day. After the performance, Miss Ward was recalled; and the American fashion of handing baskets of flowers from the boxes, and throwing bouquets adorned with long streamers of gay-colored ribbons, served to convey the admiration inspired by a performance which certainly ranks Miss Ward amongst the first Shakespearian actresses of the day."

"The Era," "Weekly Messenger," "Figaro," and others were warmly appreciative ; and "The Post" said that nothing had equalled her playing since the days of the great Siddons.

"The Court Journal" mentioned that Baring & Brothers paid a hundred pounds for a box ; Morgan & Co., fifty pounds ; Morton, Rose, & Co., fifty pounds ; Seligman, twenty pounds ; and J. P. Bigelow, ten pounds.

Soon after the Centennial Fund benefit, Miss Ward received the following letter : —

FENTON'S HOTEL, Feb. 12, 1876.

MY DEAR MISS WARD, — The proceeds of your benefit for the Centennial Fund, enclosed in your favor of this date, were immediately forwarded to the chairman of the Centennial Finance Committee at Philadelphia.

I will not stop to dwell on your splendid performance of Lady Macbeth, nor of the able assistance of your professional associates; but only add, that it is to your own energy and perseverance in organizing your noble benefit, with all the heavy details and obstacles, and to your appeals to your own countrymen to join you in a good cause, that this noble and patriotic triumph is due. With my best wishes for your success in all future undertakings, I remain very truly yours,

J. W. FORNEY.

In May, after playing in her great *rôles* in Liverpool, she received from the famous Dr. Hitchman a letter of congratulation, in which he said, —

"I think I shall give a public lecture on the tragedies of Euripides, with special reference to the Medea of your unrivalled histrionic powers. In my opinion, that is *the* character for your high dramatic walk. . . . I shall never forget your surpassing intellectual accomplishments last evening, and most emphatically your dignity of deportment as daughter of Estes, King of Colchis. You deserve to be drawn through the air upon a chariot of heavenly fire, not by Medea's winged dragons, but God's angels!"

Of Miss Ward's excellent impersonation as Mrs. Haller, and also as Meg Merrilies, the critics spoke in one accord of praise : —

"In the hands of Miss Cushman, the famous American tragedienne, recently deceased, the part of the old gypsy woman was brought into special prominence, the *rôle* being one of that great artiste's best efforts; indeed, many who have a distinct remembrance of her acting, place it first. Resembling her distinguished countrywoman in many respects, — both having overstrained their grand lyric powers, and suffered loss of voice in consequence, and both having left the operatic for the dramatic career, — Miss Genevieve Ward filled the part with great power and effect. It may be considered the least part of the excellence of the performance, but no one could fail in being struck with her wonderful 'make-up.' When she first strode upon the stage, to the astonishment of Bertram and Dandie, her appearance was strangely weird and impressive. Her face was tanned and haggard; her cheeks, neck, and arms seemed withered and shrivelled; and in the wild-eyed, wrinkled hag none could recognize the graceful and elegant Portia, or the handsome and imposing Medea. Of Miss Ward's performance, it may briefly be said that it was in every respect artistic, thoughtful, and in the highest degree picturesque; even the difficulties of the Scotch accent were sufficiently well met, although we would not have been justified in expecting this. The effect of her singing of Franco's song was indescribable; nothing could have been more true or natural. Her chanting of the prophecy had all the wild plaintiveness of an Irish *caoine*. The last act of the play was most judiciously altered. Instead of concluding with a solo for Julia Mannering, and chorus, the curtain dropped on the picture of Meg's death. Here Miss Ward made the great point of her admirable impersonation. Her acting was simply superb, intense and forceful in every particular, while her perfect taste and judgment saved the episode from exaggeration or any appearance of being overwrought. It was a magnificent piece of acting, witnessed in perfect silence by the large audience, who applauded at the fall of the curtain with significant warmth."

About this time Miss Ward received a present from the ever kind and thoughtful Ristori. It was a lap writing-desk, very handsome, with white and blue violets painted in a lovely cluster on the enamelled lid. In the note accompanying the gift Ristori said, —

" What a pleasure if you could only come here to see us, to pass days and days with us in this lovely villa! You should lead with us a country life, rising at six, and retiring at half-past nine. We have fields, a little orchard, a beautiful little house covered over with roses; and we would enjoy ourselves, and we would laugh! "

In the fall of 1876 Miss Ward, not satisfied with the great success she had achieved, and feeling she was not thoroughly mistress of her art, went to Paris, to study under Regnier, the great dramatic teacher and critic, who was the friend of Talma, the famous stage-reformer of France, and of whose reception years ago, at St. Petersburg, the following bright bit of gossip was related : —

"M. Regnier—he is the same Regnier who was the friend of de Musset — had a wonderful reception at the theatre, and soon became a lion in the capital. Every one sought him .and *fêted* him. Then he came to deliver his letters of introduction. He himself tells the story with a delightful simplicity and wit. The St. Petersburg exquisite was so exclusive that he would allow no one to touch any thing of his with an ungloved hand. Regnier unfortunately paid his visit in complete ignorance. There was the usual stiffness, and the usual insincere interest. Then tea was brought in,—at that time more of a rarity for an afternoon meal than it is now. The equipage was faultless, — curious old silver, dainty Dresden china, the furniture of a museum rather than the ornaments of a tea-table. M. Regnier was helped, and continued his conversation; but he had not sufficient sugar, so, selecting one lump out of the basin, he took it in his fingers, and dropped it into his cup. The Prince looked aghast, and exchanged a significant glance with a servant, who opened a window, and emptied the sugar-basin into the street. The imperturbable comedian continued his conversation, and finished his tea. He showed no resentment, but, when his cup was quite empty, quietly rose, opened the window, flung cup, saucer, and teaspoon into the street, observing that soon he would get accustomed to the manners of the people.

"On another occasion the emperor recognized the comedian in the street, stopped him, and had some minutes' conversation with him. They then parted; and immediately afterward the poor actor was arrested, and flung into a dungeon. He was, however, soon afterward released; and then learned that it was treason to address the emperor in the streets. The next day he again met the monarch, who sought to stop him; but Regnier was forewarned. 'Don't speak to me,' he shouted to the king: 'your majesty's conversation is compromising.'"

While Miss Ward was studying with Regnier, Mlle.

Josselin (Miss Julian), a young dramatic student of much promise, came to her in great distress : her family were opposed to her going on the stage ; and Bressants, her teacher at the Conservatoire, was ill, her lessons were stopped, and she in despair. Miss Ward, who had been rehearsing with her in the sleep-walking scene from " Macbeth " twenty-one times, Miss Josselin taking the *rôle* of the nurse, consented to teach her in tragedy, paying special attention to pose and gesture. And, at Miss Josselin's *début* at the Conservatoire, everybody was talking of her poses ; nothing had been seen like it since Rachel : and at the close the young *débutante* received the first prize in tragedy, which had not been conferred on any woman for seven years.[1]

After studying all winter, Miss Ward made her first appearance on the French stage at the Porte St. Martin Theatre, in February, 1877, as Lady Macbeth. The chief critics and famous artists of Paris were present. "The noble, deep eyes of the author of ' La Fille de Roland ' were visible in the orchestra-stalls ; and her teacher, M. Regnier, occupied one of the

[1] The Conservatoire in Paris is a national school supported by government. Its teachers for the drama are selected from the old actors of the Comédie Française, the only theatre which has lasted two hundred years. Its teachers in music are selected from the great singers of the French school. An artist receiving the first prize in the Conservatoire has a right to claim engagement at the first operas at the Comédie Française. The jury is selected by the government, from among such men as Dumas, — none of the teachers can serve, — Perrin, the director of the Comédie Française, and other great critics and dramatic authors, who pass the verdict and confer the prizes, retiring as from any other court to consult and agree. When it was announced to Mlle. Josselin, that this prize had been awarded to her, she sobbed aloud.

boxes." The play was given in French, after the translation of M. Jules Lacroix; but the sleep-walking scene was played in English at the request of Regnier, "else," said he to Miss Ward, "the critics will vow you are a Frenchwoman, and think that the announcement of your foreign nationality was only a trick to whet curiosity."

The most eminent living French dramatic critic, Francisque Sarcey, opened with a discourse on Sheridan's "School for Scandal;" then followed the first and second acts of "Macbeth," and the sleep-walking scene. A correspondent of "The London Era" said,—

"Miss Ward's French was so perfect that her American nativity was discredited until in the sleep-walking scene, given in English, she fairly electrified the house. It was splendidly rendered, with an intensity of power and statuesque grace that called forth the warmest applause, and a double recall, a very exceptional compliment here. She was afterward personally complimented in the most cordial manner, by several distinguished artists and critics. M. Victorien Sardou, who had left his sick-room to be present, and Francisque Sarcey, who volunteered to sign Miss Ward a diploma as a French actress, were among those who vied to do her honor. Needless to say that Regnier, her tutor, was in ecstasies at the triumph of his pupil, so great that she was invited to repeat the sleep-walking scene at the next Porte St. Martin *matinée*."

The French plaudit of critics and the public was one harmonious and full chord of praise, as intelligent and just as it was warm.

The London papers quoted the French journals:—

"Miss Ward's appearance at the Porte St. Martin the other day as Lady Macbeth [said a critic in "The London World"

of Feb. 21, 1877] was a genuine success. It was a difficult
undertaking to play the part of Lady Macbeth in French; and,
with that, to give more than satisfaction to an audience ill
acquainted with the piece. She was obliged afterward to repeat
the sleep-walking scene in English, and for a curious reason, —
because her French was so pure, it was necessary to give her
hearers proof that it was not her native tongue. Both representations were admirable, especially the long scene of imperious temptation with Macbeth, which occurs in the second
act.

"I was so fortunate as to witness her first appearance in
this part in England; and, much as that pleased me, I am bound
to say that her improvement under French training has been
very great indeed. She has simply had the resolution to with-
draw herself for a while from the English stage, in order to take
lessons of those masters of her art who are to be found at the
Conservatoire. I wish that others of our actresses would follow
her example; but I am sorry — and Miss Ward must be more
than human if she is not glad — to think that they will not."

Said "The Dublin Morning Mail," —

"A series of morning performances is at present being
given in the Théâtre Porte St. Martin, in Paris, called 'Mati-
nées Charactéristiques.' Their character consists in the fact,
that each one is devoted to a nationality or period: thus the
Russian, Spanish, Italian, and English authors respectively
are represented at a *matinée*, and also different centuries, — the
fourteenth, fifteenth, etc. A notable feature in each matinée
is, that at each performance is delivered a discourse by one of
the principal Parisian critics. The second *matinée* was devoted
to England, and the play was 'Macbeth.' In the latter, Miss
Ward played Lady Macbeth. The performance was in French;
and the gifted American actress, with whom Dublin is familiar,
was received by the French audience as a countrywoman; and
it was only when she spoke the sleep-walking scene in English,
that her nationality was allowed. The house was full of the
*literati* of Paris, including most of the members of the Comédie

Française, — MM. Sardou, Bornier, Dumas, etc. — all of whom applauded heartily, and recalled the artiste twice, a very rare honor on the French stage ; and a repetition of her Lady Macbeth is asked. It is pleasant to record such a distinguished success of a lady whose first efforts we witnessed with genuine delight."

A London letter to "The Dublin Telegraph" commented as follows : —

"Sarcey, the great critic, declares that Miss Ward possesses every quality necessary to insure her the most '*éclatant succès*' which has greeted any actress since the days when Alexandre Dumas created them in return for their making *him*. The French stage is sadly deficient in the tragic element just now ; and Sardou, on seeing Miss Ward's performance of Lady Macbeth, immediately seized upon her as the most fitting representative of his new play, — his *beau idéal* of the warmth and tenderness required. This striking success of a foreigner on the Paris boards is regarded as the great artistic event of the day ; and the London managers stand amazed at their own want of perspicacity, especially remembering the reception Miss Ward met with in Dublin, where she was greeted with the same appreciation of her genius as manifested by the public of Paris, — affording another proof of the superiority of Dublin in the refinement of criticism, and the higher feeling for art which exist in your city, and should force the acknowledgment of its being the artistic capital of the kingdom."

During her sojourn in Paris, Miss Ward received many distinguished proposals for theatrical engagements ; among them, one from M. Jenneval, manager of the Troisième Théâtre Français, — so called as the Odéon is considered the second, — not now in operation ; another from Jules Claretie, the same accomplished gentleman and clever dramatist now writing the brilliant *feuilleton* for *Le Nord*, entitled " La Maison Vide ; " and another from Albert Alberg, manager of the Djurgaards Theatre of Stockholm.

The celebrated and popular French actor, Pierre Berton, wrote to the critic of the " Figaro " and " Gaulois : " —

" DEAR SIR, — I have been to see Miss Ward, and I thank you for having sent me. Without your advice, I might have lost the occasion to hear an eminent artist, whose play, always natural and true even in the most dramatic situation, has carried me away ; for it is true art as I understand it, and as I try to practise it. The attitude, facial expression, and gesture of Miss Ward, are equal to her fine diction, so pliant, so varied. I am sorry I shall be unable at this time to hear her again ; for it would have been a real pleasure, and a precious study."

Some months previous to her French *début*, Lord Newry, a very clever and accomplished young man, translator of the " Danischeffs," and owner of the St. James Theatre, had written to Miss Ward : —

ASHRIDGE, GREAT BERKHAMPSTEAD, Nov. 30, 1876.

MY DEAR MADAME, — I am glad for your sake that your prospects in Paris are so good that you cannot feel yourself justified in relinquishing them under a less sum than forty pounds a week. . . . There is not a single lady in London drawing that salary ; and not more than four at the outside in receipt of even half of it. . . . I think you will show the Parisians that they are not the only artists in the world.

Faithfully yours,

NEWRY.

Miss Ward received many precious private congratulations upon her triumphs at the Porte St. Martin, — from Ristori's friend and critic, G. de Filippi ; from

the famous Madame Celeste ; from Lionel Tennyson,
son of the laureate ; from Palgrave Simpson ; and
Madame Ristori wrote : —

" Who knows what you may have been thinking of my
silence ?  But you — naughty one — have not even thought of
asking me the reason !  Your triumphs have paled my memory
in your thoughts — is it not so ?  Ah ! I am delighted with your
magnificent success in Paris, but I am not in the least astonished ; but allow me to tell you, all the same, that your English
language is diabolically diabolical !  I miss you so much !  I
kiss you with my heart ; and I love you, and am your
                                " ADELAIDE RISTORI."

Miss Ward has received letters from this dear and
generous friend from almost all parts of the world.
" Madame  Ristori  always  speaks  with  the  sincerest
kindness of artists," said Miss Ward to me, " and is
remarkably faithful in her remembrance of her friends."
This was observable in her letters.  I hardly found
one in which she did not make tender inquiry for Miss
Kate Field.

Miss  Ward's  French  triumphs  brought  her  offers
from London managers : —

" I am not astonished at the propositions made to you from
London [wrote Regnier]: the contrary would have astonished
me ; and it is equally without surprise that I hear of the French
movement taking possession of the English actors.  Last Tues-
day at the Conservatoire, an English actress imparted to me
her desire to act the *rôle* of Juliet in French.  Her accent renders the attempt impossible for her ; but I see in this the emu-
lation which your achievement has excited, and which, in my
opinion, you alone can make succeed.  If you regret our lessons, believe also that the same regret is mine.  Such pupils as
yourself are rare, or, more properly speaking, they do not
exist."

In September, 1877, Miss Ward accepted an engagement to play as Queen Catherine in the grand Shakespearian revival at the Theatre Royal, in Manchester.

"Mr. Charles Calvert, by whom the play has been arranged for presentation [said "The Manchester Courier"], and under whose care it has been produced, is already known all over Europe and America for the grandeur and faithfulness of his Shakespearian revivals; and the splendor and solidity of the scenic display will live in the memory of those who see it as one of the most elaborate and impressive performances of modern times."

The Hon. Lewis Wingfield supplied the authorities and designs for the costumes, paraphernalia, and regalia employed in the production. "His skill, judgment, and popularity, therefore," said "The Era," "were qualifications of the first order in connection with such an enterprise."

Charles Sever wrote in "The Manchester Guardian:"—

"Miss Genevieve Ward is, in my opinion, one of the most accomplished artists, both intellectually and dramatically, on the English stage. Her performance here of Lady Macbeth some time ago—to say nothing of her recent successes in Paris, in French rendering of the same—struck me as the truest, most forcible, and most finished embodiment of the part which I had seen during a period of forty years.

"Equally striking is her impersonation of the dethroned Queen Catherine, whether in the famous council-chamber scene in Act I. where she pleads before the king, or the scene with Cardinal Wolsey in Act III, or in the vision and dying scene, which is the most painfully real embodiment of gradual dissolution conceivable."

The correspondent of "The Chronicle" waxed wroth with Mr. Sever, splenetically snubbed him for the length of a whole column, and was very unsympathetic with the slow and literal death of the queen; but the press and the public were with Mr. Sever.

Her old master, Regnier, to whom she sent the Manchester papers, wrote : —

"To *you* the praise is complete; and I do not detect, in all the critics say of you, the shadow of a reticence. You are recompensed for your long, brave labors. I hope you will give me the most ample details of your success: the examination which you ought to make of the impressions made upon the public will be, I assure you, as interesting for me as for you. Continuation of success, and the warmest affection in the name of my wife, and of yours affectionately,

"REGNIER."

She attended the Church of England Temperance Bazaar, and acted with Mr. Calvert in the trial scene from "The Merchant of Venice," giving the proceeds to the society. Then followed fast upon one another noble successes in Manchester and Liverpool, as Lady Macbeth, Beatrice in "Much Ado about Nothing," and as Portia, etc. Long and able critical leaders in the papers concerning her fine impersonations were now the rule; and Regnier, delighted with her growing fame, wrote to her in reference to O'Neill's admirable review of her Lady Macbeth in "The Manchester Examiner : " —

"The author's appreciation of you is most remarkable: it is more difficult to know how to praise than to criticise; and, for the writer to justify the so well-merited praises he gives you, must make you happy and proud to be so understood. That there should have been astonishment to see you so playful and gay in a comic *rôle*, I can well understand. I did not, myself, expect it when, for the first time, we tried a comedy; but you will remember you surprised me, and fairly had my approval without reserve, nor did we long tarry over a task in which you gave me so little to do. Your success in the two styles has been complete, and it should be well established in London that you hold there a sceptre which no one can rightfully dispute with you."

In March, 1878, Miss Ward played in London at the Queen's Theatre, Emilia to the Hungarian tragedian Neville Moritz's Othello. The Othello met with some fine praise shaded by a great deal of carping and blame. The "old playgoer," Mr. Charles Sever, and his enemy of "The Chronicle," had a skirmish on the subject, Mr. Sever coming out the gentleman, logician, and critic of the two ; and his verdict in favor of the new Emilia was worthy to outweigh many adverse voices. Miss Ward was pronounced "the best Emilia of our generation."

After another successful tour of the provinces, she lent herself as Portia and Queen Catherine to the furtherance of the Shakespeare Memorial Benefit,[1] chiefly the undertaking of Miss Kate Field, but warmly seconded by the "hearty co-operation of the managers and artists who interested themselves in the carrying-out of the scheme ; and there was not a single hitch. anywhere to mar the harmony of the proceedings." The receipts were £450.

American journals were now beginning to find space

[1] For the establishment of a theatre at Stratford-on-Avon, "on Shakespeare's ground, for Shakespeare's sake."

for accounts of the foreign triumphs of their gifted
countrywoman ; and she entered into an engagement
with Messrs. Jarrett and Palmer for a tour of the States
for the winter and spring of 1878 and 1879.

Among the many congratulations Miss Ward received upon her prospective American tour, was the
following from the manager of "The New York Herald " in Paris.

Feb. 6, 1878.

DEAR MISS WARD, — I need scarcely say to you that I am
greatly rejoiced at the conclusion of your engagement. It is
what I have long been looking forward to for you. I believe it
was all that was required to crown your hopes and aspirations.
If any one ever deserved success in this world, you do. You
have struggled bravely and honestly against difficulties that
would have dismayed most women of your refinement and accomplishments. I have watched your course with interest; and
I can say to you truthfully, and without the slightest desire to
flatter you, that I have never seen any career more nobly or
more consistently played out. You are not only an honor to
your profession, but to your sex; and it is but just that you
should now meet with the rewards of your efforts, from which
you might have shrunk, had not the welfare and happiness of
others been involved in them. Your good news has made me
glad, and my hearty good wishes follow you everywhere.

Ever truly your friend,

J. J. RYAN.

From Paris, date of March 10, 1878, came the following flattering query : —

"Could you find artists, and engage to mount three or four
English plays to be performed in July at a large theatre in Paris,
probably the Italian Opera House, which will be offered for
that purpose by the French Government during the Exposition ?
Excuse me for troubling you thus, and deign to find in it, among

other motives, a sincere and earnest desire to see your great talent affirm itself again in Paris. I am also writing to the director of the Burg Theatre in Vienna, and to Madame Ristori to participate in this dramatic event.

" With best compliments,

"J. GUST. BERTRAND."

A change of ministry prevented this project from fulfilment.

On the eve of her departure for America she received the following : —

" Good-by Ristori, adieu Rachel ! — since it is thus that England speaks of you; but for me, adieu Genevieve Ward, a name which will have as great a meaning for the artists who will come after you ! My kind compliments to all your family, and to *you* the felicitations, best wishes, of your affectionate

" REGNIER."

# KATHERINE.

WE heard the eloquence that rings repeal
  Of wrongs, flagitious in a subject's sight;
We saw the gracious form consent to kneel
  To gain for Buckingham his envied right.
Like chill and rattling hail on Wolsey fell
  Her-stern anathemas 'gainst spleen and pride;
Though dark Campeius wrought a subtle spell,
  His art her nobleness and truth defied.
Most regally she stood, her brow alight
  With the mild halo that o'ertops the great,
Till Justice in habiliments of night
  For earthly honor gave immortal state.
Thus have we seen, enraptured with the view,
The queen whom Ward enacts, whom Shakspeare drew.

G. W. PETTES.

BOSTON THEATRE, BOSTON, MASS.,
    April 10, 1879.

## VI.

EARLY in July, 1878, Miss Ward with her father arrived in New-York City by the steamer "City of Berlin;" and within a very few hours after, that ubiquitous, energetic, much-abused, sometimes much-abusing, often invaluable, and always unquenchable being, the newspaper-reporter, had called on her, and propounded the question, —

"What are your plans for acting in America?"

To which Miss Ward had replied, —

"I can't say very definitely: the management is in the hands of Jarrett and Palmer, and I have scarcely seen them since my arrival. I shall go immediately on a visit to my friend Adelaide Phillips, at Marshfield, Mass., the place adjoining Daniel Webster's. It was that which brought me over so early. On Sept. 2 I shall appear at Booth's Theatre in 'Jane Shore,' which was written by W. G. Wills for Miss Heath, and has been played in England for two or three years with great success. The play has been re-written for me. Mr. Wills thought the third act was not strong enough, and has changed it in some important particulars. The penance takes place on the stage instead of off: the snow-storm scene, in which the heroine dies of hunger on the stage, I think is one of the strongest in the English drama. After 'Jane Shore,' I shall probably play in 'Macbeth,' 'Henry the Eighth,' 'Meg Merrilies,' Mrs. Haller in 'The Stranger,' Portia in ''The Merchant of Venice,' Beatrice in 'Much Ado about Nothing,' and other parts. If 'Jane Shore' should have a long run, some of the others will perhaps be postponed until my return from our contemplated tour. We propose visiting Philadelphia, Boston, and probably all the large cities. It was proposed at first that I should make my first appearance in 'Henry the Eighth.' I am glad the change of plan was made, for I should dislike to meet a New York audience first in a character which they have learned to look upon as Charlotte Cushman's. I find that I am getting a little nervous as the time approaches when I am to make my *début* here : I find that this is what I have really been working for all these years. The measure of my success abroad was valuable for its own sake and as an earnest of what I might do at home."

Jennie June, one of the guests invited to share with Miss Phillips the pleasure of Miss Ward's visit, wrote : —

"Miss Ward sailed from England a month ahead of time on purpose to enjoy a few weeks at Marshfield; Miss Matilda Phillips — whose magnificent voice has won the most unusual and extraordinary encomiums from Sir Jules Benedict and Manuel Garcia, the famous teacher — having carried over a pressing invitation to London from Miss Adelaide, whose intimate acquaintance with Miss Ward dates back to the season when they sang together in Havana.

"Can you imagine the group which poured out upon the

piazza of this pleasant house when the carriage-wheels were heard? First and foremost, Miss Genevieve Ward, who has come back to us the celebrated tragedienne, looking taller, and perhaps more stately, but beautiful, bright, and spontaneous as ever; her father, Col. Ward, so long and so well known as a representative of the United States abroad, a still handsome and dignified old man, though his hair and beard are silvery white, and he is an invalid past active service."

Referring to Miss Ward's experiences as Countess de Guerbel, Jennie June adds, —

" This romance of Genevieve Ward's life is never now alluded to by her, and does not seem to have left a cloud upon her life; for she has used it simply as the incentive to hard work in her profession. She is very young-looking for one who has won so high a place, has a magnificent figure, a manner singularly sweet and winning, yet capable of expressing great pride; a rich voice, beautiful blue eyes, which become gray when moved by thought or feeling, and a face like Ristori's, with regular features; and masses of dark hair, which she simply twists in a huge coil, through which she slips a pin or a dagger.

" I quite appreciated a remark made by Miss Emily Faithfull in regard to her, in a private letter to a friend in this country, — that she was so sorry she was not born in England : she would have been so proud to claim her as an Englishwoman. She inspires that sort of feeling. There is no nonsense about her : she is conscientious, ardent, perhaps ambitious ; but she could never be suspected of any thing mean or unworthy. I had formed no opinion of her as an artist before seeing her ; but I am inclined to think now that she will be a surprise, — that she stands alone in her own particular field of grand tragic art.

" She is rather careless about clothes, and values her wardrobe, not because it is made by Worth, but because each dress was designed by Lewis Wingfield, the great historical artist, and is strictly accurate, down to the smallest detail. There is no tinsel about them, and she wears but little jewelry ; but the fabrics are fine, and harmonious in sentiment, form, and color, and are an admirable study of effects."

All sorts of biographical sketches, inextricably con-
fusing truth with error, appeared in the journals of the
day preceding and following her visits to the chief
cities of her tour, which she began by playing as Jane
Shore at Booth's Theatre in New York on the night
of Sept. 2. Her audiences were large, and received
her with enthusiasm; and the journals, especially
the "Tribune," "Herald," and "World," praised her
performances with very high eulogium. At work
among the minor critics, however, was a detracting
spirit, moved beyond question by petty personal pique,
who wrote up a stock of spiteful comments, and succeeded in introducing them from time to time in the
columns of second-rate journals. The handiwork in
every instance was glaringly the same, and was ultimately ascertained to be that of the same person who
years before in Paris withheld from Mrs. Ward and her
daughter papers and letters *in re* the de Guerbel
marriage intrusted by them to his temporary charge
until Gen. John A. Dix's peremptory *dixit* recovered
them ! This little trail of slime among her laurels
naturally puzzled some of the fair-minded.

"The ways of critics in New York are past finding out
[said a writer in "The Baltimore American"]. For some reason or other, known only to themselves, a sort of cabal tried to
form itself against Miss Ward, and write her down. It was said
that her death-scene was too realistic (alluding to her Queen ·
Catherine), that there was no occasion to go through the death
agonies in order to die upon the stage. Now, one peculiarity of
Miss Ward's death-scene is the absence of any forced or un-
natural agonizing. As a woman said who saw her, 'she actually dies.' This same woman, a lady of great intelligence and

experience, remarked to her in my presence, ' I have seen many persons die off the stage, but I never saw one die on the stage until I saw you; and the illusion was so complete that I nearly fainted. You must have watched the phenomena very closely.' — 'No,' replied Miss Ward, 'I never saw any one die in my life. A celebrated physician, whom I consulted, advised me not to work off symptoms, but to just die ; and so natural does it seem to be, after going through the part, to yield up life and all its interests, and so absolutely am I psychologized by that idea, that I hardly know for a few moments, myself, whether I have not really given up the ghost."

One Philadelphia paper, not ill-named "The Item," busied itself in picking out and assorting single points of cavil, from among criticisms which, as a whole, broadly recognized her powers, and grouping them as the "opinions of the press." This *mélange* quoted Mr. Winter of "The Tribune" as saying, concerning her Jane Shore, —

"Those who are waiting to be entranced by a celestial visitation of overwhelming genius will probably continue to sit upon the anxious seats ; "

but omitted to include these words of Mr. Winter's discriminating pen in the same article : —

"In the intellectuality of her art, as in her personal appearance, Miss Ward awakens vivid reminiscence of Ristori ; she shows the same practical force of character, the same cold will, and thorough equipment in mechanical resources ; her presence is imposing, her countenance is splendidly expressive, her gestures are large, free, and picturesque, and her physique obeys with unswerving accuracy and instantaneous promptitude the monitions of her thought and impulse ; and she is the accomplished mistress of all her powers. A more entirely competent actress is seldom seen : she has abundant force, abundant repose, and beautiful finish. . . . In the fourth act Miss Ward rose to the height of absolutely imaginative grandeur. The theatre now rang with delighted plaudits, and there were five recalls of the tableau and the actress after the curtain fell. The success of the night stood assured at that point. It was certainly a most brilliant climax; and those who can rejoice in seeing a fine work accomplished with perfect adequacy of art will view with unqualified admiration the acting of Miss Genevieve Ward."

Miss Ward herself did not like the *rôle* of Jane Shore, preferring always tragedy to melodrama; and this fact was at the bottom of any want felt in her impersonation, which was nevertheless, as an artistic performance, without blemish, and drew large houses for the few weeks of its run.

On the 20th September she played the sleep-walking scene of Lady Macbeth, on the occasion of the "Ladies' Matinée for the Benefit of the Municipal Fund to relieve the Sufferers by the Yellow-Fever in the South;" and on the 23d received the following from the secretary of the committee appointed to take charge of such funds: —

NEW YORK, Sept. 23, 1878.

MISS GENEVIEVE WARD, — The committee desire to return to you their sincere thanks for your kindness in assisting at the *matinée* benefit given at Booth's Theatre on last Friday afternoon, in aid of the sufferers by yellow-fever in the South. The remembrance of your kindly act will always remain fresh in the memories of these poor fever-stricken people.

Respectfully,

ERNEST T. FELLOWES,
*Secretary.*

Her Queen Catherine and Lady Macbeth continued to bring the best audiences of New York to Booth's Theatre ; and her engagement there proved a genuine success.

Miss Anna E. Dickinson, who had then never met Miss Ward personally, was discussing with Mrs. Croly the relative merits of Miss Ward's Queen Catherine and Lady Macbeth, and Miss Cushman's impersonation of the same *rôles.*

Their conversation chanced to occur in the hearing of a certain reporter who had a personal grudge to satisfy against Miss Ward, and who was now engrossed in casting little pellets all along Miss Ward's victorious way. Conceiving that now indeed his hour had come, he at once stated in "The Capital," a sheet published in Washington, that Miss Dickinson had pronounced Miss Ward far inferior to Miss Cushman.

Very soon after this, Miss Ward received the following letter : —

FIFTH-AVENUE HOTEL, Nov. 5, 1878.

DEAR MISS WARD, — I trust you have been infinitely less annoyed than I, by what I find set forth of a talk of mine in the last number of " The Capital."

In a conversation I supposed strictly private, I commented on your Queen Catherine and Lady Macbeth as compared with those of Charlotte Cushman.

At the close of a great many *pros* and *cons*, what I actually said was: "The long and the short of the matter is, that I like Genevieve Ward's Lady Macbeth as much better than I liked that of Charlotte Cushman, as Charlotte Cushman's Queen Catherine seems to me greater than that of Miss Ward;" and, if I am not mistaken in you, you are quite broad enough to allow another to disagree with your conception (not with the working-out of that conception) of any given *rôle*, without thinking such an one either malevolent or a fool. It is not that I think you will specially value my opinion one way or other, but for my own content, that I want you to know the whole truth, and not the half, — which is generally the meanest of lies.

Very truly yours,

ANNA E. DICKINSON.

In accordance with one of the most blessed of the laws of life, the little seed sown in spite blossomed, despite the sower, in a warm friendship between Miss Dickinson and Miss Ward, in which each does full justice to the other's grand powers. Of Miss Dickinson's undeniable dramatic genius, Miss Ward has spoken to me in very high terms, regretting, as does many another eminent judge, that she should have received, as an actress, so little of the broad appreciation which, both as encouragement and desert, was manifestly her due.

From New York to Brooklyn, Providence (which she took by storm), Philadelphia, Washington (where she was the honored guest of Mrs. President Hayes), Baltimore, Rochester, Buffalo, Hamilton, Toronto, Montreal, Portland, Albany, Springfield, Worcester, Providence, and Boston, Miss Ward's tour was one triumphal march, the fruit, not only of genius, but of most conscientious and patiently faithful labors apart from her own noble impersonations; for Miss Ward manages all her plays, teaches, directs, superintends the rehearsals, selects even the goods for the costumes, arranges the tableaux, — in a word, carefully supervises the entire representation of which she forms the nucleus.

The following letters and quotations from letters received by Miss Ward during this tour are an unmistakable verdict upon her art.

101 EAST 59TH STREET, NEW YORK,
Oct. 2, 1878.

MY DEAR MISS WARD, — I must thank you for the very great pleasure you gave us last night, by taking us back for three centuries, and into the presence of the veritable Queen Catherine as understood by Shakespeare. Your impersonation is admirable, and will live in my memory among the great creations I have witnessed, beginning with Rachel's. You were every inch a queen: the death-scene especially was really electrifying. My friends and myself left the theatre under a spell, charmed by the wonderful art with which you recreated the proud and unhappy Aragonese princess. . . . Can you give us the pleasure of your company to dinner, *en famille*, etc.?

Yours very cordially,

MARY L. BOOTH.

456 PEARL STREET, NEW YORK,
Oct. 10, 1878.

MESSRS. JARRETT AND PALMER.

GENTLEMEN, — As an old artist permit me to give my conscientious opinion, that for originality of conception, tenderness of feeling, and startling power, Miss Ward's Queen Catherine is the finest I ever saw; and I have played with all the great representatives of that character since 1845.

Her "make-up" in the last scene was a marvel of artistic limning, and the "*mise en scène*." I have never seen equalled in this country or Europe.

Yours respectfully,

GEORGE C. BRYDEN.

The following, addressed to Miss Ward's dear friend Mrs. Sanford, is of special interest, from the fact that

the writer, a young painter of rare promise, was entirely *deaf*, and makes this beautiful and feeling tribute
through the interpretation of *sight* alone.

DEAR MRS. SANFORD, — I cannot tell you how many times
I have thought of you, and how sweet it was in you to send the
beautiful Miss Ward to see me, and to give me the pleasure I
had on Friday evening. My judgment of acting is founded on
no knowledge of it; but what sensibility I have in my own art,
I cannot help exercising upon what I see at the theatre. Miss
Ward seems unquestionably great to me. I was deeply affected
by every movement she made : every look and gesture seemed
fully charged with the mournfulness of Queen Catherine's fate,
and the beauty of the character shone out in every expression
of her noble face. In the last act, where the queen is broken
in spirit, and tremulous with suffering and age, it is the most
touching thing I ever beheld. Her costume and "make-up"
were as wonderful as her acting, and such subtle and harmonious acting I never saw. There was reason and love and beauty
and temperateness in it; it was deep, strong, and sonorous; nothing in it that I could wish otherwise. It had the solemn coloring of a Venetian picture; and her hands were a marvellous
study, a perfect revelation. I am so filled with admiration, that
I must needs write confusedly of it. . . . The costume of the
last act was a great piece of work, — a rich material of a sombre
golden tone, something like winter grass, and trimmed with
fur; and the other dresses had an artistic magnificence I have
never seen equalled. The more I think of it, the more I am
touched by your kindness; and I long to be face to face with
you to tell you *by my silence* how deeply I appreciate this
thoughtful act of yours.

Ever in great respect and affection yours,

OLIVER I. LAY.

A gentleman, formerly consul at Manchester, wrote
to Miss Ward from —

St. Louis, Oct. 15, 1878.

We were very glad to hear of your success over the water, and I read with much pleasure of the furore your last appearances in Dublin created. I only envy those who were present, and able to join in the applause. And, now that you are in this country, we seem as far from you as before, for our local papers — except in describing how Solomon in all his glory was not arrayed as you are in Jane Shore — have left us in ignorance of what you are doing. Mrs. Cabot tells us you have been received with success. Well, if Success had not tripped down Broadway, and helped you over the steamer's side, and made his best bow to you, and introduced you to everybody he knew, he would have written himself down an ass, and ought never again to have shown his welcome face among decent people! . . . The house is so large that we have two guest-chambers, one of which we call " Miss Ward's room ; " and in future ages we hope to have our boy point to its bed with pride, and tell his children that thereon Queen Catherine rested when she halted in her royal progress through the West. . . . For I take it for granted you will come to St. Louis some time during the winter or the spring. Kindest regards to your father. Tell him that I cannot get at the true inwardness of Western politics, and I think it about time we had a conference to settle the true state of the country. And now, with the Cranes' love, believe them to be your majesty's most loyal and affectionate servants,

NEWTON CRANE, *et al.*

Liverpool, Oct. 22, 1878.

DEAR FRIEND, — We have heard of your success with the greatest possible delight, although we expected nothing less than a complete triumph for you. It has indeed been achieved under adverse circumstances : the heat must have been simply awful. I knew you would like Mrs. Croly (Jennie June), and I am proud to have brought you together. You are one of the *few* women I dearly love and esteem, and we think and talk of you continually. Your photographs, which delight us, have a

place of honor on the mantlepiece : this brings your name to
many lips, among others to those of Mr O'Neill of Manchester,
who called the very day they arrived. He was all you represented, and he was charmed with " Zicka." I enclose his notice,
and also Mr. E. R. Russell's ; for, knowing the men, you will
measure their criticisms. The Kendalls are lovely to her; and,
indeed, the more I see of Mrs. Kendall, the more I admire her
as an actress, and as a woman. . . . Don't forget how welcome
news of you will always be to us. How I should like to have
an ideal theatre here, with you as *star*, and my child working
with you, — a thoroughly good company, excellent plays, and
bishops in front as well as sporting lords and newspaper proprietors ! . . . I am sorry for——, as I am for all unfortunate
women. As "Zicka" says every night, in tones which have
always riveted the noisiest audience, "Life is so hard to some
women, and men are so merciless !" She is now at the theatre,
or would send some message of her own; for you are one of
her "loadstars." God bless you !

Ever your affectionate

EMILY FAITHFULL.

OPORTO, SPAIN, Nov. 21, 1878.

DEAR FRIEND, — Forgive my delay. You know what it is
to make up a company, and put a whole *repertoire* on the stage.
Well, doing things as usual by steam, I was obliged to mount
" Marie Antoinette " in four rehearsals, and the others in the
same haste, remaining in the theatre off-nights eleven hours to
rehearse. I was afraid of falling ill, but the electricity which
always animates the artist, and me in particular, enlarged my
forces ; and the tremendous applause of the different publics
had their influence on my strength, and re-tempered me. . . .
On the 23d of December I shall again be in Rome, changing
the life of inspiration for the exactions of society, but which has
the advantage of making you enjoy repose. To me it seems
beautiful to be the artist now and then, renovating the spirit in
the emotions of glory, and then turn to enjoy the compensations
of the dear quiet of home. . . . I felicitate you on your grand

success, which will, I know, augment; and in the end your triumph will be complete over all the annoyances which, after all, you must have naturally prevised. I am sorry to hear of your father's ill health, and I understand how much it worries you. Hard, inexorable law of nature! . . . Give me, when you can, detailed accounts of yourself. How you must enjoy being in New York! I envy you: it is one of the dearest remembrances of my career. Have me in your heart with the friendship I bear you. Your

ADELAIDE RISTORI (DEL GRILLO).

Mrs. Ward received the following from an American lady : —

HAMILTON.

DEAR MADAM, — We have just parted from your wonderful Genevieve, who is making her Canadian tour, and with whom my family, including myself, my husband, children, and sisters, are madly in love. I thought you might like these few lines from across the sea, to tell you how well and how bright she looks, how every one respects and loves her, and how we would all do every thing in our power for her. She is indeed a wonderful creature, infusing life and strength wherever she goes. I was often afraid we bored her; but we love her and admire her so, I'm afraid we couldn't help it.

UTICA, Feb. 19, 1879.

MY DEAR MISS WARD, — You speak of your gratification at the approval of competent critics. It is no less a pleasure to one who is paid to sit in judgment upon the drama, to receive some sign of recognition that his work is more than the perfunctory phrases of a daily drudge. Most of all is it a delight when such tokens come in the form of such charming notes as I have the honor to thank you for. As a matter of course, dramatic criticism in the country must rest under many disadvantages — as must dramatic representation. What the latter lacks in force of surroundings, in scenery, in the spirit which a crowded and cultured metropolitan house inspires, the former also loses from lack of time, from infrequent requisition, and from the hurry of a slender-staffed daily. More than this, there is the difficulty of talking to an audience not accustomed to make distinctions between plays and players, or to distinguish with any degree of nicety artifice from art. Embarrassed thus, I am more than pleased to have pleased you. I think I can speak for Utica, in tendering to the artist whose Jane Shore is still a rich and beauteous memory with us, a cordial and hearty welcome at whatever time she may arrange to come. I remain with kindest wishes,

Very truly yours,

HAROLD FREDERIC.

Such a letter as the foregoing must have convinced Miss Ward that a "slender-staffed daily " is sometimes equipped with a pen more effective for both courtesy and capacity, and tipped with finer artistic perception, than always fills the critical departments of the plethorically-staffed metropolitan dailies.

CAMBRIDGE, April 9, 1879.

DEAR MISS WARD, — My nephew's name in full is Alexander Wadsworth Longfellow; but the first name is generally dropped by us. How very kind it is of you to offer him these letters to Paris! He is very grateful for this mark of your interest in him. So also am I, well remembering the forlorn condition of a young stranger in the great city, with no one to turn to for sympathy but his banker. I am looking forward with great impatience to Thursday and Saturday, and am, dear Miss Ward, till then and after,

Very sincerely yours,

HENRY W. LONGFELLOW.

Mr. Longfellow, Mr. O. W. Holmes, Mr. Edwin P. Whipple, and other literary celebrities, attended Miss Ward's representations during her short stay of only a week in Boston; and Mr. Longfellow told me that he considered her acting among the very greatest he had ever seen, and quite the most artistically faultless. Owing perhaps to the fact of Mr. Longfellow's appearing twice at the theatre during the week, or quite possibly to the grace and vigor of the sonnet by Mr. G. W. Pettes, published in "'The Boston Advertiser," it was supposed to be the tribute to Miss Ward of the bard of the Charles; and a raid was accordingly made on "The Advertiser," which could hardly supply the demand.

As a capable bit of appreciation, and at the same time a snub of the Hub administered by a fledged and famous Bostonian, the following is given : —

CAMBRIDGE, April 10, 1879.

DEAR MADAME, — I trust that a sincere love of the true in any branch of art will sufficiently excuse me, a stranger, for my hardihood in addressing you a few lines to express my appreciation of your acting in "Jane Shore." I have watched with interest the remarks the newspaper critics have made upon this performance, and have been more than ever convinced that those whom Bostonians call critics were more properly termed reporters. Their opinions about the loftiest grades of art have dwindled down to be the bare repetition of set phrases, "magnetism," "pose," etc., etc.

Although a native of this charmingly pedantic city myself, I hope that I have seen enough outside of its narrow streets to enable me to judge more fairly of Boston than many of my fellow-citizens; and I am obliged to confess that in our art-education we are still mere beginners. This is particularly the case with the stage; where, since the death of Miss Cushman, we have seen no first-rate artiste. Never having had the pleasure of seeing your acting before last Saturday night, imagine my surprise and delight at witnessing a performance, in many points bringing to my mind the characteristic features of the highest school of acting of to-day, — the Italian.  In many passages of that harrowing play, "Jane Shore," I fancied myself back in Rome, thrilled by Ristori herself!  I do not know whether you will agree with me in regarding Italy as the present *home* of the drama, or not : at any rate, you cannot think it a lack of appreciation which associates you with a school whose present masters are Salvini, Ristori, and Ernesto Rossi.  I am looking forward with expectation to seeing Shakespeare's heroines once more in the hands of one who I am sure will not fail to bring out their mighty lights and shadows."

Miss Ward's success in Boston was very genuine, and of that best kind that augments in the memory. If the criticism of the press was not altogether just or capable, it was seldom carping, and, on the whole, appreciative, with some instances of specially able recognition, and discriminating encomium ; and her audiences, composed of the best-qualified people of Boston and Cambridge literary, artistic, and social circles, were won to her, not only for that week of laborious and brilliant achievement, but for as often and long as Miss Ward will come to them.  She left in April for Paris, to fulfil an engagement to play Queen Catherine at the National Theatre in that capital ; and on the 2d of June she wrote to me from St. John's Wood, London : —

"I fear I shall not return to America this season.  I am obliged to produce my new play here before I take it there, or I lose the copyright in England ; and, besides, my performances in Paris are postponed until the winter.  They wished me to rehearse and mount the play of 'Henry VIII.' in two weeks, which was impossible, and therefore I refused.  A kind letter sustaining me in this refusal came from M. Regnier, who 'felicitated me on my good sense!' . . . It pleases me so much that Mr. Longfellow remembers me, and thinks to ask for my welfare. I shall always treasure the recollection of my little visit to his home in Cambridge among my happiest souvenirs. . . . A delightful testimony from Mr. Emerson, who saw me play Jane Shore, but whom I did not have the good fortune to meet while in Boston, will, I know, give you pleasure. He sent me an invitation to visit him at Concord when I return, and the lines he wrote for me were, —

> ' Oh, what is heaven but the fellowship
> Of minds, that each can stand against the world
> By its own meek but incorruptible will!
>
> RALPH WALDO EMERSON.' "

The new play to which Miss Ward alluded in the foregoing letter was written by Palgrave Simpson and Claude Templar, and was entitled "Zillah," and required Miss Ward to fill a double *rôle* as Zillah the gypsy, and again as her twin-sister the Lady Constance. This play was placed by Miss Ward on the stage of the Lyceum during Mr. Irving's vacation in August, 1879, with great care and expense as to scenic effects, and elegance and variety of costume. Her acting was pronounced worthy of all praise ; but the play was so worried and badgered and torn to pieces by the critics and the public, that after four nights representation, Miss Ward, having lost £2,800 by it, removed it without protest or complaint.

One eminent critic had written to her : —

"You did all that was possible *with the impossible ;* but no actress that ever breathed could have made a triumph of 'Zillah.' "

And Mr. Wingfield, wise and unfailing friend, wrote her these words of friendliest stern fibre : —

"What you have to do is to play *at once* something which you are sure of, to efface with all speed the recollection of a *fiasco* of which, happily, you are clearly the victim, not the cause. Should you close now, even for a night, it would be a sign of *faiblesse*, theatrically speaking, and a very grave error in judgment. If 'Lucrezia' is not possible Thursday, why then Saturday; but to the earnest and broad-shouldered all things are possible."

And Thursday it was. Without losing a night, silent as a Spartan as to the burden and strain she was enduring, she produced and appeared in " Lucrezia Borgia " with noble success.

She had received this little note : —

DEAR MADAME, — I do not leave home as often as I used; but, if you will put my name down for a quiet corner, I should like to come and see you in " Lucrezia Borgia." The situations are grand, and I shall like to see them divorced from the flimsy . . . of the Italian composer.

Yours truly,

CHARLES READE.

In view of the fact that Mr. Herman Merivale, author of the play of " Forget Me Not," now testifies, in the litigation anent .that play, that Miss Ward had never won dramatic recognition until he taught her how to play " Forget Me Not," the following letters have special interest and value.

LONDON, Aug. 9, 1879.

I must write a line to thank you for a couple of hours of immense gratification. I *have* seen you act now, and was perfectly delighted with the mingled grace, power, and tenderness of the performance. It was superb from end to end; but the transition in the third act from the imperious, domineering Lucrezia, to the soft, impassioned woman, was the gem of the part. Unstung by jealousy, what man could have said "no" to such pleading? Compliments on your profound knowledge of your art, you must be tired of; but I can honestly say that no two of your last night's audience were more pleased than Herman Merivale and myself.

Your admiring friend,

HAWLEY SMART.

Miss Patty Chapman, the niece of the famous Mrs. Charles Kean, with whom she often played, wrote, date of Aug. 9 : —

"Thank you again and again, dear Miss Ward, for the 'real treat' you afforded us last night, — my cousin, Mrs. Charles Kean's only daughter, her husband, and myself. You acted Lucrezia splendidly, with so much power, and such finish in all your great scenes; and your voice is most harmonious and telling. You often reminded us of my aunt Mrs. Kean; and Herman Merivale, who joined us during the performance, said the same thing; and many would think we could not pay you a greater compliment."

"Grace Greenwood" (Mrs. Lippincott) — whose daughter's *début* had taken place under Miss Ward's direction — wrote to her on the same date : —

"I had great delight in your superb acting last night: you remind me of Ristori in her grandest moments. I look forward to 'Guy Mannering,' your Meg is so great."

After a brilliant morning performance of Meg Merrilies, she continued to act nightly in the *rôle* of Lucrezia ; the critics hardly knowing which to applaud most, her admirable playing, or her equally admirable energy in thus quickly and competently producing play after play with a truly royal determination to satisfy the public.

Miss Ward impersonated Stephanie, Marquise de Mohrivart, for the first time, on the night of Aug. 22, in the play "Forget Me Not," which she has since rendered famous. The public was interested and puzzled, uncertain at what rate to estimate this new and complex *rôle:* the critics pronounced it superlative. Meantime a terrible blow fell on this brave woman, in the sudden news by cable of the death of her father, Aug. 28, at the home of his brother in the West, among relatives who loved him, and sought to cheer his last moments, but not, as he and she would have had it, in the arms of the daughter whose chivalrously tender friend and companion he had been for so many years, and who had loved him with a beautiful comprehension and unvarying devotion.

The very night of these tidings, Miss Ward appeared as usual in "Forget Me Not." Letters from friends came during the ensuing days, to share her sorrow, and to show her they knew what depths of tenderness bleeding in silence lay under the heroic fulfilment of her public duty. From among these tender expressions of sympathy from her venerably beautiful and gifted friend Madame Colmache, from Mrs. Louise Chandler Moulton (whose poems have shown the world glimpses of one of the most sympathetic hearts that beats), from Miss Matilda Phillips, from authors, actors, artists, critics, I have chosen this one, because of the peculiar fitness of its few strong, eloquent words.

MANCHESTER, Sept. 3, 1879.

DEAR MISS WARD,—I am deeply grieved to hear of the death of your father: you will know that I am not using the language of conventional condolence. Though our acquaintance was not long, I had learned to admire his estimable qualities, and was proud to believe that he had admitted me to his friendship. I was still in the hope that I might see him again, and not once only. I beg permission to offer you my heartfelt sympathy. It must be inexpressibly hard to pursue your task under the shadow of this great affliction. It was wiser and nobler to accept the blow as one of the inevitable sorrows of our common lot, than to obey the natural impulse to surrender yourself to your grief; and it may help you to sustain yourself in your course, to be assured that your friends, while sharing your mourning, will admire you the more for the brave front you have maintained under one of the heaviest strokes of fate.

I remain yours faithfully,

ARTHUR O'NEILL.

And this one from the world-beloved Italian : —

PARIS, Sept. 14, 1879.

MY POOR FRIEND, — Though you have long been prepared for the death of your father, I can well understand that it comes as a great sorrow. I will not repeat to you the things that are usually said in these sad hours ; but I will say to you, my Genevieve, " Courage !" and think with me that life is only a field of crosses for those unfortunates who have inherited from nature sensitive hearts. . . . I have been happy in your triumph. You have finally passed the Rubicon. I have always said, and I will always say, you deserve to win the fullest fortune for your perseverance, tenacity, and indefatigable study ; and now at last, see ! you are walking the road of the few, wearing the mantle of greatness. Courage ! These sorrows will pass : the love, the labor, and the glory will remain. Your

ADELAIDE RISTORI.

In September, just as the public began to perceive

that Stephanie was a creation, Miss Ward, resigning
the Lyceum to Mr. Irving, left London, and, in a fall
and winter tour of the provinces with "Forget Me
Not," made one of the most complete artistic and
popular successes ever recorded on the stage ; toward
the close of which she received from the gentlemen
of her company an elegant writing-case inscribed to
"Miss Genevieve Ward, in pleasant remembrance of
the 'Forget Me Not' tour of 1879 ; " also a daintily
beautiful white fan, hand-painted with forget-me-nots,
and her monogram worked in those flowers, presented
by the ladies of her company, with whom, as Stephanie, she had been so long at variance.

The following letters accompanied the gifts : —

THEATRE ROYAL, MANCHESTER, Dec. 9, 1879.

DEAR MISS WARD, — On the eve of terminating your first
"Forget Me Not " tour, we, the gentlemen of your company,
respectfully beg your acceptance of the accompanying writing-
desk as a souvenir of our sincere appreciation of the courtesy
and kindness you have invariably extended to us. We also
take this opportunity of conveying to you our warmest congratulations on the artistic success which has happily attended
you. That you may long be spared to adorn our profession, of
which you are so brilliant an example, is the earnest wish of
yours,

FRANK CLEMENTS.
F. CHARLES.
D. CULVER.
IAN ROBERTSON.
J. H. COBBE.

" Misses Foley, Alice and Rose, beg the Marquise de Mohrivart's acceptance of the accompanying fan as a peace-offering,
trusting that with the close of the present week their long dis-

agreement may come to an end. They feel that as a gift it is not all they could wish, but hope that as a slight souvenir it may find favor in her eyes, and that hereafter she will be able to say with a certain Américan poetess, —

> ' And yet, whenever I wave my fan,
> The soft south wind of memory blows.' "

"WHY may a man live two lives, while a woman must stand or fall by one?

"What was the difference between us two, Sir Horace Welby, in those bygone years, that should make me now a leper and you a saint?

"There would be no place in creation for such women as I, if it were not for such men as you!"                                           STEPHANIE.

# VII.

EXACTLY six months from the date of its first production at the Lyceum, " Forget Me Not " was reproduced at the Prince of Wales Theatre under the management of Mr. Edgar Bruce, Feb. 22, 1880, with the only Stephanie possible in Miss Ward's inimitable creation. The echoes of her provincial tour had stirred London to unwonted heights of expectation.

"The real success of the present production [said a writer in a London magazine] — for the *cachet* given by the Prince of Wales, though affecting a certain small circle, would have little influence with the general body of playgoers — lies in the fact that those persons by whose verdict dramatic fortunes are made or marred, and who are by no means the regular newspaper critics, were away from London in the autumn, and hence the 'fiery cross' which is passed from hand to hand through an enormous succession of coteries had no chance of circulation. When Miss Ward had once been seen by the *cognoscenti*, her success was achieved; and, indeed, it is very long since such a triumph of pure artistic skill and training has been witnessed on the English stage."

The little theatre[1] was crowded nightly, by the

[1] The pretty little box known as the Prince of Wales Theatre, in London, with its narrow and perplexing winding passages and inadequate exits, is by far the worst fire-trap for a complete human holocaust I have ever entered. Wherever the responsibility for the tragical risk incurred by those who enter there, rests, it is an exceedingly heavy one.

cleverest and most aristocratic, from the Prince of
Wales down through the widening network of royalty,
nobility, and wealth.

When the Prince of Wales first saw Miss Ward in
" Forget Me Not," he sent for Mr. Bruce, the manager, and asked who it was who played the part of
Stephanie. " Because," said the Prince, "she is un-
mistakably a lady: only her manner in putting the
sugar in Sir Horace's cup, shows the lady bred. She
has hardly an equal on the London stage. Where has
she been? Why have I never heard of her?"

" Her mother is in the opposite box: I will go to
her, and bring your Highness word," said Mr. Bruce.

" She is of a very old American family, and the
widow of a Russian officer," was Mrs. Ward's simple
reply to Mr. Bruce's inquiry.

After the play, the Prince went to the green-room,
and sent to Miss Ward, asking permission to see her.

Complimenting her warmly upon her performance,
and especially noting her pronunciation of French in
certain phrases and songs belonging to her *rôle*, he
asked, " You are a French woman, are you not?"

" No, your Highness: my family have been for two
hundred and sixty years in America, but were originally from London." — " Ah !" said the Prince, " you
speak French marvellously well ; but I have always
thought the women of America the cleverest in the
world."

He then asked her if she would not like to play a
French drama in London, and, when she assented,
suggested " L'Aventurière."

"Is not that your mother?" said the Prince, seeing a lady passing the green-room door. "Will you present her?"

He complimented Mrs. Ward upon the grand talent her daughter displayed, and tendered the most graceful compliments from the Princess of Wales upon the same theme.

On another occasion, when calling upon Miss Ward in the green-room after the play, he was accompanied by the Duke of Edinburgh, Prince Teck, and a Russian nobleman. The Prince of Wales showed to Miss Ward some fine portraits of herself which he and the Princess of Wales had selected, and begged she would do him the honor to write her name upon them as a souvenir of the pleasant hours passed in witnessing her performance.

While they were conversing, Miss Ward, hearing the jingle of the bells worn by her tiny pet dog who accompanies her everywhere, and fearing he might stray off, called out, "Come here, Teck!"

The gentlemen started; and Miss Ward hastily apologized, recollecting the name of one of her distinguished visitors, —

"My little dog's name is Teck, — short for Thecla, a German character in one of my plays."

They all laughed heartily ; and in came the little fellow with the princely name, and straightway rushed at the Duke of Edinburgh, who had shaken his hat in token of friendly intentions.

"She will bite me!" exclaimed the Duke.

"Basket, Teck!" cried Miss Ward reprovingly ; and

the little creature, who is as obedient to her mistress as she is haughty and unapproachable to others, ran out of the room, and curled up in her basket.

As the gentlemen were descending the stairs after having taken their leave, Miss Ward heard them laughing again, and plainly distinguished the voice of the Prince of Wales saying merrily to his cousin, " Basket, Teck ! "

Scarcely had they gone, when the Russian nobleman who had been with them returned, and, bowing to Miss Ward with an expression of great respect, said, " I dare not tell you my name or nationality, for fear you will hate me ; but I wish once again to express my great admiration of your genius."

"You need not hesitate to admit yourself a Russian," replied Miss Ward. " I am the widow of a Russian, but I love your emperor for all his kindness to me."

One of the London journals had the following : —

"Genevieve Ward continues to delight the lovers of good acting by her marvellously artistic personation of Stephanie, in ' Forget Me Not,' at the Prince of Wales's. The clever actress has twice within a fortnight been honored by the patronage of H. R. H. the Prince of Wales, who has been liberal in his compliments respecting a performance which, we have before said, he characterizes as the most perfect he has witnessed apart from the French stage. On Thursday evening a splendid audience included Mr. and Mrs. Bancroft, Mr. and Mrs. Kendal, Mr. and Mrs. Hare, Mr. Tom Taylor, and Mr. Forbes Robertson. At the close of the play Mr. and Mrs. Bancroft, Mr. and Mrs. Kendal, and Mr. Forbes Robertson congratulated Miss Ward in the green-room upon her success, and warmly complimented her on her grand performance. This little scene was

6

happily described by Mr. Kendal as 'the fourth act of " Forget
Me Not," with a full cast.' "

At the request of the Prince of Wales, Hamilton
Aïdé, his personal friend, and well known as novelist,
poet, and musician, arranged a private entertainment
at his own residence, at which Miss Ward played in a
French drama with M. Marius, with her usual brilliant
success.

Miss Ward had greatly improved upon the original
version of "Forget Me Not," in many little points of
adaptation called for by her own conception of her
*rôle*, and notably strengthened the effect of the last
scene. This gave rise to murmurs from the authors,
but the critics upheld the artist. Further trouble was
occasioned by her elimination of the acting character
of Rose, the piece being manifestly improved thereby.

Meanwhile a proposal, likely to have proved very
interesting had it been carried into effect, was made to
Miss Ward by Mrs. Sabine Greville, a lady of much
æsthetic cultivation, and fine critical taste, and a
cousin of Hamilton Aïdé's.

This lady having seen, and like every one else been
greatly impressed by, Miss Ward's Stephanie, wrote to
her : —

MILFORD COTTAGE, GODALMING.

DEAR MISS WARD, — Mrs. Lewes is a great friend and near
neighbor of mine ; and, in telling her this afternoon of your marvellous talent and innate genius, I was reminded of à piece she
wrote some years ago, " Armgart," which I imagine you could
appreciate. Mr. Lewes, who was certainly the greatest dramatic authority in Europe, has often said " Armgart " would
have succeeded in Paris. . . . I remember Rachel and Désolée,

and, until I saw you, never imagined I should have the happiness of looking on their like again. . . . If you should ever play "Armgart," I am sure Mrs. Lewes's highest aspirations for her piece would be satisfied.

Very sincerely yours,

Sabine Greville.

Later Mrs. Greville wrote : —

"I have been talking again with my dear neighbor Mrs. Cross (George Eliot); and yesterday she spoke so anxiously about 'Armgart,' that I thought I would venture to ask you if you had any thought of it. It seems to me, it would have a tremendous *succès de curiosité*, apart from its literary merit, and you could make it almost a monologue."

"The London Observer" of April 25, 1880, stated : —

"A mistake underlies the statement that Miss Genevieve Ward's intended performance of Angier's 'L'Aventurière' at the Prince of Wales Theatre was in any way suggested by Madame Bernhardt's recent assumption of the *rôle* of Clorinde, at the Théâtre Français. The experiment which is to be tried here next month owes its origin to a suggestion made by the Prince of Wales that Miss Ward should act here in a French play, with the support of English artists."

At that time Miss Bernhardt had not played "L'Aventurière," nor was it known that she was intending to do so : in accepting the Prince's suggestion, Miss Ward could not, therefore, have been influenced by a wish to institute a comparison between her own powers and those of the French artiste. Before Miss Ward appeared as Clorinde, however, Miss Bernhardt had attempted and failed in that *rôle* in Paris.

"The Prince of Wales advises you to play in French in London? [wrote M. Regnier.] I find his advice very good, and I also think that 'Forget Me Not' in English might have a great success in Paris. 'L'Aventurière' is a piece which suits you exactly."

Most of the critics in debating this novel undertaking predicted failure ; and a writer in " The Standard " singularly enough predicted it on the one point where there could be no two opinions, — her French pronunciation. Miss Ward sent the paper to M. Regnier, who replied : —

RUE DE ROME, PARIS,
May 6, 1880.

MY DEAR FRIEND, — When the talent of an artist is attacked, the best thing for him to do is to answer with the talent itself, and in no other manner. Do you remember the philosopher in whose hearing movement was denied, and who, instead of answering, began to walk? A journalist considers it impossible that you should play in French. Is not French your own language? And when, in Paris itself, you played one whole act of a tragedy in French alexandrines, at the Porte St. Martin, was there one person in the house who could have suspected that it was not a French actress whom he beheld on the stage? Play in French in London, and no English ear will have the right to reproach you with your pronunciation or your accent, since the subtlety of our own organs never permitted us to do so. Indeed, I do not understand the criticism of the writer in " The Standard ; " for he is not serious when he imputes to you and to your English companions the absurd idea of wishing to teach Frenchmen at once their own language, and how to play their own comedies in it. In my opinion, on the contrary, the experiment you are about to make is a most remarkable one, which cannot fail to be flattering to English *amour-propre.* Nor can it fail, in my opinion, to pique the honor of the comedians of my own country. I can assure you, that if it were to be announced in Paris that "The School for Scandal" was to be played in English by Got, Coquelin, Delauney, and Mlle. Croizette, no one would laugh at the attempt, no one would believe that Molière was insufficient for them, no one would tax them with a ridiculous vanity: it would be considered a proof of the spirit, of the knowledge, and the intelligence of those eminent actors. It is thus, my dear friend, that you should ask some one of your friends to reply to the critic of "The Standard." Let the question be discussed, but do not, on any account, take part in the discussion. An artist — and, above all, a lady — can never, with a good grace, make a matter of this kind personal. If, as I do not doubt, the critic of "The Standard" wrote in good faith, when he is once enlightened on the real nature of your enterprise he will come and hear you, will recognize that you speak French as I do, or rather like a *Parisienne;* and, if he once feared ridicule for you, he will be all the more disposed, having heard you, to give you the praise you merit."

The young poet whose verses are at this time of writing provoking both trenchant criticism and recognition on both sides of the Atlantic, — the son of Lady Wilde, herself a poet of high repute, and a firm friend of Miss Ward's, — wrote the following note to the tragedienne : —

St. Stephen's Club, Westminster.

Dear Miss Ward, — I suppose you are very busy with your rehearsals. If you are not too busy to stop and drink tea with a *great* admirer of yours, please come on Friday at half-past five to 13 Salisbury Street. The two beauties — Lady Lonsdale and Mrs. Langtry — and mamma, and a few friends are coming. We are all looking forward to "L'Aventurière" so much : it will be a great era in our dramatic art.

Yours most sincerely,

Oscar Wilde.

On the Sunday previous to her appearance as Clorinde, Miss Ward went to Paris, rehearsed her part to
Regnier, and, returning to London the next day, went
direct from the depot to the theatre, and played that
night, Monday, May 10, with a success confessed on
all sides to be complete. The following quotation
from a leading London journal is a fair illustration of
the full chorus of applause : —

"Miss Genevieve Ward, whose performance of the hunted
and strong-willed Stephanie in the new play ' Forget Me Not '
has so astonished and excited the students of dramatic art,
stands sponsor for an experiment that we believe to be as original as it is interesting.  Not only England, with its traditional
honesty and occasional self-depreciation, but the great dramatic
France herself, and indeed every nation that has a drama of its
own, will be astonished to hear that ' L'Aventurière ' of Emile
Augier has been played in this country, by English artists, in
its original language.  French actors and actresses have come
to England, English actors and actresses have struggled to
obtain a footing in France; but now for the first time a French
classical play has been given in French by English artists, and
with such success, that, if we mistake not, the art world, hungry
for novelty, will demand an instant repetition of this valuable
curiosity.  Much is constantly said in depreciation of the English school as compared to that of Paris; but, however sincerely we may admire the facility of our neighbors, it is impossible to believe that a picked troupe of the comedians of Paris
would do as much justice to, say, ' The School for Scandal ' of
Sheridan, as has been done to the work of Augier by Miss
Genevieve Ward and her clever companions.  They could
scarcely dare attempt what has not only been tried here, but
has succeeded ; and, looking at the matter purely as a commer-
cial speculation, the rendering of Augier's ' L'Aventurière ' by
English-speaking artists, if it could be transferred bodily to
Paris to-morrow evening, would probably do more to honor the

credit of English art across the Channel than any thing that has been done in the matter of persuasion for many years. Miss Genevieve Ward, fortified by the advice and encouragement of her master Regnier, has left nothing undone that would make the experiment fail for lack of endeavor. She wanted to show what England could do, and she has fairly proved her case. She wanted, in no spirit of affectation or vain-gloriousness, to show how much the best teachings of the French dramatic masters are valued in this country, how we can sift the good from the bad, how we are able to discriminate and select between soundness and artificiality; and now the only regret is, that the dramatic doctors of Paris will only hear second-hand of the unquestionable success of this interesting experiment. Miss Ward, in the character of Clorinde, may be criticised in comparison to the first French actresses of her time. In this play she is, to all intents and purposes, a French woman, faultless in accent, and with all the traditions of the old classical school. Her master is Regnier; her diploma of excellence has been presented to her by Sarcey; and it was Got who offered her a position in the Comédie Française, saying she had less to unlearn than her companions, seeing that her accent was free from the provincialisms that hampered the first artists in Paris. If there is one actress recalled more than another by Miss Ward, it is Favart in her earlier and more impulsive days, before she was hindered by the artificiality acquired by a training in old comedy. Those who go to see 'L'Aventurière,' as acted at the suggestion of his Royal Highness the Prince of Wales, and expect simply a curiosity, will be agreeably mistaken. They will find a French play acted as is seldom found even in Paris. One question remains. What is there in the French language, its flow, its point, and its adaptability for dramatic action, that so fascinates and grips the auditor? These artists have all caught the echo of the Parisian dramatic manner, and consequently they all seem to be better actors than they were before. When they speak English, why are we so deceived?

" The enthusiastic applause of the fashionable audience fill-

ing the theatre yesterday afternoon attested at every opportunity
the high gratification derived from this remarkable performance; and the presence of the Prince and Princess of Wales,
with the Grand Duke of Hesse, added to the interest of the
occasion.

The London correspondent of the "Gaulois" wrote
to that journal in Paris a just and eloquent tribute to
Miss Ward's successful undertaking. But a French
actress, who had just failed in " L'Aventurière," not
finding this eulogium of Miss Ward to her taste, pre-
vailed on the editor of the " Gaulois " to cut it short ;
and the article appeared with Miss Ward's name
erroniously printed " Harel." The writer of the notice
wrote at once to Miss Ward, explaining the case : —

"I have remonstrated [said he]; and they answered, ' Ne-
cessity of printing, Grève is in France, death of Flaubert,' etc.,
etc. I have re-remonstrated, and have at last enforced the
little rectification which I send you."

And which consisted in a small paragraph giving the
name correctly.

From masses of congratulatory letters I have selected : —

8 CHESTER PLACE, HYDE PARK SQUARE, W.<br/>May 11, 1880.

DEAR MISS GENEVIEVE WARD, — We thought your experiment most interesting; a bold one unquestionably, but a *har-
diesse justifiée* by the result. I should not have thought it possible to get even a nominally English company together, capable
of doing so well. We all knew beforehand that your own
French was perfect, but the risk lay in the support, of course ;
and, much as some of your comrades may be criticised, it went
well to the end. Some of us found your Clorinde perhaps a

little more hard and tragical than she would be on a second
performance, but full of power, and with many fine points; and,
as one much indebted to you for the pleasure of witnessing it,
believe me,

Yours sincerely,              .

G. W. SMALLEY.

An artist who made his "hit" as Green Jones in
"Ticket-of-Leave Man," and who has played the Fool
in "King Lear" with Booth, and went to the provinces
as Prince Malleotti in Miss Ward's "Forget Me Not"
tour, wrote this : —

45 RATHBONE PLACE, W.
May 11.

DEAR MISS WARD, — I cannot resist the temptation of adding my congratulations to those which are upon everybody's
lips to-day.   Your performance in French is, in my opinion, the
greatest triumph an English actress has ever achieved, or a
French one either.   You are at present the sensation of London, and I hope we may be fortunate enough to retain you as
such for a long time to come.   Mrs. Charles joins me most cordially in congratulations upon your last victory, and I am

Very truly yours,

F. CHARLES.

The friend and patron of Irving, and mother of
Kate Bateman, asked to be allowed —

"To offer my best congratulations on your achievement in
not only placing *yourself* on a level with the best French artists,
but presenting an entire performance, which, I am told, com-
pares favorably with any thing the French company here give
to the London public.   All this speaks volumes, not only for
the ability, but the energy, that has secured such a triumph, as
legitimate as it is unprecedented."

MILFORD COTTAGE, GODALMING.

DEAR MADAM,— You are doubtless overwhelmed with congratulations, but I cannot help adding mine. Clorinde was so absolutely perfect, one forgot the tremendous *tour de force* you accomplished working up the whole play. I could not help wishing, all the time, you could remember Racine.

Most truly and admiringly yours,<br>SABINE GREVILLE.

DEAR FRIEND,— Every one has been telling of you, and praising you. One critic said you had the finest voice on the English stage, the most capable of the subtlest, swiftest changes and modulations of passion and power. I was at Mr. May's studio; and there your Cleopatra head, your splendid eyes, your perfect artistic movements which yet seemed so natural, were all discussed, and keenly appreciated. In your Lucrezia you realize all that Victor Hugo could have dreamed : I wish *he* could have seen you. In the new play you are also the *vrai Parisienne femme du monde :* every movement arid gesture was so French. . . . I hope you will take young —— into favor : he is anxious to act with you, and with his delicate Italian face he would make such a *gennaro.* Mr. Forbes Robertson was here yesterday. He is very charming, and admires your genius enthusiastically. Mr. G. W. Wills was also here, and spoke much of you. . . . You have waked me to new life with all your splendid manifestations of genius and beauty. . . .

Affectionately,<br>" SPERANZA" (LADY WILDE).

9 ROCHESTER SQUARE, LONDON.<br>May 27, 1880.

DEAR MISS WARD, — Words would not convey my feelings, therefore I will not say any thing; and yet I must say I shall always feel so proud to have been connected with the first attempt of French plays by English artists. I have not only to thank you for your beautiful and artistic present, but for your kindness toward me during our rehearsals ; for whatever success I may have met with at the performances, I owe you a great part of it, if not all, as I learned more from you in three weeks than I would have done in three years from a less competent stage-manager than yourself. Once more, *thank* you, and believe me most sincerely yours,

D. MARIUS.

The success of "Forget Me Not" continued unabated, the last performance being given on the night of the 24th of July, to one of the finest audiences ever crowded into the Prince of Wales Theatre ; and never did English press and public unite to pass more capable and copious praise upon a dramatic representation.

The dramatic critic Davey wrote : —

"*You* make 'Forget Me Not' great, for it is not a great play. I have never seen any thing finer than your acting of the part; all the more remarkable and interesting to me, because I have known a woman of this class, who might have sat for the model of the Marquise."

The following came from the distinguished pianiste Mlle. Laure Colmache : —

"What immense pleasure last night! I have joy and pride in your talent and your triumphs; and with what satisfaction did we see that room well ornamented, and the beautiful public worthy of you! R—— was breathless all the time, but almost cried to see her 'cousin Jenny' in so cruel a *rôle*. I do not know if there be a little grain of ferocity in your composition : but it is certain that the *rôle* suits you admirably, and that you throw out your little wickednesses with a spirit and naturalness that renders the illusion complete ; but I think that in depositing your famous blonde wig on your own toilet-table, you also deposit therewith your tiger's claws!"

The pretty and deservedly popular English come-

dienne Mrs. Kendall sent this little tender ejacula-
tion : —

> DEARIE, — I'm so glad of your big success ! Will come and
> see you the first minute I have to myself.
> Kind love from
>
> MADGE.

Miss Ward thinks Madge Kendall is the greatest
English actress. " She is an honor to the stage in
every way," said Miss Ward to me. " She is the sister
to Robertson, who wrote all the comedies for the Prince
of Wales Theatre, and was the original Galatea of Gilbert's comedy. Her Rosalind and Pauline, and Susan
in ' William and Susan,' are marvellous performances.
As woman, wife, mother, and friend, she has every
quality, and is lovely and true in all."

> 8 CHESTER PLACE, HYDE PARK SQUARE, W.
>
> I was surprised and delighted by your performance on Sat-
> urday. Pardon me if I say surprised : it is only because I had
> not seen you earlier in this piece ; for though I go nightly to the
> theatre when in Paris, there is little in London, as a rule, that
> I care for, and it is long since I have seen any thing here so
> finished and admirable as your Marquise de Mohrivart, which
> I mean to see again at an early day.
> Yours sincerely,
>
> G. W. SMALLEY.

A little book of plays sent by the author to Miss
Ward was accompanied by the following : —

> 3 SNOWDON VILLAS, KILBURN, N.W.
>
> DEAR MISS WARD, —Will you kindly accept the accompa-
> nying little book as a small token of my admiration for your
> great talent ? I am not of the number of those clergymen who

ignore the stage, and place the pulpit immeasurably above it. Each may in its way contribute to the general enlightenment of the human race. I venture to hope that you are as little antagonistic to my profession as I am to yours; and that I may subscribe myself very truly your friend,

F. W. B. Bouverie.

An actor in Madame Modjeska's dramatic company wrote to Miss Ward : —

"I have just left the 'Prince of Wales,' and I don't know when I have been so honestly moved. Praise from a mere tyro like myself, after all you have received, would be almost an impertinence; still you will let me tell you that I saw the performance to-day with two other actors, and not one of us had dry eyes at the end. It is such performances as yours which give hope and encouragement to young actors. I sincerely trust you will not think this an impertinence, but find in it a respectable and humble tribute to a consummate mistress of a noble art.

"Obediently yours,

"Arthur Dacre."

"You have given a depth and pathos to the character" [wrote Lady Wilde] "of which, from the text, I did not think it capable ; and we see revealed in a most subtle and admirably artistic manner that most touching of all dramas, the striving *upward* of a woman's soul, through all the sin of the past and the degradation it brings. I do not wonder at tears : they were in my own eyes last night, as I witnessed the bitter and terrible sorrow over her own fallen self that lay under all the simulated levity and light coquetry of the unhappy Stephanie. You have re-created the character, and given it a diviner soul."

Mlle. Zara Thalberg, daughter of the great pianist and a successful singer at Covent Garden, sent a little message of delighted appreciation from herself and her grandmother, the great singer Dangri.

" What *shall* I say ? " [wrote Mrs. Louise Chandler Moulton.] " You electrified me I It was throughout a wonderful impersonation, but the last act thrilled me as I have seldom been thrilled in my life. It is not in my power to express the extent to which you moved me : praise seems so weak beside the passionate strength of that grand last act."

The popular English novelist Farjeon said in his meed of praise : —

" Mrs. Farjeon was delighted, — and frightened too, — and I enjoyed it more than I did at the Lyceum. There's not an actress here, and certainly none in America, who could create and play Stephanie with such appropriate power."

The eminent and clever critic Mr. Richard Whiteing, who wrote in " The Manchester Guardian " — and before ever having met Miss Ward — the first appreciative and adequate review of her Lady Macbeth, wrote to her from Paris concerning her Stephanie : —

" It is of course in one sense entirely superfluous to praise your art in ' Forget Me Not; ' but as with a great picture, so with a great piece of acting, — every critic naturally likes to say something about it, and to study it over and over again in new lights. You have one of the most appreciative critics in Mr. E. R. Russell,[1] of whose praise I will go so far as to say even you may be proud, and that is indeed saying a good deal. I could almost wish for my own selfish sake that you were not winning such triumphs in England; for I suppose we shall see you even more rarely than ever on this side of the Channel, unless you allow yourself to be tempted to come over and take that place at the Théâtre Français which I am sure will always be open to you."

[1] Author of a celebrated pamphlet on The Place and Power of Criticism.

Perhaps that laurel which binds permanently and indisputably the bays of fame upon her brows may be said to have come to Miss Ward with this letter : —

PARIS, July 18, 1880.

DEAR MADAME, — Have you arranged for next season? If not, would you feel disposed to accept an engagement of four months, with the right of extension on my part, for the United States, commencing about the end of November next, to play your piece, "Forget Me Not," and other pieces, four times a week? The limited number of performances may surprise you; but, having engaged Signor Salvini to play three times a week, I would like to make a combination, you to play alternate nights; and as Madame Ristori gives me to understand you speak Italian fluently, I think it it would be possible to arrange — you being willing to do so — that you should play Macbeth and some of his other pieces with Salvini.

You know, America is the country for such combinations; and your name with that of Salvini would, I feel sure, prove a great attraction.

The company to support you, travelling, theatres, etc., etc., would be paid by me. Please let me know if you are disposed to accept, and on what terms, sharing or certainty. I am not personally known to you; but my name must be, as Madame Ristori and Signor Salvini have both been to America under my management. What is still more to the purpose, I am ready to offer you any reasonable guaranty you may require for the fulfilment of the agreement.

Have the kindness to answer me at once, as I am dependent on your acceptance or refusal to arrange other matters.

Yours most respectfully,
C. A. CHIZZOLA.

Miss Ward's engagements prevented her acceptance of this offer, but the tour with Salvini will probably be made in the course of a few months.

During the summer the Rotterdam company had produced in London the drama, "Annie Mie," for which its author, Rosier Faarsen, had received the competitive prize for dramatic literature in Belgium. "Annie Mie" had been a triumph on the Holland stage : in England, though admired by the best judges, it had not been remunerative ; and, just as the Dutch company were about leaving London, the following letter came to Miss Ward : —

47 MECKLENBURG SQUARE.

DEAR MISS WARD, — I should take it as a great favor if you would oblige me by throwing over any engagement you may have for next Thursday, and dining here at *three*. The fact is, the Dutch company are going away, having been very unsuccessful ; and I don't like it to be said, that such good artists came to England, and received no civility. Hence I have thrown myself into the breach, and asked them here on Thursday. But I must have a lady to do the honors ; and I expect Stephanie de Mohrivart to help me out of the difficulty.

Ever truly yours,
L. WINGFIELD.

Towards the close of Miss Ward's provincial tour, the journals began to publish announcements to the effect that Miss Ward had bought the Dutch play, "Annie Mie," and was having it translated, adapted, and revised for representation in English at the Prince of Wales's Theatre in November.

" Miss Ward herself stage-manages the piece with a view to proving — what will not be easy — that the Dutch performers can be excelled in this important matter. The part played by Miss Beersmans is so different from those Miss Ward has played in this country, and the interest is so entirely domestic and pathetic, that her performance will be watched with much interest. If it is marked by the same fidelity to nature as that of Stephanie, it will simply prove Miss Ward one of the most versatile, as she is known to be one of the most talented, actresses living."

On the 25th of September Miss Ward re-appeared at the Prince of Wales's in " Forget Me Not," with the part of Rose excised : the critics approved the change. Mr. Merivale complained in an open letter to the press : he had rented a house, and the tenant had coolly knocked out one room in it which didn't happen to strike his fancy ! Hence — damages, my lord, damages !

Somebody, struck with this argument, intimated the presence of a flaw therein ; declaring that the tenant did not knock out the room, but simply turned the key in the door, and declined to use it.   Dion Boucicault, scenting the fray, whipt nimbly to the front, and shouted encouragingly to Mr. Merivale, "Steboy ! St !   St !   At him ! that's a good fellow ! " and tendered to Mr. Merivale, in an open letter to the press, the Disraelian advice, —

" Let's have a congress, — of dramatic authors, — to settle the yeasting question of English playwrights' interests," etc., etc.

The newspapers wheeled into line on both sides of the Atlantic, and contributed an able running comment of query and suggestion.   Punch waxed funny with imaginary dialogues on the matter : nothing was settled ; Miss Ward continued to play to crowded and admiring houses ; and "The Daily Telegraph" of Sept. 30 had the following : —

(*Before* LORD COLERIDGE.)

MERIVALE *V.* WARD.

This was a motion for an injunction to restrain the defendant from performing, or allowing to be performed, the play of " Forget Me Not," with the omission of one of the characters. It appeared that the plaintiffs, Messrs. Merivale and Grove, are the proprietors of the play, and the defendant, Miss Genevieve Ward, had purchased from them the sole right of representation for five years from 1879.

Mr. Woodruffe appeared for the defendant, and objected that the matter was not vacation business.

His lordship said the motion was for an injunction to restrain a performance now going on, and in his opinion was properly vacation business.

Mr. Woodroffe contended that the character omitted was not an important one, and that the plaintiffs had sustained no damage whatever. The learned counsel handed up a copy of the play, in which the part in question was struck out in pencil by the plaintiff Merivale himself. A letter was also produced, in which Mr. Merivale said the play was much too lengthy, and was improved by the omission of the character Rose.

Mr. Ford said that Mr. Grove, the joint author of the play, did not agree with this view.

Lord Coleridge observed that Mr. Grove had made no affidavit in the case.

Mr. Ford said this was owing to his absence on the Continent, and asked that the motion might be adjourned.

His lordship refused to adjourn the motion, and, in delivering judgment, said that before the plaintiffs could be entitled to the injunction asked for, they must show, first, that there had been a breach of the agreement; secondly, that they were suffering serious damage by such breach; thirdly, that the damage would be irreparable if the court did not grant the injunction. Upon none of these points had the plaintiffs succeeded; and it was therefore his duty to refuse the motion, with costs.

On the 1st of November Miss Ward appeared as
Annie Mie at the Prince of Wales's Theatre ; the Prince
and Princess of Wales were present (which they are
not usually on a first night), and the Princess warmly
applauded the tragedienne, as did also the large and
eclectic audience ; and Miss Ward played with admirable artistic fidelity : yet something was felt to be
wanting ; and an adverse verdict was pronounced by
the press with almost the unanimity which had char-
acterized the praises of " Forget Me Not." As George
Augustus Sala observed in an early note of comment
to Miss Ward : —

"Though *you* are admirable in Annie Mie, the part is not
suited to you: it is a great way below your artistic capacity; and
in the play there are gallons too many of tears, and at least
eight mourning coaches too many. I have been obliged to say
this in my published criticism, — doing justice to your own
genius and dramatic insight, — but into the part itself I have
been bound to pitch, and I hope you know I am too true a
friend of yours to say what I do not mean."

Many deemed the piece too intrinsically Dutch to
be susceptible of successful adaptation in English. Yet
the condemnation of the critics met with some distinguished protest, as the following letters will show.

4 HOWLEY PLACE, MAIDA HILL.

DEAR FRIEND, — I was delighted with your performance of
Annie Mie: everybody around exclaimed with pleasure. An
elderly critic seated next to me had come a long distance to see
you in your new *rôle:* half afraid, he confessed, that, after a
piece demanding such violent emotion as " Forget Me Not,"
you would never be able to subdue your tone to that of such
deep tenderness as required in " Annie Mie." You should

have seen his delight when he found his fears groundless. In every situation you came out beautifully, and the sense of art which made you keep back your powers till the situations came made them of the more value. . . . The only fault to me is, that there is too little of you.

Ever affectionately,

(MME.) G. COLMACHE.

THE GARDEN MANSION, QUEEN ANNE'S GATE,
ST. JAMES PARK.

DEAR MISS WARD, — I write to tell you what cordial pleasure and admiration your performance elicited from Mrs. Fanny Kemble and myself. I thought it quite admirable, so measured, so free from exaggeration, so profoundly touching. In short, I desired nothing altered as regards yourself. . . . But the last act is terribly too long, and the repetitions of the fiend's story. For a permanent success you must cut, cut, cut!

Ever with true regard, yours

HAMILTON AÏDÉ.

DEAR MISS WARD, — I thought your acting last night the perfection of sweetness, but I do fear the piece is disappointing: *the action is not close enough*, and it's too long. This is only my humble opinion, but that which was pretty generally expressed last night around me (in the pit) was very similar. I never met an artist who deserved success so much as you do.

Faithfully yours,

F. CHARLES.

" Annie Mie [wrote Mrs. Clarke, wife of the equerry of the Prince of Wales] is certainly the most beautifully expressed idyl I have ever seen on the English stage, delicate in its treatment, and dainty in all its details. It is an enchanting series of pictures, and its tenderness and simplicity ought to come like a new and refreshing draught to the jaded appetite of London playgoers. You achieve every thing by your inimitable acting as the loving mother, obedient daughter, and outraged and forsaken woman.

And these letters also : —

DEAR GINEVRA, — I have had my mind full of the play and
your acting ever since. I am *enraged* with the critics who have
done it so little justice I It is full of the most varied interest
and charm, and all so softly harmonized in the end, leaving a
final impression of pleasure and content. It has a far finer
moral and mental power than "Forget Me Not," and there are
many fine subtle effects in your acting not lost on me. All
your movements and expressions are true to the character.
There is nothing of the regal Lucrezia or the audacious Stephanie; but the simple peasant grace, a grace that seems all
of feeling, not of art. . . . It is a powerful study, a poem and
picture in one ; and I am amazed that the public have not taken
to it warmly. Good wishes, best wishes, dear, beautiful, brilliant Ginevra, from your affectionate friend,

"SPERANZA" (LADY WILDE).

KEATS HOUSE, CHELSEA.

DEAR MISS WARD, — I *must* see the last night of "Annie
Mie!" Might I ask for the same box mamma and I had? or,
if that is taken, any box will do. I should like to be there to
show how much I appreciate your noble acting, and how much
I admire a play the critics have so misunderstood.

Your sincere friend and admirer,

OSCAR WILDE.

"Annie Mie" was played for the last time on the
night of Dec. 10 ; and the day after Miss Ward sailed
for America, and on her arrival immediately issued this
notice in the leading journals of the United States : —

TO MANAGERS, ACTORS, AND THE PUBLIC.

I have crossed the ocean at this inclement season to protect
my purchased right of exclusive production of "Forget Me
Not," against the deliberate piracy of Lester Wallack and

Theodore Moss. I am preparing papers for an injunction against them, and shall push my legal redress with vigor. Meanwhile I beg to say that neither •Mr. Wallack nor Mr. Moss has any right to "Forget Me Not;" and, further, I will enjoin every manager and actor in the country who attempts to play my piece. I have this day concluded to play the piece in all the large cities, beginning in the city of New York, at an early date, under the management of Col. William E. Sinn.

GENEVIEVE WARD.

DEC. 27, 1880.

Messrs. Wallack and Moss received tidings of Miss Ward's departure from England, and made haste to present "Forget Me Not" at Wallack's Theatre, removing a successful play in order to accomplish this feat. Her suit for an injunction was pressed with skill and vigor, and won;[1] and she immediately made a tour with "Forget Me Not," of the chief cities of the Union and the Provinces, beginning with the city of Boston.

In "The New York Tribune" for Feb. 18, 1881, there appeared a critical review of her acting, which, aside from the moral deduction drawn, is a masterpiece of dramatic criticism, as finished as the performance it describes ; and as it expresses so admirably the sum of intelligent opinion on both sides of the water, on this consummate performance, it is given entire : —

BOSTON, Feb. 16.

Miss Genevieve Ward lately ended her engagement, of one week, at the Globe Theatre. It was a brilliantly successful engagement, and might advantageously have lasted much longer. Miss Ward acted Stephanie in "Forget Me Not," —

---

[1] The whole story is exceedingly well told in Miss Ward's concise and masterly affidavit, for which I refer the reader to the appendix.

the play that was the subject of her recent law-suit against Mr. Wallack. She first appeared here on the 7th inst., giving her first performance of Stephanie in this country; and she was welcomed by a numerous and brilliant audience. The attendance on the second night was still larger, and each night throughout the week the theatre was crowded. Even the tempest of the 12th inst. [the rain fell here in torrents that day] could not keep an eager multitude away from the theatre. Neither at the matinee nor again in the evening was it possible to obtain a seat in the house after the curtain had risen. The success of Miss Ward is beyond question; and it is of a most exceptional character. After seeing her performance of Stephanie, no one can feel surprised at the intrepid and determined energy with which she contested Mr. Wallack's infringement upon her right of property in the play of "Forget Me Not." To her the opportunities provided by the character are special, peculiar, unique, and of absolutely vital import. No dramatic artist was ever better fitted by a part than Miss Ward is fitted by Stephanie; and no other actress on the stage of to-day could act it as well as she does. Those who saw "Forget Me Not" at Wallack's Theatre would scarcely know it for the same piece, on seeing Miss Ward as its heroine. The skill and the charm of Miss Rose Coghlan are not, indeed, forgotten, and of course they are not undervalued; but, as Cardinal Wolsey remarks, "there's more in't than fair visage." Miss Coghlan's performance of Stephanie was charming for its piquancy and for its volatile, sensuous, mischievous vitality. Miss Ward's performance is brilliant with intellectual character, beautiful with refinement, nervous and steel-like with indomitable purpose, fearfully intense with passion, painfully true to an afflicting ideal of reality, and at last splendidly tragic. And it is a shining example of ductile and various art. Such a work easily takes its rank among the great achievements of the contemporary stage.

It is not meant, in thus defining the nature of Miss Ward's success, to intimate that Miss Ward is destitute in actual life of those qualities — fair, lovable, and sweet — of which Stephanie is destitute in the play. It is simply meant that Miss Ward possesses in copious abundance certain peculiar qualities of power and beauty, upon which mainly the part of Stephanie is reared. The points of assimilation between the actress and the part consist in an imperial force of character, intellectual brilliancy, audacity of mind, iron will, perfect elegance of manners, a profound self-knowledge, and unerring intuitions as to the relations of motive and conduct in that vast net-work of circumstance which is the social fabric. Stephanie possesses all these attributes; and all these Miss Ward supplies, with the luxuriant adequacy and grace of nature. But Stephanie superadds to these a bitter, mocking cynicism, thinly veiled by artificial suavity, and logically irradiant from natural hardness of heart, coupled with an insensibility to gentleness that has been engendered by a cruel experience of human selfishness. This, with a certain mystical touch of the animal freedom, whether in joy or wrath, which goes with a being having neither soul nor conscience, the actress has to supply — and does supply — by her art. As interpreted by Miss Ward, the character is reared, not upon a basis of unchastity, but upon a basis of intellectual perversion. This Stephanie has followed — at first with self-contempt, afterward with sullen indifference, finally with the bold and brilliant hardihood of reckless defiance — a life of crime. She is audacious, unscrupulous, cruel; a consummate tactician; almost sexless in fact, yet a siren in knowledge and capacity to use the arts of her sex; capable of any wickedness to accomplish an end, yet trivial enough to have no greater end in view than the re-investiture of herself with social recognition; cold as snow; implacable as the grave; remorseless; wicked; but, beneath all this depravity, capable at least of self-pity, capable of momentary regret, capable of a little bit of human tenderness, aware of the glory of the innocence she has lost, and thus not altogether beyond the pale of compassion. And she is, in externals, — in every thing visible and audible, — the very ideal of grace and melody.

In the presence of an admirable work of art, the observer, of course, wishes that it were entirely worthy of being performed, and that it were entirely clear and sound as to its applicability — in a moral sense, or even in an intellectual sense — to human life. Art does not go very far, when it stops short merely at the revelation of the felicitous powers of the artist; and it is not altogether right, when it tends to beguile sympathy for an unworthy object, and perplex a spectator's perceptions as to good and evil. Miss Ward's performance of Stephanie, brilliant though it be, does not redeem the character from its bleak exile from human sympathy. The actress, to be sure, has managed, by a scheme of treatment which is exclusively her own, to make Stephanie, for two or three moments, piteous and forlorn; and her expression of this evanescent anguish — occurring in the appeal to Sir Horace Welby, her friendly foe, in the great scene of the second act — is wonderfully subtle. That appeal, as Miss Ward makes it, is begun in artifice, is allowed to become profoundly sincere, is stunned and startled into a recoil of resentment by a harsh rebuff, and subsides through hysterical levity into frigid and brittle sarcasm and gay defiance. For a while, accordingly, the feelings of the observer are deeply moved. Yet this does not make the character of Stephanie any the less detestable. The blight remains upon it, — and always must remain, — that it repels the interest of the heart. The added blight likewise rests upon it (though this is of far less consequence to the spectator), that it is burdened with moral sophistry. Vicious conduct in a woman, according to Stephanie's logic, is no way more culpable or disastrous than vicious conduct in a man; the woman, equally with the man, should have a social license to sow the juvenile wild oats, and effect the middle-aged reformation; and it is only because there are gay young men who indulge in profligacy, that women sometimes become adventurers and moral monsters. All this is launched forth in speeches of singular terseness, eloquence, and vigor; but it is hardly necessary to point out that all this is specious and mischievous perversion of the truth — however admirably in character from Stephanie's lips. Every observer who has looked carefully upon the world is aware that the consequences of wrong-doing by a woman are vastly more pernicious than those of wrong-doing by a man; that society could not exist in decency, if to its already inconvenient coterie of reformed rakes it were to add a legion of reformed wantons; and that it is innate wickedness and evil propensity that make such women as Stephanie, and not the mere existence of the wild young men who are willing to become their comrades, and generaily end by being their dupes and victims. It is natural, however, that this adventurer — who has kept a gambling-hell, and ruined many a man, soul and body, and now wishes to reinstate herself in a virtuous social position — should thus strive to palliate her past proceedings. Self-justification is one of the first laws of life. Even Iago, who never deceives himself, yet announces one adequate motive for his fearful crimes. Even Bulwer's Margrave — that prodigy of evil and great type of infernal, joyous, animal depravity — can yet paint himself in the light of harmless loveliness and innocent gayety.

It is but a little while since "Forget Me Not" was seen in New York, and readers and playgoers are familiar with its story. It is a thin story; but, in the handling, it has been made to yield some excellent dramatic pictures, some splendid moments of intellectual combat, and some affecting contrasts of character. The dialogue, particularly in the second act, is as strong and as brilliant as polished steel. Here, in this combat of words, Miss Ward's acting is marvellous for trenchant skill and fascinating variety. The easy, good-natured, bantering air with which the strife begins, the liquid purity of the tones, the delicate glow of the arch satire, the icy glitter of the thought and purpose beneath the words, the transition into pathos and back again into gay indifference and deadly hostility, the sudden and terrible mood of menace, when at length the crisis has passed and the evil genius has won its temporary victory, — all these were in perfect taste and consummate harmony. Seeing this brilliant, supple, relentless, formidable figure, and hearing this incisive, bell-like voice, the spectator is repelled and attracted at the same instant, and thoroughly bewildered with the sense of a power and beauty as hateful as they are glorious. Not since Ristori acted Lucrezia Borgia in this country has our

stage exhibited such an image of imperial will, made radiant
with beauty and electric with flashes of passion. The leopard
and the serpent are fatal, terrible, and loathsome; yet they
scarcely have a peer among nature's supreme symbols of power
and of grace.

Into the last scene of " Forget Me Not," — where, at length,
Stephanie is crushed by physical fear, through beholding,
unseen by him, the man who would kill her as one kills a
malignant and dangerous reptile, — Miss Ward has introduced
certain illustrative " business " not provided by the piece, but
such as greatly enhances its final effect. The backward rush
from the door, on seeing the Corsican avenger on the stair-
case, with the incident yell of terror, is the invention of the
actress; and from this moment to the final exit she is the very
incarnation — thrilling and even agonizing — of abject fear.
The situation is one of the strongest that dramatic ingenuity
has invented; and Miss Ward invests it with a coloring of truth
that is pathetic and awful. Wherever this piece of acting is
seen, accordingly, the lovers of true art will have an enjoyment
such as is seldom vouchsafed upon the stage.

An eminent London physician, whose writings are
much admired for their deep thought, powerful logic
and humanity, wrote to Mrs. Ward the following pleasant letter : —

LONDON, March 10, 1881.

DEAR MRS. WARD, — I have to thank you much for letting
me see the criticism on Genevieve Ward and " Forget Me
Not," in " The New York Tribune." It is indeed a remarkable
article ; and if " Forget Me Not" were published it might
preface it as Schlegel and Coleridge combined preface Shakespeare. There is spiritual clairvoyance in its perception of Miss
Ward's intellectual personation, and a now rare knowledge of
the rights of good and evil, in both the personation and the
drama itself. It is seldom that one meets in criticism with

such a satisfactory wholesome wholeness. To you it must give the gratification of something like a final certificate of your gifted Genevieve's powers. And I am grateful to the writer for also, in his ardent admiration, being so far master of his reason as to be able to declare that human good is the last attainment of the drama in both its parts.

Your old doctor,

GARTH WILKINSON.

Miss Ward appeared in New York in March; and a friend wrote to her : —

"The sure prospect of the triumphant settlement of the Moss-Wallack suit in your favor gives me unfeigned pleasure, since you are unquestionably in the right, morally and legally. . . . Stephanie, as you create her, is a pathetic, thrilling lesson and example in social ethics; and so, strikes deep into the sympathies, and teaches moral and social wisdom in a new and original manner."

"It is very easy to see," wrote Mrs. Anne L. Botta, "how much the play owes to you, and what it would be in inferior hands."

Mrs. George Vandenhoff wrote : —

"I thank you with my whole soul! Your wonderful Stephanie will remain engraven on my memory while I *have* a memory. You turned for me a chapter in the history of a woman's heart which I had never read before. Was it an inspiration that named the play 'Forget Me Not'? Surely to all and every woman who shall see you in that character, you will remain a never-to-be-forgotten revelation! It was not acting: it was living, being, doing, suffering, and agonizing! She was bad — wicked — lost! But your genius so elevated and redeemed her, that my feeling about her is one of regret, of sorrow that the chance she so longed for and prayed for was denied to her. . . . The mingled pathos and scorn with which you appealed to this *man!* the wonderful recovery of your bravado and insolent nonchalance, the grandeur of your defiant and just accusations, and then at last your abject fear — it makes me shudder even *now!* I have always admired you as woman and artist, but in this new creation you rise above my feeble praise."

DEAR MISS WARD, — I am compelled by sheer admiration of your wondrous creative power to say that " Forget Me Not " took us all by storm. The play is not well constructed, but you have made it full of points, creating a character at once true and striking; and I am more than ever your friend and admirer,

R. SHELTON MACKENZIE.

And this from the clever editor of " Harper's Bazar : " —

MARCH 26, 1881.

DEAR MISS WARD, — I think you will like to hear what was said of you last night by Mr. Salvador de Mendoza, consul-general of Brazil, whom we met with his wife on our way home, after leaving you. He declared that he could not understand why the Americans made such a fuss about Sara Bernhardt, when they had so much greater an artist among them in their own countrywoman, Miss Ward. The Mendozas had stopped to talk with Madame Gerster, who expressed herself delighted with your powerful impersonation; and they say she is not easily pleased. These things were so pleasant for me to hear, coinciding so fully with my own opinion, that I feel like telling you of them, though I doubt not they are only echoes of what you hear continually. I was charmed, indeed, with such a subtle and lofty conception of such a complex character as Stephanie; and your countrywomen may well be proud of your success.

Affectionately your friend,

MARY L. BOOTH.

In June of this present year, 1881, Miss Ward returned to London, and devoted herself to her friends, and to her beloved occupation of modelling, at which, as well as in painting, she is very skilful.

In his article on the Dramatic Fine-Art Gallery, Mr. Forbes Robertson said, —

"Here also is a vigorously treated miniature bust of the late Col. Ward, executed from memory by Miss Genevieve Ward, the greatest of our living tragic actresses. She has been blessed with a wonderful diversity of gifts, — a linguist, a musician, an actress in the very highest sense of the term, and, if we may judge by the bust before us and by the pictures she has sent to the exhibition, it is manifest she would have been supreme in these walks also had she turned her attention to them. Her 'Sheep, after Verboeckhoven' (34) would make even an expert hesitate to say that they were not from the pencil of the Flemish master himself. Whence this lady inherited her gift of the pencil, is made abundantly manifest by the exquisite miniature (112) which her mother painted of her when a child. Sir William Ross himself might have stippled this portrait."

"Who taught you to model?" I asked her one day this summer, as she sat working with light and sure touch on the bust of her friend Col. Sanford.

"No one taught me," she replied: "it 'growed' like Topsy; but I ask the best critics to sit in judgment on my work."

But acting, painting, modelling, and talking all tongues, do not complete the list of Miss Ward's accomplishments. She can write. M. Regnier says that her letters would make a second edition of "Madame de Sévigné;" and her "Côtelettes á la Pojarsky," published in "The Theatre" for March, 1881, is a perfect literary *ragoût* of Russian gastronomic novelties.

Her personal friends are the noblest and cleverest men and women of the time ; and I have read and heard abundant and glowing testimony to her personal qualities from those of her own profession, not a jealous note of discord anywhere.   Madame Colmache, critic of "The Court Journal," and author of "The Life of Talleyrand," is one of the most venerable of her friends, a lady who looks like an empress in her own right, needing no crown but her own soft white tresses, and no jewels but the lustre of her serene and loving eyes.

Another of her friends, Miss Elizabeth Philp, the eminent balladist, who wrote the music of "Genevieve," which appears early in this volume, and is also the original of the "English Amazon" figuring in Mr. Sala's brilliant book on the late American Rebellion, is an English lady of most charming character, whose acquaintance is a never-failing source of delight to all who meet her.   Annie Thomas describes her : —

"A distinguished ornament of the musical world, and one of the most perfect hostesses in society, who has risen to a high place among our female composers, and has made her mark by her own unassisted efforts.   Thoroughly impregnated with the real artist spirit, she has set herself resolutely to conquer every difficulty that arises in the artist's path, in the most honorable and legitimate manner.   Clever, painstaking, persevering, and sensitive to an extraordinary degree, she is her own most severe critic ; while her prompt recognition of talent and thoroughness in others, and her hearty appreciation of whatever is worthy in her compeers, render her opinion of their achievements as valuable as it is sought after."

The critic of an authoritative London journal says, —

"Her music is always melodious, intelligent, and unforced. She selects a poem with taste, and interprets it with respect. A poem in her hands remains a poem, and does not become a mere peg on which to hang a melody. This is true art, and real feeling, and is a quality as invaluable to the balladist as it is unfortunately rare. From the long list of a hundred songs which she has composed, it is difficult to select a few for special mention, when all or nearly all of them are of exceptional merit. For pathos, 'Airlie Beacon,' 'Marguerite's Letter,' the grand 'Story of a Year,' and 'Younger Years,' may be fairly quoted; in passionate feeling 'The Poacher's Widow' stands unrivalled among modern English ballads; and 'Lillie's Good-Night' finds an echo in the heart of every mother who hears it. In addition to her great musical gifts, Miss Philp is a profound thinker, a careful reader, and a brilliant conversationalist. She has the art, so rare among women, of telling a story well, and of coming up to her point in a way that compels her most obtuse auditor to see it. Her house in London is the popular head-centre where musical, dramatic, literary, and artistic people (most of them celebrities) delight in meeting on those well-known Thursday afternoons which she commenced some twenty years ago, and has kept going with signal success ever since."

Which is all perfectly true; for I have heard her sing some of her own delightful songs, — one particularly fine in interpretation of Mr. Lowell's "Moonlight deep and tender," — and I have eaten "chicking" at her house, and found it "ospitally"!

As I draw this sketch to a close, the great tragedienne is sailing toward her native land, wearing near her heart the one amulet that never leaves her when she enters into her ideal life of art, — the silver lock of the great Siddons linked with the dark tress severed by Ristori from her own classic temples for a token of love, companionship, and God-speed to the gifted

American woman she so nobly and generously loves. With her go the clever artists, and firm personal friends, who will share with her in the labor and honors of the dramatic representations which many of my readers will be enjoying when these leaves are fresh from the press ; and with her goes also the warm good-will of hosts of friends, and the blessing of the invalid brother and venerable mother who remain behind waiting, with how much love and faith and justified pride, to catch the echoes of the new plaudit from across the sea.

A beautiful light is thrown on the private character of Miss Ward, in a little incident made known to me since her departure for America. A dear friend asked Mrs. Ward how soon they could hope to hear from her daughter.

" I have had a letter from her every day since she sailed ! " was the reply.

Miss Ward had written beforehand letters for each day of her journey, marked them all " per Sea-Gull express," and left them with a friend in Liverpool, to be posted to her mother daily, according to their dates. In these letters Miss Ward's imaginary descriptions of the daily occurrences at sea, not omitting to mention the latitude and longitude they were in, and the progress made, were delightful for originality and humor ; and the whole act was one of the most graceful filial tenderness.

# APPENDIX.

GENEVIEVE WARD,

*Plaintiff,*

*against*

THEODORE MOSS AND LESTER WALLACK,

*Defendants.*

CITY AND COUNTY OF NEW YORK, *ss.:*

GENEVIEVE WARD, being duly sworn, says : I am the plaintiff. I was born in the city of New York, and am a citizen of the United States of America. I am an actress, and am dependent upon the practice of my profession for a livelihood. My attention was first drawn to the play of "Forget-Me-Not" by one of the authors thereof, Mr. Herman Merivale. Messrs. Merivale and Grove were the authors of the said play. Mr. Merivale requested me to read it, and I did so. I was greatly impressed with the dramatic power of the play upon my reading thereof; and I thought I saw that the principal character, Stephanie, Marquise de Mohrivart, was exactly suited to my professional capacities. Not willing to trust to my own judgment, I submitted the play to my good friend Bram Stoker, then and now the acting man-

ager of Henry Irving, Esq., at the Lyceum Theatre, London. Mr. Stoker confirmed my impression of the play,
and of my adaptability for the principal part thereof. I
was in August, 1879, and am still, known in London as
an American actress. Mr. Stoker advised me to secure
the play. I accordingly sent for Mr. Merivale; and he
came to the Lyceum Theatre, Aug. 12, 1879, and we
talked over the terms of the purchase of the play. I
was informed by him that he had never sold the play to
anybody, and that he and Mr. Grove were the authors
thereof, and that they only had one hundred copies of
the play printed; that they had never published the
play, nor sold, nor authorized to be sold, any copies
thereof, and that said play had been printed exclusively
for private circulation. I told said Merivale that I was
about arranging for an American tour, and that I desired
to get a good play for the United States. It was distinctly understood by all parties that I was buying the
piece for representation at any place on the inhabitable
globe. We especially spoke of the United States; and
Mr. Merivale never, prior to the signing of the contract
hereinafter mentioned, by word or action, led me to infer
that aught else was contemplated. Mr. Merivale wanted
some limitation as to the number of times that I should
play the piece within a given time. I told him I did not
think it necessary, as I intended to produce the play in
London, in the Provinces, and in the United States, and
that I had no doubt that I should pay him the whole of
the consideration money within one year from the date
of the production of the piece in London. There were
present at the time of this conversation, besides Mr.
Merivale and myself, my brother Albert Lee Ward, and
Mr. Stoker. Nothing, it seems to me, could have been
better understood than that I was negotiating for the

purchase of the right of the exclusive production of the play everywhere, and that said authors were to sell me such exclusive right of production everywhere, and certainly most especially for the United States, as I had positively stated I was especially desirous of getting a successful play for America. At that interview the terms were fully settled; and it was verbally agreed that I was to have the exclusive right to produce the play for a period of five years, for the sum of three pounds for every time it was produced by me in London, and two pounds for every occasion during said period in which the play was produced by me elsewhere. As soon, however, as I had paid the sum of three hundred pounds, I was then to have the exclusive right of production of said play anywhere during said five years without further payment. I was also to have a right to a further period of five years upon the same terms, providing I gave three months written notice of such being my wish.

The terms being agreed upon, I arranged with Mr. Merivale that he should come to the theatre, and read the play to my company. He came on the thirteenth day of August, 1879, and read the play to the members of the company. All were delighted with it. I at once assigned the different characters, and put the piece in rehearsal. Mr. Merivale gave me three printed copies of the play. He said he could not give me any more, as he had none. Upon the title-page of the play were the words, " Printed for private circulation." I was advised then, and am now, that an author had, and has, a right to print a limited number of copies of his play for his own and friends' use, without thereby dedicating it to the public. I agreed to make the large payment of three hundred pounds for the piece in that belief, and the authors took my money in the like belief. I found my original im-

pression of the play intensified by the rehearsal thereof.
It had been agreed between Mr. Merivale and myself,
that I should have my solicitor prepare a written agreement embodying the above understanding between the
authors and myself. I desired my said brother to so
instruct Mr. Coe, whose affidavit is hereunto annexed.
Mr. Coe prepared the agreement; but what with rehearsing, and one thing and another, I could not get the
authors together to sign it until about five o'clock P.M.
of the twenty-first day of August, 1879. They then went
very carefully over the contract so prepared by Mr. Coe,
in the presence of my brother and Mr. Stoker. The
authors made many suggestions, and desired a very
material amendment thereof. I had agreed to purchase,
and they had agreed to sell to me, the exclusive right,
without restriction, to produce the play anywhere. This,
I am advised, would have given me the right to sell to
others the said right of production. The authors desired to change this so as to limit my right of sale, and
compel the performance by myself. As the piece was to
be played that night, I consented to that important alteration from our understanding. The contract was then
signed by the authors in the presence of my brother and
the said Stoker. Hereunto annexed, marked "Exhibit
A," is a copy of the contract as finally concluded and
signed between us. I have never heard of the authors
disputing this contract. I have understood that they
now affect to interpret it differently from its plain meaning, and from the usual import attached to the language
employed in the contract. Indeed, the authors have,
since the execution of the contract, fully satisfied and
confirmed the same in all its features by bringing an
action thereon in a court of England, before Lord Coleridge. · His lordship, Sept. 29, 1880, denied the authors'

motion, with costs. Hereunto annexed, marked "Exhibit B," is a report of the case as it appeared in "The Daily Telegraph," a newspaper printed in the city of London, Eng., on the thirtieth day of September, 1880.

The play, from the night of its first production, on the said twenty-first day of August, 1879, was a great success. The papers, with one accord, spoke very highly of it; and the London managers all believed in its being destined to a long and prosperous career. Prior to its first production, Mr. Merivale had induced me to permit a sister-in-law of his to appear in the part of Rose de Brissac. Notwithstanding I had a lady of my company well suited to play the part, I yielded to his request, the more so as I desired to remain upon good terms with Mr. Merivale. Unhappily the young lady proved herself inadequate to play the part. I called Mr. Merivale's particular attention to the shortcoming; and he begged me to retain her, and that he would coach her so as to play the part acceptably. She showing no improvement, for managerial reasons I was compelled to substitute a daughter of Grace Greenwood in her place. By this necessary act, I incurred the malignant hatred of Mr. Merivale. So bitter was his resentment that he published cruel lies of me, and sent defamatory circulars wherever he thought he could do me harm. He has publicly threatened I should never play the piece in America. Regarding him as an unaccountable being, after advising with my friends, I have taken no notice of him, but have done all in my power to make his play a success. I trust I do not offend good taste when I add that the unhappy man, Mr. Merivale, was for several years in an asylum of restraint, where he had been placed by his own mother for an assault upon her. This is a fact of open, common notoriety in England; and I refer to it

principally because the defendant Moss claims to have
had a verbal arrangement with Mr., Merivale about the
play. At that time I verily believe he was in an insane-
asylum. The instantaneous success of the play, and the
difference above mentioned with Mr. Merivale, led the
authors to refuse to receive the first payment of compen-
sation due under the contract. They continued to refuse
for several weeks. They sought to have me break the
said contract; but I was careful to fully keep its terms,
and I made all necessary tender of the amounts legally
due thereunder. I finally, and on the eighth day of
April, 1880, paid to and the said authors received from
me the full balance of the said three hundred pounds
mentioned in the said contract; and I now allege I am
the sole owner of the right to produce said play for my
exclusive performance for the period of five years from
the twenty-first day of August, 1879, without further
payment.

I solemnly aver, that, at no time during the negotiations
between the authors and myself, did I ever hear the said
authors say, suggest, or intimate that they had, at any
time prior thereto, made any sale of said play to any
person whomsoever, either in Europe or America. I
never heard the names of Lester Wallack or Theodore
Moss mentioned by said authors, or either of them. I
remember saying to Mr. Merivale, prior to signing of the
contract, that I should produce the play in France. He
said it was a good idea, and that he would translate it for
me. Before the signing of the contract, I only had
casual conversations with Mr. Grove. Mr. Merivale represented him with full·powers. Afterwards, and when
the play had run about eight days, Mr. Grove called upon
me at my residence in St. John's Wood, London, and,
after referring to the unhappy difference that had arisen

between Mr. Merivale and myself touching the want of
capacity of the sister-in-law of said Merivale to fill the
aforesaid part of Rose de Brissac, stated to me that the
executed agreement was all on my side ; but that he had
submitted it to his solicitor, Mr. Martineau, and that the
said Martineau had stated that the contract was perfect
and valid. But that he, Grove, hoped I would change it
to the one that he had prepared. He then handed me
the paper hereunto annexed, marked " Exhibit C." We
discussed its terms. He said it was not fair; that I
might go to America, and stay there a year, and that
it would injure the piece greatly not to have it performed meanwhile in England. He therefore proposed
the alteration contained in subdivision three of said
Exhibit C. I talked freely to him of playing the piece
in the United States. He never even hinted that I
had no right to do so. Indeed, the judge, hearing this
motion, will find that in exact words, in subdivision four
of said Exhibit C, he includes the United States. This,
I think, quite disposes of the asserted claim of Mr.
Moss, that the authors had already verbally sold to him
the right to produce the play in the United States. Mr.
Grove urged upon me that I ought to make these proposed changes, as the play was very successful. I informed him that I had made the play a success; that
they had tried for years to sell the play to managers,
both in England and America, and that no one of them
could be induced to undertake its production. He did
not deny this statement, but insisted that I ought to
change the terms. I told him we had already agreed upon
our terms; but that, if I found the play was a great success in the United States, I would send him a further
check as a matter of good feeling. He still urged me to
sign Exhibit C. Finally he threatened me, that, unless I

signed, they would write a novel upon the play, that somebody would dramatize it, and thus I would be injured without my being able to prove that they did it. I told him, in conclusion, "that I should consult my solicitor, and, if I found that they had a knife at my throat, I would sign it; otherwise, not." He then handed Exhibit C to my brother, and left. Mr. Grove, after said interview on the fifteenth day of September, 1879, sent to me a letter in his own handwriting, which is hereunto annexed, marked "Exhibit D." He simply claims therein that I have no right to produce a translation of the play. I have never modified the agreement, and it remains as it was executed. After the contract had been signed between the authors and myself, two engrossed copies thereof were made, and sent to the authors for execution, which they never executed, but proposed in lieu thereof the said Exhibit C. I first heard in January, 1880, from Mr. Bird, my attorney herein, of the claim of Mr. Moss to produce the play in the United States. I tried to learn from the authors whether or not they had sold the right to the United States prior to selling it to me. I could not learn that they had. Mr. Grove indignantly denied, on the 31st of January, 1880, to my brother, as mentioned in his affidavit hereunto annexed, that he had made any such sale, not wishing to run any risk; and on the fifth day of February, 1880, my brother, at my request, wrote to Mr. Grove, requesting an answer in writing as to whether the authors had sold the play for the United States to Mr. Moss, and received in reply from the solicitors of said Grove an answer hereunto annexed, marked "Exhibit D, No. 2," wherein Mr. Grove indignantly spurned the imputation of an earlier sale than the one to me. I then requested my attorney, Mr. Bird, to call upon Mr. Moss, and have him show him his alleged contract

with the authors. Mr. Bird did so, and informed me that
it was without date, but that Mr. Moss had stated to him
that he would swear that he had had it in his possession for two years. I then directed Mr. Bird, as I was
under contract with Col. Sinn, of the Brooklyn Park
Theatre, to come to America and produce " Forget-Me-
Not," to call upon Mr. Moss, and see what compromise
could be made with him. None was made with him. I
was, however, involved in such doubt, distrusting the
authors, and believing the statement made to my attorney
by said Moss to be true, and being threatened by Mr.
Moss with injunction proceedings if I came to America
to play " Forget-Me-Not," that I had to abandon my engagement at heavy loss to myself and Col. Sinn. I
advised in London with Mr. Judah P. Benjamin ; and he
counselled me to have an action, brought in America
against Moss, and compel him to show his contract, so
that, if it should appear that the allegation of the defendant Moss was true, and that he really had a contract prior
in date to mine, and taking precedence of mine, I could
bring on action against the authors in England, where I
then was, for damages, and I would be spared the further
damage of coming to the United States, and asserting a
right which I did not have. I directed my attorney, Mr.
Bird, to bring this action, and examine Mr. Moss herein.
Mr. Moss was examined, and then produced his alleged
contract, a copy of which is hereunto annexed, marked
" Exhibit E." This contract was not acknowledged until
the tenth day of March, 1880. It is only an assignment
of the authors' right, title, and interest in and for the
said play in said United States. Mr. Moss has sworn
in this case that he received the contract, Exhibit E, after
the tenth day of March, 1880, although I understand he
had told Mr. Bird that he had had possession of it for two

years. When Mr. Merivale was accused of double-deal
ing with regard to this alleged contract with Mr. Moss,
he published in a London paper, called "The Era," a
letter over his signature, which is hereunto annexed,
marked "Exhibit F." I was advised by my attorney that
the defendant Moss would claim that "Forget-Me-Not"
had been published and sold by the authors, both before
and since my purchase as aforesaid. This greatly astonished me, and prepared me for the present contract.
I have caused diligent search to be made at all places in
London where the said play would be exposed for sale if
the same had been published, and could not find that such
had been or was the case. I know, when I purchased the
right of production aforesaid, I applied to the authors for
additional copies of the play, and Mr. Merivale informed
me that he had none. I asked him if he did not know
where I could find some, and he answered no. I further
asked him if he thought the printer might not have some
copies. He said he did not know, so I called upon him;
but he informed me that only one hundred private copies
had been printed, and that he had none on hand. I am
quite sure that I should have heard of the fact if the play
had been published and sold in London and the British
Isles. I am also convinced that the copies referred to by
Mr. Moss, if they are in existence, have either been
printed since my purchase, or else refer to the limited
edition printed as aforesaid but not published.

Had the play been published and sold at the time of
my purchase of it — thus making it public property,— in
this country, I certainly would not have paid the large
sum of three hundred pounds for it. It would, under
such circumstances, have been dishonest in the authors
to have taken my money, as they knew I was buying a
play for America. I was advised, that, by the law of

England, the play must first be produced there, and that
it had to be entered under the act generally known there
as the Copyright Act of the 5th and 6th of Victoria, chap.
45, enacted July 1, 1842, which, amongst other things,
provides, "In case of any dramatic piece or musical
composition in manuscript, it shall be sufficient for the
person having the sole liberty of representing or performing, or causing to be represented or performed, the
same, to register only the title thereof, the name and
place of abode of the author or composer thereof, the
name and place of abode of the proprietor thereof, and
the time and place of its first representation or performance." I therefore caused the said requirements to be
duly observed, so as to protect my right of property in
said play in England, and also to prevent any dedication
thereof to the public under British laws. This was done
on or about the twenty-first day of August, 1879. The
play has never been published under the Copyright Act,
or in any way, either by the authors or myself. It was not
necessary to publish it in order to obtain the protection
thereof. The reference to the authors as owners of the
copyright of a play called "Forget-Me-Not," in the contract, had sole regard to my contemplated act aforesaid,
and was inserted by my lawyer in said contract, as a matter
of description only, at my request. The word "copyright"
in the agreement was not intended, nor does it refer to a
published play of "Forget-Me-Not." I should never
have purchased the right of production of said play if it
had been a published play. Nothing is better understood
in the theatrical profession than that an author may pre-
serve the manuscript character of his play by having a
number of copies thereof printed for private use. It saves
vast trouble, and is of great utility in the distribution and
learning of parts. I know that authors and managers,

both in Europe and America, have printed what are known as manuscript copies of an original play. Upon information and belief, I state that such is sometimes the custom and habit of both the defendants herein at their theatre, known as "Wallack's," in this city. If this play has been published, and publicly sold, as I am informed the defendant Moss, in his extremity, now claims, I then charge and aver that it has been done since I purchased my right thereto, and in pursuance of a fraudulent conspiracy between the said authors and the said defendant Moss. I deny that it has been done. I have no doubt that said Moss may have had a copy of said play in his possession at or about the time stated in his examination hereunto annexed, marked "Exhibit G." In fact, I have been informed by Mr. George Loveday of London, that, several years ago, Mr. John Clayton, a friend of Mr. Merivale's, requested him to open negotiations with Wallack's Theatre concerning the play of "Forget-Me-Not." Merivale was then not mentally capable of business. That, in pursuance of said request, the said Loveday sent to said Moss a copy of said printed manuscript play; that said Moss afterwards returned same to said Loveday, and subsequently thereto Loveday returned the same to said Moss, at his (Moss's) request. The said Loveday informed me that the said Moss thereafter declined to make any contract concerning the said play, and that the negotiation came to nought. I was advised that the defendant Moss claimed to have acquired some rights through the said Mr. John Clayton. I therefore requested my brother to ask him concerning same. The result of the investigation was, that said Mr. Clayton sent to him the letter hereunto annexed, marked "Exhibit H," which is in his, said Clayton's, handwriting. I have thus shown to the court that not only the authors, but that all the parties represented by said Moss to have been in any way connected with the alleged verbal sale to him, repudiate the same; the authors claiming that to have sold it to me when they had previously sold it to Mr. Moss, would not only have been dishonorable, but that, as a matter of fact, no contract with Moss was made until they sold whatever right, title, and interest to the play they then had, "if any there was," to him in March, 1880. This is fully shown by Exhibit E, being without date, and having been acknowledged as late as March 10, 1880. The acts and doings of said Moss are in keeping with this last stated fact. He never advertised that he owned the right to "Forget-Me-Not" in the United States until March 28, 1880, and then in "The World" newspaper of this city, just after the receipt of Exhibit E; and subsequently issued a circular to a like effect under the date of April 9, 1880. I desire to call the careful attention of the court to Exhibit E, wherein Mr. Moss claims to have purchased his right from Merivale only. This was in January, 1880. No doubt the fraud was perfected after that date and contract, Exhibit E given, without date, to bolster it up. It is incredible, if he had the right to the play at the time he claims, that he should have slumbered so long on his rights, and should have permitted the play to have been produced in California without any attempt on his part to stop it. As soon as I was notified in London that my rights were being invaded in America, I caused due and public notice of my ownership of said play to be given through the public newspapers. I also, as early as January, 1880, caused to be sent a notice thereof to every theatre in America that would be able to produce the play. One of said notices was sent to Wallack's Theatre, with the result stated in the affidavit of my attorney, John H. Bird.

This was the first time I ever heard of the asserted claim of said Moss. My rights, since said notification, have been respected by all managers in America, excepting the defendant. No one in the British dominions has dared to attempt to invade them. When I was convinced that the claim of said Moss — as to his having a contract with the owners prior in date to mine — was spurious, I then directed, as before stated, that the action brought against him should be prosecuted, and to seek, with other relief, an injunction restraining him from performing the play in the United States. The action was begun by the service of summons on Aug. 5, 1880. The said defendant Moss has been examined under an order of the chief judge of this court, and a copy of his examination is hereunto annexed, marked " Exhibit G." I never believed that the defendants, Moss and Wallack, would, in the face of the facts, actually produce the said play of " Forget - Me - Not," until I received a letter from my attorney, of the date of Nov. 26, 1880, stating that the defendants' attorney had told him that as soon as the run of " The Gov'nor " was over, the said play would be produced at Wallack's Theatre. My attorney had previously urged upon me the importance of my being here at the trial of the case; and, as I believed I was about to be foully wronged, I hastened to America with such hasty affidavits as I could collect, to vindicate, in person, my rights in a court of justice. Unfortunately, notice of my departure was cabled to the American newspapers; and, to the astonishment of the theatrical world, " The Gov'nor " was withdrawn in the midst, "as the defendants claimed," of its prosperous career, and " Forget - Me - Not " substituted. I aver that this was done so as to produce the play before I could arrive and apply for an injunction.

My attorney informs me that the play was produced in violation of a verbal understanding between counsel to the effect that after it was determined to produce the play sufficient time would be allowed him to send to Europe, and get necessary affidavits. He also tells me that he granted the adjournments of the defendants' examination from time to time, upon that understanding. That examination was only concluded on the 6th inst. I now learn that the defendants' counsel repudiates any such arrangement, and claims that my attorney is wholly mistaken. Be that as it may, when I arrived here on Wednesday, the 22d inst., I found that the defendants had produced said play of " Forget-Me-Not " at their theatre, on Saturday evening, Dec. 18, 1880. It is my firm belief, and I aver the same to be the truth, that said play was produced on that date, so as to prevent my getting an injunction in time to stop it, as the said defendants well knew I was *en route* to this country with that purpose in view. Since my arrival here I have devoted all the time that my ill health would permit, in giving my said attorney the facts to prepare the necessary papers herein. I have not delayed a moment that could have been saved. I aver that Lester Wallack is the manager, and Theodore Moss is the treasurer, of the theatre known as " Wallack's " in this city, and upon information and belief that both share as partners in the net profits thereof. That both are now producing, in violation of my exclusive right of production everywhere of said play, said play at said Wallack's Theatre in the city of New York. That I have never directly or indirectly consented thereto. That the said Wallack claims to produce the said play under a verbal license from his co-defendant and partner Moss, as appears by said examination of said Moss, hereunto annexed. That the said Wallack well

knows my rights and claims in the premises, and that the
same are prior to any pretended claim of his co-defendant. That the whole has been done by the said defendants, each and both of them, in pursuance of a conspiracy
between said defendants and the authors of said play to
rob me of my exclusive right to produce the play in these
United States. That the said Moss further threatens,
and says he is now in negotiation with other managers,
to sell to them licenses to produce said play throughout
the United States. That the said Wallack is a party to
the said scheme, and is, and will be, interested in the
profits thereof. That the right to the exclusive production upon the stage of said play is of great value to me.
I verily believe that during the time I am entitled to it
under my contract it will be, if I am protected in my
rights, worth upward of the sum of one hundred thousand
dollars. That I created the part of Stephanie, and have
played it nearly three hundred times in the kingdom of
Great Britain and Ireland. That I have acquired by
hard work, and the expenditure of a vast deal of money,
exceeding the sum of five thousand dollars, great artistic
notoriety in the part of Stephanie, and have made the play
of " Forget-Me-Not " one of the pecuniary successes of
the age. That hereunto annexed, marked " Exhibit J,"
are transcripts from the leading London papers concerning my production of said play, and my representation of
the leading character thereof. That, without vanity, I
verily believe the success of said play depends upon my
creation of the part of Stephanie. That, if said play is
permitted to be played, my right of property therein will
be greatly injured, and the said play will become valueless
to me. That no amount of damages that the defendants
are able to pay would repay me for the time and money
I have spent in introducing this often-rejected play to

the public. That the said play is announced for nightly performance at said Wallack's Theatre, and that, as deponent is informed and believes, the said defendants are now arranging a company to play said piece in all the principal cities of the United States; that the production of said play at said Wallack's Theatre, its continued performance thereat, and the threats to license others to produce the same, in violation of my rights respecting the subject of the action, and tending to render the judgment to be recovered herein ineffectual, have all occurred during the pendency of this action; that final judgment has not been rendered herein; that I never intended that the said play of "Forget-Me-Not" should be published in America, and I do not now so intend. In fact, I do not claim the right to copyright said play, as I am not the author thereof, and I have never had any authority or permission from said authors to copyright said play; that my object in depositing the title-page of said play was to secure the title to said play, and the manuscript thereof. I never deposited with the librarian of Congress any of the printed books of said play. I was subsequently advised that the play, being the composition of foreign authors, could not be the subject of a valid copyright, and that publication was a condition precedent to obtaining the same; and, further, that I must rely upon my common law rights, which would afford me adequate protection.

That the production of said play at said Wallack's Theatre has already done me great pecuniary injury, and if continued during the pendency of this action the injury will be irreparable.

GENEVIEVE WARD.

Sworn to before me, this thirty-first day of December, 1880.

MILES F. POWERS,

*Notary Public,* Kings County

Certificate filed in New-York County.

## Superior Court of the City of New York.

GENEVIEVE WARD *against* THEODORE MOSS.

I, FREDERICK CHARLES of the city of London, England, being duly sworn, say and declare, that I have inquired at Stationers' Hall, in the city of London, where all plays or publications are recorded (if published or printed), if the play "Forget-Me-Not," by Herman C. Merivale and F. C. Grove, had been recorded or registered as printed and published for public circulation or sale, and found that it has not been done. I have also inquired at the several printing-offices where plays are printed and published, if said play had been printed or published for public sale, and found it had not been. I certify that to my certain knowledge, Miss Genevieve Ward has expended much time, money, and assiduous labor, in making the play "Forget-Me-Not" a success, and that it is due to her personal energy and acting such success is chiefly due.

In witness whereof I have hereunto set my hand, this tenth day of December, A.D. 1880.

FREDERICK CHARLES.

Sworn by Frederick Charles, at the Consulate-General of the United States of America, No. 53 Old Broad Street, in the city of London, this the tenth day of December, 1880, before me,

.          T. NUNN,

*Vice and Deputy Consul-General and ex-officio a Notary Public of the United States at London, and a Commissioner to administer oaths in the Supreme Court of Judicature, in England.*

[L.S.]

## Superior Court of the City of New York.

GENEVIEVE WARD *against* THEODORE MOSS.

I, BRAM STOKER of the city of London, England, do solemnly swear and declare, that, at the time of making the arrangement for the purchase by Miss G. Ward from Herman Charles Merivale and Florence Crawford Grove of the play of " Forget-Me-Not," no mention was made to me or to my knowledge that the piece or any of the rights thereto had been in any way previously disposed of; and I was all along convinced that Miss Genevieve Ward was purchasing from Messrs. H. C. Merivale and F. C. Grove the sole and entire rights of the play for the time and under the conditions specified in the agreement.

In witness whereof I have hereunto set my hand this tenth day of December, 1880.

BRAM STOKER.

Sworn by Bram Stoker, at the Consulate-General of the United
    States of America, No. 53 Old Broad Street, in the city of
    London, this the tenth day of December, 1880, before me,

T. NUNN,

*Vice and Deputy Consul-General and ex-officio a Notary
        Public of the United States at London, and a Com-*
[L. S.]  *missioner to administer oaths in the Supreme Court
        of Judicature in England.*

[EXHIBIT A.]

*Memorandum of agreement made the twenty-first day of
August, one thousand eight hundred and seventy-nine, between
Herman Charles Merivale of Barton Lodge, Kingston-on-
Thames, and Florence Crawford Grove of 4 Bolton Row,
Piccadilly (hereinafter called "the authors") of the one part,
and Genevieve Ward, of No. 10 Cavendish Road, Saint
John's Wood (hereinafter called "the purchaser") of the other
part, whereby it is agreed as follows : —*

1. The authors who are the owners of the copyright of a play called " Forget-Me-Not," hereby agree that the purchaser shall have the sole right to produce for her own performance the said play for performance for a period of five years from the date hereof. The purchaser agrees to pay for such right the sum of three pounds for every occasion during the aforesaid period on which the said play shall be produced by her in London, and two pounds for every occasion during the aforesaid period in which the play shall be produced by her elsewhere.

2. So soon, however, as a sum of three hundred pounds shall have been paid by the purchaser to the authors, under the first clause of this agreement, she shall from that time have the sole right, until the expiration of the said term of five years, to produce for her own performance the play at any place, without making any payment to the authors.

3. Upon the expiration of the said term of five years, the purchaser shall (provided within three months from that time she intimates in writing to the authors addressed, and sent by post to their last known places of abode, of her wish to do so) have the sole right to produce for her own performance the said play for a further period of five years upon precisely similar terms as regards payment to the authors as those mentioned in this agreement; the meaning and intention of the parties hereto being that the purchaser shall in fact have a right to renew this agreement for a second or further period of five years.

4. Nothing in this agreement contained shall affect the right of the authors to use the story for other than dramatic purposes.

HERMAN C. MERIVALE.
F. C. GROVE,
GENEVIEVE WARD (Per A. L. W.).

[EXHIBIT B.]

"THE DAILY TELEGRAPH," LONDON, SEPT. 30, 1880.

BEFORE LORD COLERIDGE — MERIVALE *v*. WARD.

This was a motion for an injunction to restrain the defendant from performing or allowing to be performed the play of " Forget-Me-Not," with the omission of one of the characters. It appeared that the plaintiffs, Messrs. Merivale and Grove, are the proprietors of the play, and the defendant, Miss Genevieve Ward, had purchased from them the sole right of representation for five years from 1879.

Mr. Woodroffe appeared for the defendant, and objected that the matter was not vacation business. His lordship said the motion was for an injunction to restrain a performance now going on, and, in his opinion, was properly vacation business. Mr. Woodroffe contended that the character omitted was not an important one, and that the plaintiffs had sustained no damage whatever. The learned counsel handed up a copy of the play in which the part in question was struck out in pencil by the plaintiff Merivale himself. A letter was also produced, in which Mr. Merivale said the play was much too lengthy, and was improved by the omission of the character " Rose." Mr. Ford said that Mr. Grove, the joint author of the play, did not agree with this view. Lord Coleridge observed that Mr. Grove had made no affidavit in the case. Mr. Ford said this was owing to his absence on the Continent, and asked that the motion might be adjourned.

His lordship refused to adjourn the motion, and, in delivering judgment, said that before the plaintiffs could be entitled to the injunction asked for they must show, first, that there had been a breach of the agreement; secondly, that they were suffering serious damage by such breach; thirdly, that the damage would be irreparable if the court did not grant the injunction. Upon none of these points had the plaintiffs succeeded, and it was therefore his duty to refuse the motion with costs.

[EXHIBIT C.]

*Memorandum of agreement made the twenty-first day of August, one thousand eight hundred and seventy-nine, between Herman Charles Merivale, of Barton Lodge, Kingston-on-Thames, and Florence Crawford Grove, of 4 Bolton Road, Piccadilly, London (hereinafter called "the authors") of the one part, and Genevieve Ward, of No. 10 Cavendish Road, Saint John's Wood (hereinafter called "the purchaser") of the other part, whereby it is agreed as follows:—*

1. The authors, who are the owners of the copyright of a play called "Forget-Me-Not," hereby agree that the purchaser shall have the sole right to produce, for her own performance, the said play, in English, as written by them, for a period of three years from the 21st August, 1879. The purchaser agrees to pay for such right the sum of three (3) pounds sterling for every occasion during the aforesaid period in which the play shall be produced by her in London, and two (2) pounds sterling for every occasion during the aforesaid period in which the play shall be produced by her elsewhere.

2. So soon, however, as a sum of three (3) hundred pounds sterling shall have been paid by the purchaser to the authors, under the first clause of this agreement, she shall, from that time, have the sole right, until the expiration of the said term of three years, to produce for her own performance the play, at any place, without making any payment to the authors.

3. In the event of the purchaser ceasing to perform on the stage in England for a period of three consecutive months during the said term of three years, the authors are to have the right to license any one else to produce and perform the play, at any royalty they think fit to take; but accounting and paying to the purchaser one-half of whatever royalty they do so take.

4. During the said period of three years the authors shall have the right to license translations of the play into a foreign language, for performance in any country except Great Britain and Ireland and the United States.

5. During the said period of three years the authors shall not use the story for any purpose whatsoever.

In witness, the hands of the parties, the day and year first above written.

### [EXHIBIT D, No. 1.]

4 BOLTON ROW, MAY FAIR, W., Sept. 13, 1879.

DEAR MADAME, — In order to prevent any possible misunderstanding, I write to say that I do not at all admit that you have the right to produce a translation of "Forget-Me-Not." I regret having to trouble you, but I think it best to have no doubt on this point.

I am faithfully yours,

F. C. GROVE.

### [EXHIBIT D, No. 2.]

36 THEOBALD'S ROAD, GRAY'S INN, W.C.,
7th February, 1880.

SIR, — We are requested by Mr. Crawford Grove to acknowledge the receipt of your letter to him of the 5th.

He is much surprised that a question which imputed dishonorable conduct to himself and Mr. Merivale should be repeated; and, having regard to the way in which they have been treated, he is not inclined to assist you in asserting an alleged right, the evidence of which he does not admit.

We remain your obedient servants,

WALKER, MARTINEAU, & CO.

A. LEE WARD, ESQ.

[EXHIBIT E.]

We, Florence Crawford Grove, of 4 Bolton Row, Mayfair, London, and Herman Charles Merivale, of Barton Lodge, Kingston-on-Thames, England, do, in consideration of the sum of one dollar, hereby transfer, assign, set over, and convey to Theodore Moss, of Wallack's Theatre, New York, all our right, title, and interest in and for our play of "Forget-Me-Not," in and throughout the United States of America, and we do hereby authorize him to take any and all steps necessary for the defence of the said right, title, and interest.

FLORENCE CRAWFORD GROVE. [L. S.]
HERMAN CHARLES MERIVALE. [L. S.]

Signed, sealed, and delivered in presence of

T. W. VRIGON,
*Consulate General U.S.A., London.*

H. H. NERDMAN,
*Consulate General of the United States of America for Great Britain and Ireland, at London.*

On the tenth day of March, 1880, before me, Joshua Nunn, Vice and Deputy Consul General and Notary Public *ex-officio* of the United States of America, residing at London, England, personally appeared Florence Crawford Grove and Herman Charles Merivale, to me known to be the persons of that name severally described in, and who have executed, the foregoing assignment or instrument, and then and there acknowledged the same to be their free and voluntary act and deed, for the uses and purposes therein contained; in testimony whereof I have hereunto set my hand and affixed my official notarial seal, at London aforesaid, the day and year above written.

[L. S.]                                              J. NUNN,
    *Vice and Deputy Consul General, U. S. A., London.*

[EXHIBIT F.]

"THE ERA," LONDON, OCT. 3, 1880.

"FORGET-ME-NOT."

*To the Editor of the Era.*

SIR, — There is a paragraph in your American news with reference to this play which I am obliged to notice. It throws doubt upon the "good faith" of Mr. Grove and myself, states that our contract contains a clause selling the play for "Great Britain and elsewhere," and that "unquestionably Mr. Moss's contract with us was made prior to the other" — as your correspondent "hears" — a year or more.

Imputations upon our good faith do not much trouble men of Mr. Grove's character and mine; but we are not good at what is known and admired in the modern dramatic world as "smartness," and it will probably be some time before we have thoroughly sifted and exposed a very discreditable affair, which, having begun with it, we now intend to do.

There is no clause about "Great Britain and elsewhere;" and, if there had been, it would have exposed its own futility, as, being British authors, we had no rights outside our own country to give. The contract described us as "owners of the copyright," and let the play for so much a night in London, and so much elsewhere, — a word which does not mean the moon. "Owners of the copyright" limits the operation of the contract to places where we possessed it, — the Islands and possibly the Colonies, about which last I don't know. As for an "American right," people do not usually give, or intend to give, what they haven't got. We might just as well have let Buckingham Palace. The difficulty of all English authors is to secure a right in America. If it could be done by the very simple process of omitting allusions to America in the agreement, that difficulty would be strikingly simplified. I do not understand how such a claim can be seriously put forward; but no doubt the American courts will know how to deal with it.

As to our agreement with Mr. Moss, we might, I presume, have made it when we liked, on principle of doing what we please with our own. As a matter of fact, and in spite of your correspondent's "unquestionable" information, we made the assignment to Mr. Moss in the only legal way we found practicable, six months or more after the first contract, for no consideration in money whatever, and in simple self-defence against the extraordinary tricks then being practised on us and our play, both in England and America.

While I am upon the subject, I may as well·allude to this morning's decision in the matter of the injunction for which we applied to prevent the mutilation of the play. I was myself in Leicester, and came up too late, under the impression the case was to come on in the afternoon. I therefore had no opportunity of explaining what I must now reserve for a later period. That the "letter" produced, without any statement of the circumstances which followed, makes the matter, in my opinion, infinitely worse with reference especially to Mr.

Grove. But for all further action I shall wait till Mr. Grove's return from the Continent, where he is at present travelling. You will now have published "both sides of the question" in a preliminary form, and will, I hope, refrain from further discussion till the whole matter has been the subject of inquiry.

Meanwhile, it is as well that authors and actors, from their different points of view, should be thoroughly aware that an original English play is now being acted in London with the omission of a character in the mature and deliberate judgment of both the authors essential, after an express prohibition addressed to the responsible manager of the Prince of Wales, three weeks before its production, and by him deliberately disregarded.

Faithfully yours,
(Signed)     HERMAN MERIVALE.

SEPT. 29, 1880.

[EXHIBIT G.]

## New York Superior Court.

GENEVIEVE WARD *against* THEODORE MOSS.

*Examination of Theodore Moss, in pursuance of an order made herein by Mr. Justice Sedgwick, on the fifth day of August, 1880.*

I reside in the city of New York, and have resided here for forty years past; have been engaged in the theatrical business for a number of years; have been, and am now, engaged as a manager; I know the play of "Forget-Me-Not;" I know that Merivale and Grove are the authors of the play; Mr. Merivale's first name is Herman Charles, and Mr. Grove's full name is Florence Crawford; I do not know them personally.

*Q.* Do you claim an interest in the play of "Forget-Me-Not"?

Objected to, and answered subject to objection.

*A.* I do claim the entire and exclusive right and ownership of the play in the United States of America, to do just as I please with it.

*Q.* When did you acquire that right?

Objected to, and reserved.

*A.* Verbally in 1878. When I was notified by Col. Sinn that Miss Ward claimed some rights in the play, I notified Mr. Sinn that I owned the play; and I then sent to the authors for a written contract, which I received, and a copy of which has been furnished to plaintiff's attorney.

*Q.* Does your title to the play in question arise by a purchase thereof?

Objected to, and answered subject to objection.

*A.* It does.

*Q.* From whom did you purchase it?

Objected to, and answered as above.

*A.* From the authors above named.

*Q.* Was such purchase evidenced by any memorandum in writing?

Objected to, and answered as above.

*A.* The purchase was both verbal and written.

*Q.* Have you now got possession of the written part of that agreement?

Objected to, and answered subject to objection.

*A.* It is in the hands of my counsel, Mr. Dittenhoefer.

*Q.* Will you produce it on this examination, and show it to me, as counsel to Miss Ward, and submit it for my examination?

Objected to, and answered subject to objection.

*A.* I will not, unless ordered to by the Court.

*Q.* When did you receive this written paper?

Objected to, and question reserved.

*A.* I must have received it after the tenth day of March, 1880. I have no present recollection.

*Q.* Have you made any arrangement or contract for the production of the play of " Forget-Me-Not "?

*A.* I have made no arrangement, but have had some negotiations for its production ; but have made no licenses nor granted any permissions for its production.

*Q.* Do you intend to produce the play?

Question objected to, and answered subject to objection.

*A.* I do.

*Q.* Have you got a copy of the play in your possession?

Objected to, and answered as above.

*A.* I have a copy, received from the authors themselves.

*Q.* Is the copy in your possession in print, or manuscript?

Objected to, and question reserved.    .

*A.* It is in print.

*Q.* When did you receive the copy of the play that you have in your possession?

Objected to, and question reserved.

*A.* The first copy that I had was in 1876, and that was in print.

*Q.* Did the copy in your possession and the memorandum in your possession come to you at the same time, or at different times? and, if at different times, which came first?

Objected to, and question reserved.

*A.* At different times, and a copy of the play came first.

*Q.* Were your negotiations for the purchase conducted by correspondence with the authors, or conducted through the medium of a third person?

Objected to, and question reserved.

*A.* I received the play first through my agent, Mr. Floyd: the negotiations were partly conducted by him and partly by myself.

*Q.* Have you in your possession any letters from the authors, or either of them, upon the subject of the purchase, or of acquiring your title to this play?

Objected to, and answered as above.

*A.* I have a number of them.

*Q.* Who are those letters from?

Objected to, and question reserved.

*A.* From Mr. Merivale.

*Q.* About when are those letters dated, and about when were they received?

Objected to, and declines to answer.

*Q.* At the time you purchased the play of " Forget-Me-Not," or the right to produce it in America, or whatever proprietary interest you may have therein, were you informed by any person that the plaintiff, Genevieve Ward, had an interest in the play?

Objected to, and answered subject to objection.

*A.* When I first received the play, Miss Ward had never heard of it, as I am informed; since that I have been informed by the authors that she never had any rights in the United States.

*Q.* When the authors so informed you, did he or they inform you what rights Miss Ward had?

Objected to, and reserved.

*A.* No.

*Q.* When you were informed by the authors that the plaintiff had no rights in the United States, was it before, or after, your purchase?

Objected to, and reserved.

*A.* It was after.

*Q.* Was the information you speak of respecting Miss Ward's want of right in the United States conveyed to you in writing?

Objected to, and answered as above.

*A.* It was.

*Q.* Will you produce that letter, and allow me, as counsel for Miss Ward, to examine it?

Objected to, and answered as above.

*A.* I will not, unless ordered by the Court.

*Q.* Why will you not produce it?

*A.* Because I am advised by the counsel that is not proper.

Adjourned by consent to Aug. 31, 1880, at 12 M.

Adjourned by consent to Sept. 7, 1880, at 12 M.

JOHN H. BIRD,
*Plaintiff's Attorney.*

I sold the right to produce the play to Mr. Wallack for the city of New York. I did that before my examination in this cause; but I did not think, when I was inquired of respecting transfers, that you meant to refer to Wallack's Theatre. The license to Wallack is verbal, and made ever since I have had the play.

*Q.* What consideration, if any, did you pay for the assignment of the play to you?

*A.* An agreement to pay royalties. The agreement as to royalties was by correspondence. I don't remember the date. I don't know when the play will be produced at Wallack's.

*Cross-examined.* — I first got a printed copy in December, 1876, or January, 1877. I returned the play to the authors. In 1878 we telegraphed or wrote to send the play back, as we had a chance to produce the play. In December, 1878, got a printed copy of the play back. About the time I received the written contract, I got three or four copies from the authors.

THEODORE MOSS.

Sworn to before me this sixth day of December, 1880.

A. A. CAULDWELL,
*Notary Public, New-York Co.*

[EXHIBIT H.]

VAUDEVILLE THEATRE, Feb. 7, 1880.

MY DEAR MR. WARD, — I am in the middle of rehearsal, so please excuse my writing in great haste with such material as I can find.

I have seen your letter to Mr. Grove, in which you used the word " sold " in regard to " Forget-Me-Not." I never asserted in any way the play had been *sold* to me.

What I informed you was, that, by Mr. Merivale's desire, I some years ago caused the right to be registered in America in my name and that of an American citizen, to produce a propriety right for the authors. It appears Mr. Grove was never told of this: he now knows this fact. In haste,

Yours truly,

JNO. CLAYTON

[EXHIBIT I.]

## WALLACK'S.

MR. LESTER WALLACK . . . . . . *Proprietor and Manager.*

MEMORANDUM.

With the compliments of Mr. Theodore Moss, Treasurer.

NEW YORK, Jan. 14, 1880.

JOHN H. BIRD, ESQ.

*Dear Sir,*—I am in receipt of a circular from you relative to the play of "Forget-Me-Not;" and I would notify you in return, that, whatever rights your client may possess in the piece for Great Britain, she has none for America. For your further information, I would state that I acquired the only legitimate right to "Forget-Me-Not" for this country direct from Mr. Herman Merivale, as I shall be prepared to show when occasion demands.

Yours sincerely,

THEO. MOSS.

[EXHIBIT J.]

## MISS GENEVIEVE WARD.

"FORGET-ME-NOT."

PRINCE OF WALES'S THEATRE, LONDON.

A success upon which Miss Genevieve Ward and playgoers are equally to be congratulated. The acting of Miss Ward is beyond question fine: her manner is excellent. Through all her banter and her fencing with her opponent, which is expressed with admirable point and vivacity, she never permits one to lose sight of the terrible earnestness of her purpose, and her resolve to push the weapon chance has put into her hands home to the very hilt. The first dawn, too, of that sheer physical fear to which she is eventually to succumb, and her efforts to suppress it, are very finely marked. — *The Times.*

Miss Genevieve Ward's Stephanie, Marquise de Mohrivart, gambler, adventuress, false friend, and pitiless enemy, may fairly take rank among the most powerful impersonations the modern stage has seen. Although Stephanie is shown chiefly as a woman of invincible determination, working out her own plans with an utter disregard of the feelings of those in her power, and doing all this under cover of an imperturbably sarcastic and polished manner, the character is an extremely difficult one to play. The woman, wicked as she is, and relentless as she glories in appearing, is not wholly lost to softer emotions. She has her brief flashes of tenderness, and her equally transient sensations of shame, to express. While at war with all the world of respectability, she has to make her abject appeal to be allowed a place in that world; and these alternations of feeling are presented by Miss Genevieve Ward with a power and truthfulness we have very rarely seen approached. Her appeal to Sir Horace Welby when, wishing to lead a new life, she implores him to be silent as to her disreputable antecedents, is as quietly touching and pathetic as her sudden outburst of indignation after he has, by way of answer, threatened her with exposure is impressive in its concentrated passion. Miss Ward plays this scene of the appeal and the defiance very finely. The reception given to " Forget-Me-Not " was nothing short of enthusiastic. — *Morning Advertiser.*

No spectator can fail to admire the power and intensity of Miss Genevieve Ward's impersonation of the heroine. — *Daily News.*

Of Miss Genevieve Ward's fine performance of Stephanie we have had occasion before now to express our hearty admiration. It is a brilliant impersonation, carefully thought out, artistically finished, and intimating in the actress not alone poetic imagination and histrionic passion, but also that mental culture which gives to acting a certain intellectual charm not very easy of definition, but irresistible in its influence. It is high praise, but no higher than she deserves, to say of Miss Ward, that in the subtlety of her by-play and the general refinement of her execution she at times reminds us of Madame Ristori. — *Morning Post.*

A signal success in the present instance is obtained, and the enthusiasm aroused was of a kind that can scarcely fail to spread to succeeding audiences. Miss Genevieve Ward has thoroughly mastered the character of Stephanie, the heroine, and gives in it an example of art equally remarkable for breadth and delicacy. Not a movement, not a gesture, is there which is not carefully thought out. The whole affords an instance of that patient elaboration to which the highest results in art are due. In appearance, and in every other respect, the performance is a masterpiece of exposition, establishing the position of the actress, and rendering as interesting as possible a character which from the first is intended to be anti-pathetic. — *Globe.*

I would earnestly advise all those who are interested in the higher phases of dramatic art to pay a visit to the Prince of Wales's Theatre. It is a long time since I have seen such an actress as Miss Genevieve Ward; and in her knowledge of her art, and her power of giving expression to it, she has certainly no rival at present on the English stage. Of drawing-room charade acting, of carving on cherry-stones, and the representation of society

prettiness, we have had in all conscience enough.  Such a
performance as that now given by Miss Ward reminds
us pleasantly that acting is an art, and comforts us with
the feeling that in our day it has still an exponent.  The
interest centres in Miss Ward; and the subtlety and
power of her acting haunt the memory when all else is
forgotten. — *World.*

Without a doubt, the best performance of last year
was the Stephanie of Miss Genevieve Ward, a study of
female character so nervous, forcible, and expressive, so
different from the fastidious littleness and faded prettiness that occasionally elbow their way into the companionship of art, that all who saw it last autumn recorded their favorable impression of it without hesitation,
and wished that London had been at home to see that
rare combination, a good play thoroughly well acted.
Good as was Miss Genevieve Ward at the outset, she is
far better now.  The study of the fated Stephanie is
rounded, finished, polished, and made more thoroughly
convincing.  Fanciful people will complain that Stephanie is a bad woman, and, as such, has no right to pose as
the heroine of a drama: they will gather up their moral
skirts, and wonder what interest can be attached to the
ambition, the hesitation, the defeat, and the despair of
this proud, cold, passionless beauty.  But those who love
bold acting and good art will here find a study most
worthy of contemplation, from the time when Stephanie
bursts upon the scene to the saddened hour when crushed,
humiliated, broken, and paralyzed with fear, she crouches
at the presence of the instrument of her doom, and totters
from the scene a wreck and a ruin.  In cold and defiant
sarcasm, Miss Ward is excellent to a fault; in the expression of a just and righteous indignation, as when she
lashes with her tongue the selfishness and cowardice of

her arch-enemy, man, she is exalted and absolutely convincing. In her physical fear she is horribly true; but
it is in the passages when a better nature is struggling
with a studied indifference, when acting is fighting with
reality, when the woman is wrestling with the fiend, and
the heart is striving for mastery with the manner, that
Miss Genevieve Ward gives her best contribution to art.
The expression of the face shows what a mental conflict
is raging, and there are countless instances where the
woman's nature changes at the dictation of art. Acting
so striking as this seldom fails; and we seem to perceive
in the surprise and content of the audience a recognition
that is seldom delayed. — *The Daily Telegraph.*

Miss Genevieve Ward's performance of the Marquise
is a singularly forcible conception, carried out with rare
art. At times the actress rises to a height of passion and
emotional power seldom seen upon our stage. — *Standard.*

Miss Genevieve Ward plays the adventuress, Stephanie, with an elaboration of detail, and a finish, both of
which are remarkable. A performance with more that
is genuine, original, and powerful has not recently been
seen on the stage. — *Athenæum.*

In the present instance a portrait, as shown us by Miss
Genevieve Ward, stands out in such rich and glowing
colors as are rarely to be seen on the canvas of the
English stage. A more magnificent performance than
that of Miss Ward has not been witnessed for years. A
public which greeted Sarah Bernhardt with adulation,
and applauded her with effusion, cannot fail to recognize
that in Genevieve Ward stands, not the rival of the
French woman, but her superior. Miss Ward gains her
triumph by no *bruyant* effects, no coarse exaggeration,
but by subtle touches, the grand passion, and the dramatic force which are the characteristics of a true artist.

In her great scene with Mr. Clayton (who plays Sir Horace Welby) the way she turns upon him, the former companion of Madame de Mohrivart's vices, but now the defender of injured innocence, is not less fine in its treatment than her abject terror when the image of the avenging Corsican in the garden is disclosed to her. The insolence and the bravado of the notorious adventuress in Act II. have changed in this last scene to the utter helplessness of the horror-struck woman, and bring down the curtain upon a faultless display of the histrionic art. — *Life.*

The actress who plays the Marquise de Mohrivart finds provided for her by the authors of " Forget-Me-Not" a character drawn with a firm hand, with unflinching consistency, and with a general feeling for dramatic effect. The *rôle* is in many ways a repulsive one, and calls for no little courage, as well as ability, on the part of the actress who would do it full justice. This courage is not lacking in Miss Genevieve Ward, who never wavers in her determination to present to us the painted adventuress, hard, selfish, cruel, and subject only on the rarest of occasions to spasms of womanly feeling. The art by which the actress gives to her embodiment a power akin to the fascination of the rattlesnake, by which she makes Stephanie's baleful influence felt in every tone of the smooth, calm voice, in every smile of the glittering eyes, and, most of all, in the woman's resolute repose, is unmistakable. The traces of humanity in the fiendish nature are indicated with consummate tact; bursts of eloquence come without apparent effort when they are called for, and not a single point of the difficult study is missed. The performance was a fine one when Miss Ward first attempted it; now that she has many times repeated it, it has gained in fulness and ripeness, without any ap-

proach to over-emphasis or to staginess. It should on
no account be missed by those who can enjoy watching
a powerful dramatic conception, powerfully worked out.
The success of "Forget-Me-Not" was last night even
more pronounced than on the occasion of its original
production. — *Observer.*

Miss G. Ward acts, with much power and great finish,
a part that would be worthless in the hands of a less-
practised artiste. It is not a character which creates the
slightest sympathy, and consequently her success is more
difficult to attain, and more creditable when reached.
There was great applause at the end of each act, and
Miss Ward, in the second act, was applauded from all
parts of the house with a heartiness and persistence that
seldom occurs. — *Weekly Times.*

The great theatrical hit for which we have been waiting so long has come at last! The re-opening of the
Prince of Wales's Theatre with Miss Genevieve Ward's
"Forget-Me-Not" has fulfilled all the anticipations which
had been formed of its success. Of Miss Ward's magnificent impersonation of the heroine, it need only be
said, that it is one of the finest pieces of acting on the
London stage. The immense talent displayed by Miss
Ward in the character of Stephanie will be long remembered. — *Court Journal.*

Miss Genevieve Ward assumed her original part of the
vindictive, scheming woman, who has attained the cog-
nomen of "Forget-Me-Not." Her acting is certainly
artistic and finished, and she met with well-deserved
success in a character which is all "against the audience." — *Lloyd's Weekly.*

"Forget-Me-Not" is decidedly the best original drama
written last year, and Miss Genevieve Ward is decidedly
the only actress I know of on the English stage fitted to

grapple with the terrible central character of the play.
She is an actress of intense power and passion, and she
has made a marvellously close and artistic study of this
wonderful character. Stray depths of possible tenderness and gentleness are curiously suggested in Stephanie's character. Under all the icy sarcasm and jarring
levity of her words we see the workings of a woman's
heart, a yearning for something better and purer in her
life, that shines up through all the sins of the past. The
sin is all but redeemed by the strong shame that breaks
upon her as she thinks of the absolute wreck of her life.
You see it in the working of the face, in quivering lips
and close-clasped hands ; you hear it in the sudden break
that comes in the clear, pitiless voice. It is acting of the
very highest order, and nothing so strong or so passionate is to be seen on any stage in London. — *Vanity Fair.*

" Forget-Me-Not " gives Miss Ward an opportunity for
acting which recalls the triumphs of Madame Ristori,
and should not be missed by any genuine play-goer, for
it is as powerful as it is rare. — *Victoria Magazine.*

In the comedy scenes, that is to say, throughout the
first two acts, Miss Genevieve Ward is perfect. " Forget-Me-Not " is worth seeing for the sake of the principal
part, and the principal part is worth seeing for the artistic
style in which Miss Genevieve Ward fills it. The result
of so perfect a representation of a really interesting play
was seen in the abundant applause at the fall of the
curtain. — *Pall Mall.*

In the Marquise, Miss Genevieve Ward has a splendid
opportunity, and she rises to it; the result being a most
finished and elaborate portrait of the scheming adventuress. Every look, every word, every tone, has all the
significance imparted to it, which long artistic training,
combined with talent of a high order, can bestow; and it

would be well-nigh an impossibility to find a better exponent of the character than Miss Ward has proved herself to be. — *Sporting Opinion.*

In Stephanie de Mohrivart, Miss Genevieve Ward has a part which fits her like a glove, and in the stronger scenes she played with a singular power. Her performance was throughout a consistent one, and to a high degree artistic, and she well deserved the lavish applause with which her efforts were greeted. — *The Scotsman.*

The consummate art displayed by Miss Genevieve Ward has led us on from one scene to another, until the catastrophe happens in its own good time, to release us from the weird thraldom in which she had held us. It is long since we have seen such a frank success upon the London boards. — *Dublin Evening Telegraph.*

Miss Genevieve Ward's impersonation is one to be seen, and will not readily be forgotten. — *Sporting and Dramatic News.*

To Miss Genevieve Ward the play belongs. Of her impersonation of Stephanie we have already spoken in terms of the warmest eulogy. We have recognized in this embodiment, artistic skill, grace, animation, vigor, pathos, and in certain scenes genuine comedy power. We have told how the caustic, sarcastic utterances of the beautiful merciless woman of the world were given with such keen point, variety, and expression, that they fell from her lips like sparks of fire; we have said how grandly was presented the transition from sparkling badinage to vehement scorn which marks the great scene of the second act, where Miss Genevieve Ward's tones were scorching in their fierce invective, where her attitudes were majestic, and where the facial expression magnificently indicated the supposed turbulent working of Stephanie's soul; and further, we have commented upon the tragic force of the final situation, where the terrors of a violent death are upon the guilty woman, where the horrors of remorse rack her conscience, and where, almost swooning with fear and palsied with fright, she crawls from the presence of her foe, who is waiting to take her life. Miss Ward's acting in this scene, we have been bold enough to say, might without exaggeration be compared with the grandest efforts of a Ristori or Rachel. This is high praise, but it is thoroughly well deserved. The actress last Saturday seemed to cast a spell over her audience. Pulses beat fast in that encounter with Sir Horace, where, having been stung by his bitter words, Stephanie turns upon him with vindictive scorn and flashing eyes; recalls the dissipation of the past, and cries aloud, "There would be no place in creation· for such women as I, if it were not for such men as you;" while the effect upon her spectators in the last act was manifest by the breathless silence which reigned, a silence which denoted awe as well as interest, and which gave unmistakable proof of the actress's power. Cheers and floral compliments were not wanting, but this marvellous silence was the best compliment that could be paid to the artiste. — *Era.*

Meanwhile, as the principal combatant, for such she is in a play made up of combat, Miss Genevieve Ward is superb. We can recall few performances on the modern stage that are finer, more artistic, more careful, more conscientious, more thoughtful, more sustained; whether in the insolence of triumph or the despair of defeat, the performance is alike powerful. Her appearance, as she enters the house she has determined to make her own, is perfect, and during her stay on the stage she fills it. Even in her concluding cowardice and abjectness she still triumphs, and she departs bearing our enforced homage. The acting is quite enough to make a reputation. — *Sunday Times.*

What shall I say of Miss Ward? Such acting as hers, as the Marquise, must either be analyzed for pages by Balzac, such is its astonishing fidelity to nature, its marvellous subtlety and attention to the minutest details, — or dismissed with one word — perfect. I prefer the last alternative. I repeat the word, perfect, most perfect. It is superfluous to compliment so very great an artist. Strange! Miss Ward looks, as Stephanie, the exact image of the Empress Eugénie as she was before her misfortunes. — *Town and Country.*

Miss Ward has no equal in her profession as an exponent of the strongly defined, passionate heroines of the stage. — *Sketch.*

Miss Genevieve Ward is an actress of very remarkable power. She has a fine figure and voice, a quiet power in every line of her face and in every gesture; and that itself is one of the highest requisites of an actress, for it makes every thing she does interesting. Again, she is perfectly simple and refined in her manner, and her playfulness has an air of distinction: it is that of a woman in whom playfulness is the unbending of strength, not the dissipation of all the little energy of character there is. And what is more, perhaps, than any of these characteristics, Miss Ward is not absorbed in her own part. She is anxious to give full effect to the parts of the other actors as she is to her own. Her power was so singular and so remarkable, and it was the power of so much mental culture, that we may fairly congratulate the English stage on the presence of a new actress of the first class amongst us. — *Spectator.*

Miss Genevieve Ward, as Stephanie, shows herself to be a true artiste. The strong dramatic power which she exhibits is no less admirable than the ironical tone of comedy, which is the main characteristic of the part. In the last scene, Miss Ward's performance is of the highest order. If the gradual escape from the room were done with the least want of force or artistic feeling, it might go hard with the play. In Miss Ward's hands the situation becomes thrilling. — *Saturday Review.*

[EXHIBIT K.]

"NEW-YORK HERALD," DEC. 28, 1879.

*To Managers and the Theatrical Profession generally.*

Miss Genevieve Ward hereby gives notice that she is the owner, and has the sole right to produce the play of "Forget-Me-Not" in the United States and elsewhere; that she has duly copyrighted same, and will prosecute all infringers by injunction and otherwise.

JOHN H. BIRD,
*Attorney in fact,*
137 BROADWAY, NEW YORK.

[EXHIBIT L.]

To......................................................

Notice is hereby given, that the undersigned did, on the twenty-first day of August, 1879, at the city of London, England, purchase from Herman Charles Merivale and Florence Crawford Grove, the authors of the play called "Forget-Me-Not," the exclusive right to produce the same in the kingdom of Great Britain, in this country, and elsewhere, for a period of years; and that the same was duly copyrighted at Washington on the thirtieth day of September, 1879.

This notice is given because of information, just received by me, that Miss Jeffreys Lewis, and others, are endeavoring to secure engagements to produce this play in the principal theatres of the United States.

I trust that my rights of ownership will be readily respected by all managers and members of the theatrical profession generally.

If, however, notwithstanding this notice, you should proceed, and attempt to produce the play, in defiance of my exclusive rights in the premises, then I will resort to the courts, and protect those rights by injunction, and all other protective and compensatory measures known to the law.

GENEVIEVE WARD,

By John H. Bird, *Attorney*,

137 BROADWAY, ROOM 5, NEW YORK.

NEW YORK, Jan. 2, 1880.

N.B.— I am about concluding a contract with Col. William E. Sinn, sole lessee and manager of the Brooklyn Park Theatre, for the production in the United States and Canada of the above play of "Forget-Me-Not," for the season of 1880–81. For terms and dates, please address him at Brooklyn Park Theatre, Brooklyn, Kings County, New York.

[EXHIBIT M.]

"FORGET-ME-NOT."

THE NEW PLAY, BY HERMAN CHARLES MERIVALE AND FLORENCE CRAWFORD GROVE.

*To Managers, Owners, and Proprietors of Theatres throughout the United States.*

The undersigned gives notice that he is the sole and exclusive owner for the United States of this play, with the sole and exclusive right of representing the same, by purchase and assignment from the authors and proprietors, and that he will prosecute all parties infringing on his right of property in the said play.

THEODORE MOSS.

*Dated* NEW YORK, April 9, 1880.

[EXHIBIT N.]

CABLE MESSAGE.

NEW YORK, May 3, 1880.

BIRD, 137 *Broadway, New York.*

Can do nothing here now. Find out what royalty Moss would take.

WARD.

17, PARIS.

[EXHIBIT O.]

JUNE 16, 1880.

MR. THEODORE MOSS.

*Dear Sir,* — Miss Ward writes me from London, requesting that I procure from you a copy of the agreement between the authors of " Forget-Me-Not " and yourself. Will you kindly comply with her request, or advise me at what time and place I can send, and have a copy made ? I sincerely trust you may feel at liberty to grant this courtesy.

Very truly,

JOHN H. BIRD.

# INDEX OF NAMES

OF FAMILIES THAT HAVE INTERMARRIED WITH THE
WARD FAMILY AND ITS DESCENDANTS OF VARIOUS
NAMES, AS GIVEN IN "THE WARD FAMILY," PUBLISHED
BY SAMUEL G. DRAKE, BOSTON, 1851.

| A. | B. | |
|---|---|---|
| | | Beaman. |
| | | Bean. |
| Abbe. | Babcock. | Bedford. |
| Abbey. | Bacheller. | Bellows. |
| Abbott. | Bacon. | Bemis. |
| Ackley. | Bagley. | Bennet. |
| Adams. | Bailey. | Bently. |
| Ainsworth. | Baird. | Bickford. |
| Albee. | Baker. | Bidwell. |
| Alden. | Baldwin. | Bigelow. |
| Aldrich. | Ball. | Bird. |
| Alexander. | Ballard. | Bisbee. |
| Alfrey. | Bancroft. | Bishop. |
| Allen. | Bannister. | Bixby. |
| Ames. | Barber. | Black. |
| Amsden. | Barnard. | Blackman. |
| Andrews. | Barnes. | Blake. |
| Angier. | Barnum. | Blanchard. |
| Appleton. | Barrell. | Blodget. |
| Aravello. | Barrett. | Blood. |
| Arnold. | Bartlett. | Bond. |
| Ashley. | Barton. | Booth. |
| Atherton. | Bascom. | Bouker. |
| Atwater. | Basset. | Bowman. |
| Atwood. | Bates. | Boyenton. |
| Austin. | Bathrick. | Bracket. |
| Avery. | Battle. | Bradish. |
| Ayling. | Bayley. | Bray. |
| Ayres. | Beade. | Breck. |

Brewer.
Brewster.
Bridges.
Briggs.
Brigham.
Brookins.
Bromly.
Brown.
Broughton.
Brownell.
Bryant.
Bucknam.
Buffington.
Bullard.
Burchard.
Burgess.
Burnham.
Burnap.
Burnet.
Burns.
Burrage.
Burroughs.
Burt.
Bushnell.
Busnam.
Butler.

**C.**

Cabot.
Caldwell.
Cady.
Call.
Callender.
Cameron.
Canfield.
Carpenter.
Capron.
Carey.
Carlton.
Carrington.
Carruth.
Carter.
Castle.
Caswell.
Chadwick.
Chambers.

Chamberlain.
Chandler.
Chapin.
Chapman.
Chase.
Cheesbrough.
Cheney.
Chesmore.
Child.
Childs.
Church.
Churchill.
Cilley.
Claflin.
Clapp.
Clark.
Clary.
Cleaveland.
Clough.
Coates.
Cobb.
Coe.
Coggin.
Cole.
Colman.
Columbia.
Comins.
Conant.
Converse.
Cook.
Cooley.
Coolidge.
Cooper.
Corbett.
Cornell.
Cornish.
Corthell.
Cotton.
Covil.
Cowdin.
Cowles.
Cox.
Craft.
Cranston.
Crosby.
Crossman.
Crouch.

Croxford.
Cudderbuck.
Cummins.
Curtis.
Cutler.
Cutting.
Cutts.
Cuzzens.

**D.**

Dakin.
Dalrymple.
Dame.
Danforth.
Daniels.
Darling.
Davenport.
Davids.
Davis.
Davison.
Dawes.
Day.
Dean.
Dehanne.
Delano.
Demond.
Dennehe.
Dennis.
Dennison.
Denny.
Denzelo.
Derby.
Dewey.
Dexter.
Dibbell.
Dickinson.
Dike.
Dix.
Doan.
Dodge.
Dole.
Doolittle.
Dow.
Drake.
Draper.
Drew.

Drury.
Dryden.
Dudley.
Duger.
Dunklee.
Dunton.
Durgen.
Dyer.

**E.**

Eager.
Eames.
Earle.
Eastman.
Easton.
Eaton.
Eddy.
Edmands.
Edson.
Elder.
Elkins.
Elliot.
Ellis.
Elmes.
Emerson.
Emery.
Enos.
Este.

**F.**

Fairbank.
Farley.
Farnsworth.
Farwell.
Fay.
Fennell.
Ferrin.
Ferry.
Fessenden.
Field.
Fife.
Finney.
Fitch.
Fisher.
Fisk.

Fiske.
Fitts.
Flagg.
Flint.
Fload.
Flowers.
Fosket.
Fowler.
Freeman.
French.
Fuller.

**G.**

Galbraith.
Gardner.
Garfield.
Gates.
Gay.
Gaylord.
Gerald.
Gilbert.
Gill.
Gilmore.
Gillet.
Gillis.
Glazier.
Gleason.
Goddard.
Godfrey.
Goodale.
Gorham.
Goss.
Gould.
Goulding.
Gove.
Graham.
Granger.
Grant.
Green.
Greenwood.
Grosvenor.
Grover.
Guliker.
Gunn.
Gurney.

**H.**

Hall.
Hamilton.
Hammond.
Hanks.
Hannum.
Hapgood.
Harback.
Hardy.
Harman.
Harris.
Harrington.
Harroon.
Harper.
Hart.
Hartwell.
Harvey.
Harwood.
Haskell.
Hastings.
Hawes.
Hayden.
Haynes.
Hays.
Hayward.
Hazeltine.
Head.
Heald.
Heath.
Hedge.
Hemphill.
Henry.
Henshaw.
Herbert.
Herrick.
Heywood.
Higbee.
Higgins.
Hill.
Hilton.
Hinman.
Hitchcock.
Hobbs.
Hobart.
Hodge.
Hoit.

Holbrook.
Holcomb.
Holden.
Holland.
Hollis.
Holmes.
Holt.
Hook.
Houghton.
Hovey.
Howe.
Howard.
Howell.
Hoyt.
Hudson.
Hull.
Humphrey.
Hunt.
Hunter.
Hunting.
Huntington.
Hyde.
Hubbard.

**I.**

Ingalls.
Ingersoll.
Ingraham.
Ingram.
Ireland.

**J.**

Jackson.
James.
Jameson.
Janes.
Jenkins.
Jennison.
Jewett.
Johnson.
Jones.
Janord.
Joy.

**K.**

Kassan.
Kasson.
Keet.
Keith.
Kelton.
Kendall.
Kendrick.
Kennedy.
Kenney.
Kenrick.
Kerley.
Ketchum.
Keyes.
Kibbe.
Kidder.
Kimberly.
King.
Kingman.
Kingsbury.
Kinne.
Knapp.
Knight.
Knowlton.

**L.**

Ladd.
Laffin.
Lake.
Lamb.
Lamson.
Langdon.
Lathe.
Lawrence.
Lazell.
Leach.
Lee.
Leet.
Leffingwell.
Leonard.
Lewis.
Libbey.
Livermore.
Livingston.
Locke.

Loomis.
Lord.
Lothrop.
Lounsbury.
Love.
Lovering.
Lowe.
Lowell.
Lyon.
Lyscom.
Lull.

**M.**

Mace.
Mack.
McLennan.
McElroy.
McFall.
McFarland.
McIntyre.
Macumber.
Mallory.
Manning.
Marble.
Marsh.
Martin.
Martyn.
Mason.
Mather.
Mattocks.
Maynard.
Mayo.
Mellen.
Melvin.
Merrick.
Merritt.
Messer.
Millard.
Miller.
Mills.
Minchent.
Mirick.
Mitchell.
Mix.
Mixer.
Mixter.

Monefeldt.
Montague.
Montandon.
Montgomery.
Moore.
Moores.
Morey.
Morgan.
Morrill.
Morris.
Morse.
Morton.
Mossman.
Mower.
Munsell.
Munson.
Murdock.
Muzzy.
Myers.

### N.

Nelson.
Newell.
Newhall.
Newton.
Nichols.
Nicholson.
Norcross.
Northup.
Norton.
Notewaire.
Nourse.
Noyes.
Nurse.
Nutting.
Nye.

### O.

Oaks.
Oliver.
Orcutt.
Osborne.
Osgood.
Overbaugh.
Oviatt.
Owen.

### P.

Packard.
Page.
Paine.
Palmer.
Park.
Parker.
Parks.
Parmenter.
Parsons.
Patten.
Peabody.
Peache.
Peake.
Pease.
Peckham.
Peirce.
Pelton.
Pendleton.
Pepper.
Perkins.
Perry.
Phelps.
Phillips.
Pigeon.
Pike.
Pinney.
Piper.
Pitkin.
Pond.
Pool.
Porter.
Post.
Potter.
Powell.
Powers.
Pratt.
Presby.
Prescott.
Priest.
Proctor.
Prouty.
Purdy.
Putnam.

### R.

Ralston.
Ramsdell.
Randall.
Ransom.
Rawson.
Raymond.
Raynsford.
Read.
Reed.
Reese.
Remick.
Retts.
Rhodes.
Rice.
Rich.
Richards.
Richardson.
Richmond.
Rider.
Rising.
Robinson.
Rockwood.
Rogers.
Rood.
Root.
Ross.
Rowley.
Roy.
Ruggles.
Russell.
Rust.
Rutt.
Ryan.

### S.

Sacket.
Saddler.
Safford.
Salisbury.
Samuels.
Sanders.
Sanderson.
Sandin.
Sargeant.
Sarvey.

Sawtell.
Sawyer.
Scott.
Scribner.
Seagraves.
Seely.
Selfridge.
Sewall.
Sexton.
Seymour.
Shattuck.
Shaw.
Shed.
Sheffield.
Sheldon.
Shepard.
Sherman.
Sherwin.
Sherwood.
Shumway.
Shurtliff.
Shute.
Sibley.
Simonds.
Sinclair.
Skinner.
Slater.
Smith.
Snelling.
Snow.
Soule.
Southworth.
Spaulding.
Spencer.
Spinney.
Spokesfield.
Spring.
Spurr.
Squiers.
Stacy.
Stafford.
Staples.
Stearns.
Stebbins.
Stedman.
Steele.
Stevens.

Stickney.
Stimpson.
Stocking.
Stockwell.
Stoddard.
Stone.
Storrs.
Storer.
Stow.
Stratton.
Streeter.
Strong.
Symonds.

**T.**

Taft.
Taintor.
Talbot.
Tappan.
Tatman.
Taylor.
Temple.
Tenant.
Tenny.
Thayer.
Thomas.
Thompson.
Thornton.
Thurlo.
Thurston.
Tileston.
Tinkham.
Tobey.
Tomlin.
Toombs.
Torrey.
Town. .
Townsend.
Tracy.
Trask.
Trowbridge.
Trusdale.
Tucker.
Tufts.
Turner.
Tuttle.

Twitchell.
Tyler.

**U.**

Underwood.
Upham.

**V.**

Van Horn.
Vickery.
Viles.

**W.**

Wadleigh.
Wadsworth.
Wait.
Walbridge.
Wales.
Walker.
Walter.
Warden.
Warner.
Warren.
Warrick.
Washburn.
Waters.
Watkins.
Watson.
Webb.
Webster.
Weeks.
Wellington.
Wells.
Whalan.
Wheeler.
Wheelock.
Whipple.
Whitaker.
White.
Whittelsey.
Whittemore.
Whiton.
Whitney.
Wiggins.

Wilder.
Wiley.
Wilkinson.
Willard.
Williams.
Williamson.
Wilmot.
Wilson.

Winchester.
Winslow.
Wiswall.
Witherby.
Witherell.
Witt.
Wood.
Woodbury.

Woodcock.
Woodward.
Wyman.
Wythe.

**Y.**

Yearo.

www.ingramcontent.com/pod-product-compliance
Lightning Source LLC
Chambersburg PA
CBHW021054030726

47496CB00006B/1833